S0-EIJ-308

White Butterflies

White Butterflies

AND

Other Stories

BY

KATE UPSON CLARK

Framingham State College
Framingham, Massachusetts

Short Story Index Reprint Series

 BOOKS FOR LIBRARIES PRESS
FREEPORT, NEW YORK

First Published 1900
Reprinted 1969

STANDARD BOOK NUMBER:
8369-3247-1

LIBRARY OF CONGRESS CATALOG CARD NUMBER:
75-103505

PRINTED IN THE UNITED STATES OF AMERICA

PS
3505
L 352
W 45
1969

To

E. P. C.

THIS BOOK IS DEDICATED

Framingham State College
Framingham, Massachusetts

Contents

	PAGE
WHITE BUTTERFLIES	1
"RALDY"	27
THE CHARCOAL BURNERS	49
CUPID AND MINERVA	74
THE CASE OF PARSON HEWLETT	88
"FOR LOOLY"	103
TOMLIN DRESSER'S DISAPPEARANCE	142
DAFFODILS	158
"SOLLY"	173
TID'S WIFE	198
"YE CHRISTMAS WITCH"	209
DIREXIA	244
LYDDY WASHBURN'S COURTSHIP	266

White Butterflies.

IT was a large, bare house—the only one on the sandy Pine Hill road. An air of desolation surrounded it, which young Mrs. Collis Wood felt painfully, as she reined up her gentle pony in front of it. Gloomy evergreen forests covered the hill, and even the little opening around the house looked dark, though the sun was shining.

She knocked at the door, and a stout, middle-aged woman responded. Mrs. Wood introduced herself, and the woman gave her own name as "Mrs. Keasbey—Mrs. Thomas Keasbey"—with an air of pride.

"Perhaps you may know, Mrs. Keasbey," Mrs. Wood proceeded, when they were seated in the plain little parlor, "that I have a class of girls which meets every Sunday afternoon in the school-house just at the foot of the hill here. Some of us enjoy driving out the two miles from the village, and staying there an hour then, and we hope it is a good thing for this neighborhood. I have noticed, when I have been driving past here, that you have a very bright, pretty girl. Wouldn't she like to join my class?"

In spite of the gratified expression which the easy compliment brought to Mrs. Keasbey's flabby, but not uncomely face, a flush of displeasure accompanied it.

"It was our Dorilla you saw, probably," she said, with a nervous little laugh, "but she's been to school a sight. Mr. Keasbey and I have traveled mostly during the last three or four years, and Dorilla has been in a convent down South—not that we're specially religious, for we

7

ain't—but it was a good place for her, and she liked it. She took all the prizes there—and she reads most of the time now. She's 'most seventeen, and we think maybe she's gone to school enough. She's sort o' odd, and we want to get her out of the way of it."

"Then wouldn't this be a good thing for her?" urged the visitor. "There are several nice girls in this neighborhood who go there, and it would be pleasant for a stranger like your Dorilla to get acquainted with them."

"N—no," dissented Mrs. Keasbey. "We may not stay here very long. I guess it ain't worth while."

There was a pause. Mrs. Wood felt as though she were expected to go, but she decided to make another attempt.

"Perhaps Dorilla would really like to come," she suggested. "Won't you let me ask her?"

"I don't know where she is. She may be off in the woods somewhere, and I can't very well leave to hunt after her, for Mr. Keasbey is home now, and I've got work to do. I reckon she don't care to go."

At this moment the front door opened, and Dorilla herself entered. Her attire, like her mother's, was soiled and tawdry, but beyond this there was little resemblance between them. Dorilla was tall, and slender, and fair. Her black hair was as soft as silk, and hung in a long braid down her back. Her eyes were dark, and their expression was almost wild, but her rather large mouth and nose were well-shaped and firm, and her whole bearing was quiet and pleasing. It was no wonder that Mrs. Wood had observed Dorilla Keasbey, when passing the lonely house on Pine Hill.

"See," said the girl, smiling, as she stood in the doorway.

White Butterflies.

She held out her round arm, from which the loose sleeve fell away at the elbow. Three palpitating white butterflies were ranged in a row upon the delicate, blue-veined flesh. A fourth was fluttering around the girl's head.

"Don't!" cried the mother, with a half shriek. "Push 'em off, Rill! Put 'em out doors!"

"Why?" asked the girl, pulling away, as her mother tried to push her. "They like me, and I like them—and they are the sweetest things in the world."

At this point, she saw Mrs. Wood for the first time, and Mrs. Keasbey performed the necessary introductions, in a reluctant manner which the daughter could not fail to observe. She listened with interest to the scheme which the sweet-faced visitor proposed, only breaking in when the advantages of knowing the "other girls" were mentioned.

"I don't think I care much about them," she said, with a warm gleam in her dark eyes, "but I know I should like you—and I think I will go."

"You better ask your father first," her mother warned her.

"I think I can manage him."

"And you may bring your butterflies with you," Mrs. Wood said, smilingly.

"I always carry one," said the girl, soberly. She rolled up her loose sleeve, and showed, just above her elbow, a singular birthmark. It stood out white, even against Dorilla's white skin and was of the general shape of the common white butterfly.

"How strange!" murmured the gentle visitor.

"Yes," said the girl, "and I have always chased white butterflies ever since I was born. I feed them and keep them in my room—and I suppose I tame them—and make them like me in that way. But I believe they would like me anyway—that there is something between us. Don't you think that that might be?"

"Perhaps so," replied Mrs. Wood, slowly. "At any rate, it is a beautiful omen. It betokens a white soul."

"In me?" questioned the girl, half-mockingly.

"Yes, you."

"Oh, you don't know!" she murmured, bitterly.

"What did you say, Rill?" demanded her mother, suspiciously. "Take care!"

Mrs. Collis Wood felt uncomfortable, and rose to depart, more interested in this strange girl than ever.

"Then you will come on Sunday?" she said.

"No," muttered the woman, thickly. "She can't go, and she knows she can't."

Dorilla said nothing until she handed the reins to Mrs. Wood. Then the girl intimated that she might appear at the school-house on Sunday afternoon, after all, and only laughed at the rather shocked and doubtful expression which, at these expressions of disobedient intent, appeared on her visitor's face. She drove away, with the vision in her mind of Dorilla standing there in the sunlight, with the delicate, white-winged things settling down upon her. Beside that picture, the sordid, shackly house, with its vulgar mistress and its sinister atmosphere, sank into insignificance.

Sure enough, on the following Sunday, the girl appeared at the school-house, and after the lesson was over and the others had left, she explained to Mrs. Wood that she had come without the knowledge of her parents, "but," she went on, "it didn't make any difference. A lot of my father's friends came from the city last night, and we had to get a big dinner for them this noon. Father does some of the cooking, and Mikey and the others help. Mother doesn't like to have me spoil my hands. She and my father care a great deal more about keeping them white than I do—and while they were eating, I just crept away. They think I am in the woods— for I go off there by myself a great deal. It's no matter, anyway."

"Oh!" breathed Mrs. Wood, still somewhat dubious as to the propriety of receiving Dorilla into her class under the circumstances, and wondering why these strange parents should wish to keep the girl cooped up by herself on Pine Hill; but her delight in the class, her evident love for her young teacher, and, as the Sundays went by, and she still came, her high ethical perceptions and her thrist for spiritual light, determined Mrs. Wood to let things go as Dorilla wished. She said one day to her: "It is just as I said, Dorilla—the omen is true—you have a white soul. You always know what is right, and see it more quickly than any of the rest of us."

Again the mocking, half-distressed look came over the girl's face, and her eyes filled.

"You don't understand," she repeated, in a voice full of misery.

Mrs. Wood did not call again at the house at Pine Hill, but sometimes she drove past it, on the chance of catching a glimpse of Dorilla. One day she had seen a man there who was undoubtedly Mr. Thomas Keasbey. He was short, thick-set, slovenly, yet flashy, like his wife.

Occasionally Mrs. Wood managed to get Dorilla to spend an afternoon with her in the village. Then they had long, affectionate talks, in which each told the other of the chief events of her life, though Dorilla was rather provokingly reserved in her accounts. Mrs. Wood gathered, however, that she had been born on her grandfather's farm, a little way from New York City; that later the family had removed to the town, where they had lived above Mr. Keasbey's locksmith shop; that they had had periods of prosperity, during which they had traveled abroad, dressed well and had everything. These had been succeeded by times of poverty. Dorilla spoke most lovingly of the sisters at the convent where she had been so long. "I had been sick, but I grew well and strong there," she said. "Oh, I loved the convent so! If I were only there now!" She burst into tears as she spoke, and sobbed long and passionately.

"Don't! Don't, Dorilla!" begged her gentle hostess. "You shake so and sob so, you frighten me."

"Oh, you don't know!" wept the girl.

"Don't know what? Aren't they kind to you at home?"

"Oh, yes. My father is good to me, and proud that I have had some education. He somehow expects to become rich again, and then he will make a fine lady of me, he says."

As Mrs. Wood stroked the girl's silken head, she cast about in her mind for threads of recollection which might unravel the mystery of Dorilla's tears. She remembered seeing once a pleasant-looking young man sitting beside Dorilla on the Pine Hill doorstep. She had spoken often of a certain "Mikey." Could there be a love affair at the bottom of this grief?

A few questions revealed the fact that Dorilla did, indeed, cherish an affection for "Mikey," which was disapproved by her father, who said that "Mikey" had no "nerve," and would never "amount" to anything.

"But he is a gentleman, through and through," Dorilla concluded, with dilating eyes and blazing cheeks, "and I shall never like anybody else half so much. I know his name isn't pretty—but neither is mine. Dorilla! It is the softest, sickest name I ever heard of. My mother got it out of a novel. But I must go." Dorilla had stolen away from home as usual.

"I wish they would not keep you so closely," sighed Mrs. Wood. "Why do you suppose they won't let you have any friends?"

The girl's eyes assumed their most unhappy and inscrutable look.

"I—I don't understand it myself," she stammered. "Maybe it is because we are so poor now—and my father wants to wait until we can live better, before we have friends. Good-bye."

The girl stooped her beautiful head to receive the kiss which her young teacher offered her. As she walked swiftly away in the direction of Pine Hill, a white butterfly went dancing along after her.

"I wonder," speculated the happy young wife, as she stood watching the fair figure of the girl, and thinking of the secret just revealed, which she fancied explained Dorilla's excitement, "I wonder if I am doing right in asking her so much to come here—and all. It seems as though it couldn't be wrong. At any rate, I will think about it a little longer before I make any change."

One day, late in September, Thomas Keasbey, who was at home oftener now than during the summer, asked Dorilla to do a strange errand, strange even to her, who was accustomed to strange errands. She was expert with her pencil. He wished her to visit the rooms of the Woman's Exchange in the village, buy a few articles there, and take such notice of the rooms that she could make an accurate plan of them afterward.

The Woman's Exchange rooms were situated on the second and top floor of what was called "the Bank Block" in the village. They were three or four in number, and were under the charge of a charitable organization of women, prominent among whom was Mrs. Collis Wood. Preserves, sweetmeats and needle-work were sold there, as in most such places. In one room there was a sort of an intelligence office—in another, a small public library. In the summer there were a good many city boarders in the vicinity, who patronized the exchange. It had been well-managed, and had more than paid for itself, besides aiding many poor women.

Directly underneath these rooms was the village bank, one of the richest and best-conducted country banks in the State. Mr. Collis Wood was the cashier. He was a young man, but he had grown up in the business and understood it thoroughly. He had married the daughter of the bank's president. Altogether, he possessed a social and business standing second to none in the place.

Through a man who had assisted in the building of the bank, Thomas Keasbey had ascertained that a steel ceiling just above it was topped by a layer of cement, three feet in thickness. This cement was as hard as marble. Weeks might be required, with the limit of available hours per night, and with the only tools which could be used in such a case, to cut a hole through such a ceiling, large enough to admit the body of a man— yet such a hole Mr. Keasbey proposed to make. He had secured a complete plan of the bank. Now he must get the exact plan of the rooms above it. His daughter, with her refined face, quick eye and skillful hand, was just the one to do the work unsuspected—if he could only get her to undertake it.

It was on a Saturday afternoon that Dorilla's father asked her to make herself ready to go to the village. When she had her hat and gloves on, he briefly outlined her errand.

"I am thinking of putting up a block of buildings myself," he concluded, with a wink at his wife.

"Then why don't you go to the people who built this, and ask them for the plan?" she inquired, with the cloudy look in her eyes which always came when she was deeply moved.

"I can't afford it, you little goose," he answered with a laugh. "They would charge me big money."

Dorilla turned; slowly walked over the hill to the village; did her errand, and gave the plan to her father, having finished it as soon as she was well concealed by the trees on her way home; but she felt vaguely uncomfortable over what she had done, and she went back into the woods, after a little, and sat there on a rock. thinking for a long time.

In her thought she lived over her life again. She remembered how fondly she had adored her father before she went to the convent. During the years there, she had seen little of him. She had usually spent her vacations with the sisters, who had made a pet of her. Now and then she had staid with her father and mother at some hotel. The quality of these hotels had declined steadily during the last two years, and Thomas Keasbey had grown gloomy and irritable. Still, when he had come to the convent to see her, he had brought her beautiful presents, and at the hotels he had been fond and proud of her, and she had still loved him.

This summer, however, during the ten or twelve weeks since the Keasbeys had moved into the Pine Hill house, Dorilla's feelings toward her father had undergone a change. He was still kind to her and to her mother, when he was himself; but he often drank deeply—especially when the five or six friends, whom he called his "business partners," came out to spend the night with him. Dorilla could dimly recollect such scenes far back in her childhood, but she had not known them in recent years, and they shocked her. Her lessons in the schoolhouse had lent a new force to moral convictions formed in the convent. They and the indirect influence of Mrs. Collis Wood, in those long, delightful talks which Dorilla contrived to steal now and then on a weekday, were insensibly altering the whole current of the girl's thoughts. The squalor and confusion of the shackly house on Pine Hill annoyed and chafed upon her more and more. The atmosphere of tobacco smoke and rum which filled it when the "friends" had been there nauseated and disgusted her. Her quick intuition led her to believe that her father's "business" was not strictly legitimate. The awful truth was only just beginning to dawn upon her, but all summer, since she had come away from the convent in early June, she had felt that matters were not right. The drunken carousals, the oaths and allusions to crime—which her father always tried to stop in her presence—all of the circumstances which surrounded her, distressed and mystified her. Mrs. Collis Wood often felt as though the girl had in her an element of the supernatural; but to Dorilla herself this element seemed even stronger. She felt like two people. She could not realize that she was the same girl who had chased the white butterflies in the convent garden, studied her lessons in the quiet school-room, and built her fondest hopes on the winning of first medals. Now there was this awful secrecy —these coarse men coming to the house at night—always by night—the constant injunctions to her to repeat nothing which she heard said—to make no acquaintances —these expectations of wealth in the near future—and then—there was Mikey, with his handsome face, the love which he had declared for her and which she herself saw no harm in returning—and yet to which her father was so unalterably opposed. It was all so deeply confusing and bewildering that it seemed to her like a horrible nightmare.

That Saturday night, five of the "friends" had come for Sunday, and there was a great supper to clear away. Dorilla wiped the dishes in the kitchen for her mother, saying little or nothing. Then they both sat down for a moment on the cool back steps. Presently Mrs. Keasbey spoke chidingly.

"What was you whispering and talking so with Mikey for, Rilla? You know——"

"Yes, I know," interrupted Dorilla, impatiently. "I'm tired of hearing about it. I wish you would never mention Mikey to me again."

Mrs. Keasbey fumed and fretted on weakly, but the girl made no further reply. Suddenly a great white moth came fluttering down out of the darkness and settled upon her ruffled hair, swaying his velvet wings back and forth. The mother started as she saw it.

"Where did that come from, Dorilla?"

"Where they always come from when I'm around," laughed the girl, with a little note of triumph in her voice.

Mrs. Keasbey got up and went into the house. She was half afraid of Dorilla when she was in this mood.

2

White Butterflies.

Two terrible weeks followed. The men remained at the house all the time, sleeping by day and roaming abroad by night. Two or three times the girl questioned her mother, but Mrs. Keasbey either answered nothing at all, or in meaningless general terms. The housework, even when performed after that lady's easy methods, was a heavy burden, though the men attempted to help, and one of them, who was a baker by trade, rendered considerable assistance. They drank more than usual, and Mr. Keasbey was taciturn and morose. Even Mikey was nervous, and drank too much. Dorilla could not get away on Sunday for the class at the school-house, nor any visit with her teacher during the week. She was inwardly excited to the highest pitch. It seemed as though she must go crazy.

On a certain Friday night the crisis came. For two weeks, every evening, Thomas Keasbey and his men, gathering singly, from different directions and at different hours, had effected, by means of skeleton keys and other simple tools, an entrance into the room which lay above the vault of the bank. They had raised the carpet there, removed some planks, and bored into the adamant cement below them. By cautious and persistent labor, they had now hewn out a jagged hole in it, large enough to admit them, one by one, into the bank below. The steel ceiling had been partially drilled through. Every night, the dust and fragments had been neatly swept into bags, the planks and carpet had been replaced, the doors and windows had been securely relocked, and the great burglary had been a little nearer its consummation—and Thomas Keasbey had as yet no reason to fear that the slightest suspicion had fastened upon their movements.

That day the men slept long and soundly. It was

after six when they assembled for their evening meal. The October night was warm and close, but they dared not have a curtain up nor a window open. Dorilla and her mother waited on them in silence. The men were nervous and thirsty, but Thomas Keasbey would not let them drink much.

"We want clear heads to-night, boys," he said. "Dorilla, fill the glasses once out of this bottle. When we get back, maybe we'll have a little more."

They did not sit long at the table, and Mrs. Keasbey and Dorilla, assisted by Mikey, cleared up after them in a few minutes. Mikey was very gentle that night. Even Mrs. Keasbey, who was always "short" with him, in spite of his solicitous efforts to please her, could not help softening a little when she saw how deft and kind he was; but when she marked the glances which passed between him and Dorilla, her anger rose again.

"It will take more than Thomas Keasbey to part those two," she mused. But in her soul she felt sure, after all, that the iron will of her husband would effect his purpose. It did not seem to her that anything could be stronger than he.

Mikey at last joined the men in the parlor, into which the door stood open. Dorilla could hear that the talking which was going on there was excited, though it was subdued in tone.

Mrs. Keasbey declared that she was so tired she couldn't sit up a moment longer, and pottered off to her room upstairs. It was only nine o'clock, but she recommended that Dorilla should go to bed also. The girl obediently followed up the stairs, and shut the door of her room behind her. She heard her mother moving about on the other side of the partition. Then all was silent there, but Dorilla herself made no preparations to retire for the night. Instead, she sat by the open window, gazing into the warm darkness, and listening to the rustling of the pines. After awhile she went out and sat on the stairway.

Thomas Keasbey had heard his wife and daughter depart for their rooms, and he supposed that by this time they were sound asleep. He was therefore talking unreservedly with the men in the parlor. Dorilla could hear almost every word which was said there. She heard directions given for the use of the explosives by means of which the bank safe was to be blown open, and what was to be done with the booty, when the job was completed and the smoke had cleared away. Then words fell from Mikey which made her blood run cold:

"The cashier sleeps there now, while all this money is there, as well as the watchman. We can manage the watchman well enough, but two of them won't be so easy—and the cashier is likely to be an ugly customer—that Wood. They say he isn't afraid of the devil himself."

"Mike, you're a —— fool!" Dorilla heard Thomas Keasbey rejoin fiercely. "What's that bottle of chloroform for? There's enough of it for four men, and it's to use. Then there is that coil of rope, and you ought to have three or four good gags in your pockets, every one of you. Tie his hands and eyes as quick as you can—and don't ask again what you will do with any man who gets in our way."

Dorilla heard allusions which showed her plainly what use had been made of her drawings. The whole terrible plot stood revealed to her in all its ghastliness. She reproached herself for a fool that she had not understood it from the first. Struck with a paralysis of horror, she sat on the stairway, as though she should never move again.

When the men began to push their chairs about on the bare parlor floor, however, she rose and fled softly into her room, closing the door and locking it behind her. Then she flung herself on her bed and wept wildly, wringing her hands and asking herself what she should do.

She heard the clock strike twelve. There was a sound of doors and windows opening and shutting. Then she heard the men tramping off. Hoarse voices uttered a few words under her window. She knew that the last details of the elaborate plot were now arranged. Then there was a dead silence. The very pines seemed to wait and listen.

Once she sprang up, determined to fly to the village and arouse her friend. She would tell Mrs. Wood of the danger that threatened her husband and the bank. Then they could go together and drive the men away. The next day, the hole which had been made through the ceiling could be filled up, and the Keasbeys and Mikey and the rest could vanish quietly from the place.

Thus reasoned the child within her, but the woman there laughed aloud at such silliness. "It would mean the whole town awake and excited," said the wiser mentor. "It would mean twenty years in prison, perhaps, for your father and for Mikey."

As she lay upon her bed, clutching the counterpane, and shuddering and groaning aloud, her father's kindness to her through all her life passed like a panorama before her. His old tenderness and goodness blotted out for a moment all his sternness and all the vices which had made her love him less this summer.

"It is for my sake that he is risking his life and his freedom to-night," she wept. "He wants to make a lady of me."

It seemed as though real and sinewy hands caught her heart between them and compressed it until it ached. She could hardly breathe. She rushed to the window for air.

"And Mikey!" she panted. "I couldn't give up Mikey! I don't so much mind the others. They are bad, through and through. But my father isn't. Anyway, he has always been good to me. And Mikey is good. That is what my father meant when he said that Mikey hadn't any nerve. Mikey said he was going to get into some sort of 'regular' business. I know now what he meant. He knows that I could never bear to have him doing things like this. He understands me. If he only gets along right to-night, he will turn over a new leaf, and become an honest man—and father, too."

Then she thought of the sisters at the convent, and their peaceful, virtuous lives. If they had quarrels or troubles, they had never let her know it. She imagined their dismay if they should learn that her father was a burglar.

She thought, too, of Mrs. Collis Wood. Her beautiful, innocent face seemed to rise out of the shadows and confront the girl only an arm's length away, and her eyes were brimming with reproachful tears.

"I loved you. I trusted you," the sweet mouth seemed to say, "and how have you rewarded me? I did everything in my power for you. I would have done more if you would have let me—and yet you have given over the one I love best to robbers—perhaps to murderers.

You have let thieves steal my property, and that of many other blameless people. Is this right?"

On the moment, the girl heard a fluttering in the darkness. Black as it was, she could dimly discern in it the shape of the great white moth, which had come to her when she had sat with her mother on the kitchen steps. She had kept it in her room, and had fed it ever since. Now it had flown away. She had never known one to fly away from her before. The superstition which had been bred in her by her sequestered life, and by the singular peculiarity which marked her, awoke with a passionate fervor.

"Come back!" she cried, with a shriek, which she instantly regretted, for she feared that it might have awakened her mother—but the moth had gone. She could hear its great wings beating the darkness, just beyond her reach.

"I must do it! It is right!" she murmured, over and over again. She ran into the hall, and listened at her mother's door. Mrs. Keasbey was breathing hard, and had evidently heard nothing. Dorilla envied her mother the power to sleep at such a time. Then the girl took off her shoes, weeping bitterly, but with unfaltering movements carrying out her determination. As she crept into the shadows of the forest and stooped to refasten her shoes, something brushed the air beside her. It was a great white moth. She felt sure that it was the one which had left her. Before she had risen, it had settled and was swaying upon the loose ringlets above her forehead.

*　　*　　*　　*　　*　　*　　*

Two hours later, she was lying, more dead than alive, upon the lace-covered bed of Mrs. Collis Wood. A serving woman stood over her, fanning her. There was a sudden rush of garments. White and startled, much as she had seen it in her vision on the hill, the face of her young teacher looked into Dorilla's.

"Can you bear it, Dorilla? Oh, I wonder if I ought to tell you! You must know it soon, but are you strong enough to bear it now?"

The girl nodded. All the fierceness and selfishness of her nature seemed gone. She was melted down to utter tenderness.

"My husband has been brought home. He is unconscious, but the doctor says that he will be all right before long—and you have saved his life!"

She could not go on for the tears which choked her.

"Well?" said Dorilla, raising herself on her elbow. Her voice showed that her nerves were strained to the last pitch of endurance.

"But your father—you know there was a hand-to-hand fight between his men and ours—and he was hurt, but not seriously. He will have to, oh, my poor Dorilla! he will probably have to serve a long term in prison. And—and—nobody was shot but one—he was shot—dead—the one you called Mikey."

Dorilla fell back on the bed. She had heard now all that she wanted to know.

Presently she sprang up and began with quivering hands to arrange her dress.

"You better lie still," the serving-woman warned her. "You don't look as if you'd oughter stand up. You'll faint away, first you know."

"Dorilla!" cried Mrs. Collis Wood, throwing her arms around the white and agitated girl, "don't think of leaving me! You are going to live always with me now!"

"No," said Dorilla, with the old dark look flashing

from her wild eyes. "I love you, and I always shall—but I can't live in the world any more. Don't you see? My heart is broken. I am young, I know—and you think I can get over things—but I can't. I have tried to do right, as you told me—and it has broken my heart."

"But you are needed in the world! We need women like you—brave and unselfish, and with quick minds to plan and do."

"No, I can't stand it," insisted the girl, wearily, but with a trace of her old fire. "I will go and get my mother. They will take us both there—at the convent. Just help me to get back to the convent. It will be the kindest thing you can do for me. I want to live there always with the sisters. You don't believe in masses for souls, or prayers for the dead—but don't you see I've got to? That's what I shall do now—offer them all the rest of my life—for—" she stopped, and the strained look gave way on her face, "I tell you my heart is broken."

She threw her arms around her friend, and they wept together.

*   *   *   *   *   *   *

When they had bound up Thomas Keasbey's wounds and led him away, it was broad daylight. His head was bandaged, and he had one arm in a sling, but he could see, and his mind was perfectly clear. Ever since the first onslaught of the constables upon them, he had been casting about for some explanation of the failure of the plans upon which he had expended his best thought for many months. He could not devise any.

The cashier's house was only a few doors away from the bank. As, held between two of his captors, Thomas Keasbey shuffled along past this house, he glanced downward. There lay a great white moth, trampled and dead.

He shook himself free for an instant, and with his sound arm picked up the soiled, exquisite thing. Then he turned furiously to the man beside him.

"It was a girl that gave us away, I reckon, wasn't it?"

The man hesitated a moment. Then he said: "Yes."

"Raldy."

A STORY OF THE WISCONSIN RIVER.

"WHAT'LL they do?"

"I'm sure I don't know."

"Sim won't work, and they're poor as poverty. It's a year since the wife died, and now the old mother's gone. She brought in the pennies right smart."

"There he is now."

The two women stopped their whispering as the tall, loosely-built figure of Sim Peebles came shambling along the ragged street of "Dearborn City."

A look of unmistakable affliction rested upon his weak but handsome face, and a rag of black stuff was tied decently about his shabby hat. Two children, little more than infants, came running to meet him from the low but fierce-fronted house, into which he finally entered with them, and then the two women went on with their interrupted conversation.

"Who's a-doin' things for them, anyhow? Who fixed *her?*"

"Him, I guess."

"Then he's smarter than I ever give him credit for."

A young woman who was walking hastily along the street had come close upon them while they were engaged in watching Sim Peebles, and had overheard these latter remarks of that gentleman's critics. She was above the medium height, and of a large and imposing figure, though far from graceful. Her large hands swung almost fiercely as she walked, and her tread was hard and masculine. With a mouth and chin handsomely and firmly though somewhat coarsely moulded, her broad and projecting forehead, and brilliant, fearless blue eyes, added to the heavy braids of flaxen hair which were wound neatly about her head, made her face striking, and even comely. The women turned with a start as they saw her, and realized that she had overheard them. Geralda, or, as she was commonly known, "Raldy," Scott was evidently a woman of whose opinion they stood somewhat in awe.

"*You* didn't offer to help Sim Peebles yesterday," Raldy Scott said disdainfully, pausing a moment in her hurried walk. "He was alone there with that dead woman and those little children, and yet you, his neighbors, women with husbands and children of your own, never offered to help him. You ought to be ashamed of yourselves," she continued, her eyes flashing, and her language, which had been much better than that of her slatternly neighbors, taking on in her excitement more of their peculiar Western twang. "And here, instead of walking up to his door and saying, 'Sim, can't we help you in your trouble?' you are standing in the street outside, wondering 'Who'll help him?' Raldy Scott despises lazy, shiftless Sim Peebles as much as you do; but she washed and dressed his dead mother for him, she fed his children, and, not being quite a brute, she proposes to take care of them till Sim Peebles can get somebody else. He swam in, when the Dells were full of ice, and got my father's body, so that his daughters could bury him decently, and Mart and I don't forget it."

Raldy Scott swung along, leaving her listeners half-stunned with her scathing rebuke.

"Humph!" said one of them sullenly; "mebbe Raldy Scott can't always carry things so high."

"But the men'll always stand up for her," said the other one dejectedly. "They think she's pow'rful smart because she's made two or three trips up in the pines and down on the rafts with the men. It must 'a' ben since you come here that she come back the last time with her drunken old father. She sorter looked after him, I reckon. He had fine airy ways, he had, and nothing but a tipsy Irishman, after all; and she with breeches and coat on, jest like the men. Oh," spitefully, "she ain't partick-eler, Raldy Scott ain't; can swim and pole a raft with any man in the Dells any day. Only since old Roy Scott died she dresses like the rest of us. Her sister Mart's goin' to get married. Likely she wants to, too"; and the two women laughed viperishly.

"Perhaps she'll get Sim Peebles," said the other, as they parted; "he's ben a likely young widower some time now," and they laughed a coarse, hateful laugh as they went to their homes.

The two or three scores of houses, many of them built of logs, which formed the homely, straggling street of Dearborn City, were inhabited almost wholly by lumber-men. During a large part of the year these men were away from their families, cutting wood in the pines; but when the ice began to break, and the great spring flood of the majestic Wisconsin rolled down from the north, they massed their logs into rafts, and came floating down the river to their homes. The village had been planted in the midst of the forest, and from many of its houses were visible the high red walls of the river, as it shot through its wonderful Dells, and the roar of its torrent rose upon their hearing perpetually. Just below the site of the village there was a break in the high red sandstone which lined the river for miles—with occasional rifts like this one—and here, when the current would permit, the rafts paused in the spring long enough for those to land who were not absolutely necessary to conduct the unwieldy argosies to the distant Mississippi. If the current were too strong for the rafts to stop, as was generally the case, the men sprang into the boiling rapids and swam ashore. Many a life, even of experienced river pilots, had been lost in the attempt, and it was in this way that Roy Scott had perished.

He had indeed been an Irishman, and a dissipated one, but he had belonged to a wealthy and honorable family. He squandered his patrimony early in life, however, emigrated to the New World, and pushed into the wilds of what was then the farthest West. There he became enamored of the exciting life of the lumbermen of the Wisconsin, entered into it, met and married a quiet Swede girl, the daughter of one of his hardy comrades, and from their strange union had sprung the gentle Martha and the large-featured, fair-haired Geralda, whose Northern phlegm and endurance were united with the quick wit and intense passion of her Irish ancestors.

Geralda Scott clung to the memory of her father with an almost sublime devotion. His varied knowledge, a certain bluff polish of manner which his wild and roving life had never entirely obliterated, and his feats of strength and bravery, which were many and remarkable, she loved to dwell upon. From the upper windows of the rude, high-fronted "shanty" in which she and her sister lived, they could see plainly, some fifty feet below the top of the red rock which bound the river, and a full two

hundred above the swirling rapids, the legend, in bold
white letters:

LEROY TALBOT SCOTT,
RIVER PILOT.
1843.

The girl never saw this without a secret thrill, for her
father, years before she was born, had climbed unaided up
the beetling crag, and had hung by one hand between
heaven and earth while he had written it.

"Humph, Mart Scott!" she had said, sharply, to her
quiet and unimpassioned sister, "what are you made of
that you can hear these things, and yet sit there like a
block?"

But Martha, with her pale Northern face and stolid
Swede manner, cared more for the stout young pilot who
was going to marry her than for all the stories of her
reckless father's exploits. To her, whose frame was less
robust than Ceralda's, and who had always lived at home
with her gentle mother, he had seemed only a carousing
debauchée, whose absence in the pines was a pleasant relief, and whose coming was dreaded like the coming of a
cyclone. To tell the truth, Martha regarded Raldy, who
at sixteen had donned man's attire, as the disapproving
neighbor had truly said, and had gone, under the leal
though maudlin protection of her father, to do lumbermen's work and share lumbermen's fare in the rough life
of the pineries—she regarded Raldy with almost as much
dread as she had had of her dead father. But Raldy Scott,
though she might be dreaded, was thoroughly respected
by every man, woman and child in Dearborn City. She
was the soul of honor, and by hard work and economy she

and Martha had managed to bury their father and mother decently, and then to pay off the mortgage on their little home. Raldy Scott had a brusque and forbidding manner, but, as Sim Peebles and many another man and woman had found out in times of trouble, underneath it beat a kind and generous heart.

Raldy Scott was as good as her word; and when the little funeral procession which followed Sim Peebles's mother to the grave moved away from the desolate hut, which Raldy's strong, neat hands had cleansed and purified, Raldy herself, with her brave, straightforward face held up defiantly to her gaping neighbors, had led one of the sobbing babies, while their shambling father, looking strangely kempt and tidy, walked beside the other. Then they had come home again to the little hut, and every day through the dreary November weather Raldy Scott had tended the orphaned children, and kept the cabin, hastening home, when the little ones were safely in bed, to Mart and her own trim, though only less humble, home.

"What you goin' to git for your pains, Raldy?" said a kindly old lumberman to her one day. He had befriended her father, and Raldy could not answer him curtly.

"Talk behind my back—and experience," said Raldy, half-smiling. But Mart was to be married at Christmas time, so that Raldy felt she could afford to earn less for a while; and, indeed, though she would not have allowed it to herself, she was becoming almost fond of the life which she was leading in Sim Peebles's cabin.

"You're a powerful hand to work, Raldy," said Sim to her one day, as he sat watching her swift and energetic movements about his cheerless little kitchen.

Raldy stopped, and squared her elbows, looking straight at him from under her great forehead.

"I'm setting you an example, Sim Peebles," she said slowly. "You're clever, and you're kind. You did me a great service once, and I'll never forget it; but if you had half the work in you that I have, you wouldn't be so all-possessed poor that you can't pay an honest woman for tending your wee bits and cooking your venison."

Raldy's tone forbade reply or argument, and Sim Peebles slunk guiltily away.

A day or two later he came in with a new brightness in his face.

"Say, Raldy," he began, half-sheepishly—for Sim Peebles had been "raised" in semi-luxury in an Eastern State, had loafed ever since he could remember, and hardly knew whether the announcement which he was about to make would be really creditable to him or not —"could you get along—I mean, would you stay and look after things here till I come back, if I go up in the pines till spring?"

Raldy laughed a rather incredulous laugh.

"What are you going to do up in the pines?" she asked at length.

"Chop," answered Sim Peebles succinctly.

"Humph! they've all gone long ago."

"No; there's a party going up to Stevens Point next week, and strike off from there."

"You can't chop," said Raldy contemptuously.

"Yes, I can, too."

"Well, then, go." Raldy spoke crustily. She would not give the peeping neighbors any chance to accuse her of spending soft words on Sim Peebles. Yet, truth to say, she no longer held him in the low respect which she had expressed in the screed delivered to her gossiping

8

neighbors, and which her language to him would seem to indicate. In these long, quiet weeks since she had come to live in his humble cabin, she had detected in the lonely, saddened man qualities which had softened her heart toward him. He loved his children, and though he knew little enough how to care for them, he yet "minded" them devotedly, in his own rough way. Then Sim Peebles's almost womanish face was yet handsome and attractive when it was clean and shaven; and one day Raldy had come unexpectedly upon him with his eyes wet with tears, gazing upon a picture, which her quick vision noted, before he could put it away, as a likeness of his old mother.

"Humph!" said Raldy to herself, quite angry at a little secret tenderness which the sight had evoked in her. "Sim Peebles puts on considerable about his mother; but I notice he didn't get her a new dress while she was here, and if she had enough to eat, it was because she hoed the clearing and dug the potatoes."

Still, it was a fact, and Raldy, in a dim, unwilling way, knew it, that she was daily growing to set a higher value upon Sim Peebles than he deserved, and she felt this more definitely than before when he told her that he was going "up in the pines." There was in her a strange, an unreasoning aversion to having him go, glad as she was to see him developing something of the courage of a man.

She had repelled so fiercely the young men who, won to admiration by her spirit and good looks, had dared to make her any overtures, that Raldy had never yet had a regular love-affair; but, as is often the case with a strong and self-reliant woman, weakness had won where force had failed. She could not help acting a little more tender and approachable than her wont as the day drew near for

Sim Peebles to go; and Sim—poor Sim, who had come to
worship the very ground that Raldy trod—Sim felt it, but
he did not dare to speak.

He was to start on a Monday, and Raldy had patched
and darned his clothes till he was fit to go. Sunday
morning she went, as usual, to the little Lutheran chapel,
the only place of worship which Dearborn City afforded,
and where her mother had been one of the most devoted
attendants; and having come home again, she got the
dinner and fed the children. Then she turned them out
to play in the clearing, and leaving the door ajar—for it
was one of the mildest and pleasantest days of early
winter—she went singing about her work. Sim Peebles
watched her as she moved here and there, and Raldy,
independent and imperious though she was, stole now and
then a furtive glance at him.

"He's handsome," she thought dreamily, as she gave
a casual glance at Sim's waving hair and large brown
eyes; "but," coming to herself a little, " how shiftless he
is! But he's kind," wandering off again, "and he's done
some brave deeds—but no pride, no ambition. Still, he's
honest," thought Raldy again; "nobody ever said Sim
Peebles wasn't honest; there's nothing mean about Sim
Peebles, and that's one reason," excusingly, "why he's so
poor." Then her thoughts drifted off to what Mrs. Jenks
and Mrs. Smith, her hateful neighbors, would say, if she
should happen, by chance—of course she wouldn't, even
if Sim should ask her—but what would they all say, what
would Mart say, if she should ever happen to marry Sim
Peebles?

Here Raldy checked herself, for she was standing absently, with a plate of butter in her hand, the butter in

great danger of slipping, and her song quite still. She had been singing the old revival hymn:

"And when I pass from here to Thee,
Dear Lord, dear Lord, remember me."

Sim saw his opportunity, and seized it, and as she hurried into the little pantry and out again, he spoke quietly and earnestly:

"That's what I've been thinking, Raldy—something like, I mean. When I'm gone away, remember me."

"I'm not likely to forget you, with the youngsters under my feet all day," retorted Raldy, with asperity.

"You have been very kind to me and mine," continued Sim, with a choice of words which proclaimed an early training greatly superior to that of the rough men around him. Raldy recognized this superiority. It was, indeed, one of Sim's strongest claims upon her favor. But she was not to be tempted from her rôle.

"I didn't suppose you had noticed it," she said tartly.

"Noticed it! Why, Raldy!" in a tone of deep reproach. "And you can't think—I wanted to tell you before I went away—you can't think, Raldy, how it kind o' spurs me up to try and be somebody. That's what makes me want to go up river now. I want to show you, Raldy—I want—." But here Sim Peebles choked up. His courage had given out. Raldy felt hers oozing out too.

"I guess I'll go home till supper," she said, and she darted away.

After supper she put the children to bed, and then brushed up the hearth and put the little cabin to rights, Sim meanwhile devouring her, as usual, with his eyes.

Raldy had captured him, soul and body, and the nearer he came to the sublime sacrifice which he felt that he was making for her sake, the more completely his passion dominated him.

Raldy moved for her hat and shawl, and murmured something, in a manner strangely unlike herself, about "going home to Mart," when Sim Peebles caught her hand—no man had ever dared to touch Raldy Scott's person before—and begged her to sit down for a moment with him by the fire.

"You know," Sim said brokenly, and with a face like ashes, "it's my last night, Raldy." With all his love, he stood in absolute terror of her.

Raldy sat down with a strange docility, but Sim could not speak, after all, and they sat for several moments in silence.

"Well," said Raldy at last, getting up in her old arrogant way, "I guess I'll go."

"Say first," said Sim, swallowing hard, and catching at her hand again, "tell me first, Raldy, that maybe, when I come home, if I do well, Raldy, and turn out better, that——," he paused.

"That what?" questioned Raldy, in so gentle a tone that Sim took heart wonderfully.

"That maybe you'll—you'll marry me, and live here always, and see to the children."

It was all out now, and Sim drew a deep sigh as he turned his handsome, effeminate face, almost strong in its expression of intense love, full upon the strangely hesitating woman.

Raldy dropped into her seat again, and buried her face in her hands. Then she let them fall slowly, and said.

with a serious and deliberative air which would have daunted a less persistent suitor:

"You're an honest fellow, Sim, and you know that's a good deal to me—and you're good-looking, but I declare I don't know of any other earthly reason why I should marry you. You couldn't support me. How you have had to fly around to get enough to eat since I have been here! And what wages have you paid me?"

Sim fairly cowered before her; but, with a woman's perversity, Raldy Scott's love only burned the more fiercely.

"It's all true," he said mournfully, "but don't you see, Raldy, I'm turning over a new leaf? I'm going to work, and I'm going to show you, and the rest of them, that I can be like other men."

As Raldy looked at him, a tear glittered in her eye.

"Well," she said, rising, and with no hint in her voice of the tear, "when you come back'll be time enough to see."

"Oh, but Raldy," cried poor Sim, who had reached just the point where "despair sublimes to power," "won't you tell me that you love me—just a little?" He fell on the floor at her feet, and buried his face in her dress. "Haven't you any thought about me," he went on piteously, "only that I'm a worthless fellow?"

"Sim, you fool," said Raldy, raising him up with more tenderness than her words would seem to warrant, "do you suppose that I would have let you go on this way if I hadn't? Good-by, Sim;" and slipping away before he could stop her, Raldy left him with such consolation as he could gather from her last remark.

Sim did not go till nine o'clock the next morning, and meant to have a few words more with Raldy before he left; but she was as cold and incisive as usual, when she came at daybreak, and she went about her work in a way that precluded further conversation. Once she colored violently when Sim caught her eye, and some tender words rose to his lips at the sight; but she looked at him again so sternly that he was glad to withdraw into himself, and dared not plead his cause any further.

The days of the winter wore slowly away, while Raldy did her self-appointed task, and bore unflinchingly the slurs of the gossips and the thousand little irksome trials of her position. At last the intense cold began to yield. March glided into April. The ice in the river thawed, and daily among its floating masses came down great rafts of logs, guided by sturdy lumbermen, whose cries echoed and re-echoed from the mighty walls of the river, and gladdened the waiting hearts in the little village.

"When will our men come?" an aged lumberman, too old to go "up river" any more, shouted as one great raft became wedged between rocks and ice, near enough for a little conversation amid the tremendous tumult.

"In a week or two," shouted back a man who lived at the next landing, and knew them well. There was no time for further talk, for the great raft just then made free, and swung into the current, and with the loud cries of the men as they plied their heavy poles, and the rescuing and clambering up of several who had been swept off, as they often were in the dipping and swaying of the raft on its perilous passage, it was carried out of sight, the echoes of the hubbub lingering long after the vision had vanished.

All along the straggling, forlorn, burned, stumpy street of Dearborn City, with its staring hotel, its half-dozen beer saloons, and its one small meeting-house,

ran the good news, "The men will be back in a week or
two." Raldy Scott sang more blithely over her work,
while visions of Sim Peebles in an absurdly glorified
aspect floated all day through her mind, though, if anybody had insinuated as much to her, she might have
raised the old shot-gun in the corner, which no man in
Dearborn City could handle better than she, and have
shot him dead on the spot. Still, she had to acknowledge to herself the alarming extent of her infatuation,
and chide herself a little. "I don't care," her heart had
answered; "there's something about Sim Peebles that I
like, and if he likes me, what difference does it make to
anybody? There's nobody in this world who can dictate
to Raldy Scott"; and Raldy drew herself up proudly.
"He needs me—I can see that I'm just the woman he
needs; and I like weak creatures. And he's honest, if
he is shiftless; he wouldn't defraud a man out of a cent."

Raldy's straightforward soul clung desperately to
that—Sim Peebles was honest. He might drink sometimes, though Raldy had never seen him the worse for
liquor, but everybody called him "an honest fellow."

"Yes," Raldy said to herself over and over again,
"he's a true, well-meaning man, and I like him; and if
I want to marry him when he gets back, I'll do it,
whether Mart or anybody objects or not."

The days dragged somewhat as a week went by and
the men did not come; but Raldy read once again the
few books which her father had left her, and which she
had already worn threadbare, did her daily work, and
tried to be patient, and every afternoon she went with the
children down to the landing to watch the rafts.

It was Friday afternoon, and the April sunshine was
warm and bright, when the noise of a great drive,

manned by strangers, having just died away, a new one was heard coming down the Dells. The voices seemed to Raldy's quick ear familiar ones. She had thrown her long, heavy red cloak, such as all the Norse women wear, around her to cover her house dress, which consisted, as her mother's had before her, of a short stuff petticoat and a black bodice over a coarse woollen waist, and she drew her cloak closer, and gazed fixedly up the river, where the rafts always shot suddenly into view around a great bend.

The voices grew more distinct: "Halloo!" "Bear a hand!" "Shove her in, boys!" "Keep her steady!" And the great drive came thundering into view, rising and sinking, creaking and rubbing, the strong poles keeping her clear of the rocks, and the shouts of the men coming down with startling clearness on the gentle wind.

A cry arose from the men on shore. Yes, there were their friends and neighbors, and there—there was Sim Peebles, straighter than his wont, standing on the very edge of the logs, ready to leap into the current and swim ashore, for it was impossible to push the raft to land. Half-a-dozen others were beside him, mostly the older ones, whose families needed them. The youngsters would see the raft safe to its destination.

On swept the great drive, the men redoubling their cries as the passage became narrower and more dangerous; and just as they shot under the great white name of Leroy Scott, the river pilot, one after another of the black figures who were waiting sprang into the water, and began to struggle for the shore.

Raldy's pulses quickened, and a longing for her old wild life came over her. She had more than once made that leap herself, and no man of them all had battled more stoutly and resolutely than she with the freezing rapids.

One after another of the swimmers came safely through
the two or three rods of foaming, icy water, which were
all that were necessary in order to reach the shore; but as
Sim Peebles sank after his plunge, a dozen floating logs
passed over him. The logs were carried on, but he did
not rise; another moment; still he did not rise.

Raldy Scott paused for no second thought. A strap-
ping fellow near her was pulling off his coat; but before
he could do it, she had flung her heavy cloak aside, bared
her arms, and dashed past him. She was a bold and
vigorous swimmer, and fought her way desperately to the
place where Sim went down. Suddenly a man's white
face glared from the water, ten feet away. His eyes were
set, and his mouth was open. Raldy struggled toward
him, seized his collar, and with the assistance of the young
man, who had reached the spot just in time to help her
bring her burden in, she towed him ashore. Once there,
she lifted him as though he had been a baby, and poured
the water from his lungs, loosened his coarse shirt,
breathed into his bloodless lips, and poured a few drops
of brandy down his throat, chafing his hands and chest
meanwhile. Then she listened for his heart-beats, and a
look of relief passed over her stern face.

"He all right, boys," she said, turning carelessly to the
breathless crowd about her. "Here, you Sam Jenks, and
the rest of you, you can carry him home. You'll find
things all right there," and flinging her cloak around her,
Raldy called the children and strode off, and by the time
the men had fairly revived Sim Peebles, and had got him
home, Raldy was at the door to meet them, her drenched
clothes exchanged for dry ones, and the wet braids of her
fair hair alone revealing that she had dared, not an hour

before, the perils of the Dells of the Wisconsin for the sake of Sim Peebles.

"I hope," said Mrs. Jenks viciously, as she passed out with the rest of the crowd that had seen Sim safe home—"I hope you'll get paid somehow, Raldy, for all you've done; and I rather guess," with a meaning, and to Raldy an utterly maddening, leer—"I rather guess you're going to get something or other."

Mrs. Jenks discreetly passed out of ear-shot as she uttered her last words, the effect of which upon Raldy was rather impaired by the noise of the clink of glasses in the dingy little saloon opposite, and the voice of Mr. Jenks, raised purposely, so that Raldy might hear it—"I give you Raldy Scott, boys, the smartest girl on the Wisconsin River."

Raldy's training had not, unfortunately, taught her, much as she disliked drinking, to feel toward it exactly as an "Ohio crusader," and she took a grim satisfaction in imagining Mrs. Jenks's wrath when she too heard the toast, as she could not well help hearing it, and in thinking that these rough men, no one of whom would dare to speak to her save in the deepest respect, yet admired her with all their souls.

In a few days Sim Peebles was all right again. He seemed in excellent spirits; but it was not until he had been at home for nearly a week that Raldy gave him any chance to "speak out." Then he contrived it only by desperately barricading the door, and sitting down in front of it, just as she was about going home for the night.

"I want to tell you something," he said piteously, for Raldy was severely on her dignity.

Raldy concluded to be cornered, and sat down to listen to him.

"I've saved up my pay," continued Sim, speaking a trifle hurriedly, "and I've done well, Raldy. I can support you well now. I got an extra job up there, and—and made some money out of that, and I've really done well, Raldy; you ask the fellows if I haven't."

Something in his manner made the quick-witted woman pause and look at him suspiciously; but as she looked, she saw nothing but Sim Peebles's handsome face, and great pleading brown eyes full of adoration for her, and she flung her suspicions to the winds.

"Well," she said calmly, "if you have money, you'll find use for it. I suppose you know by this time that I've run up quite a bill at the store since you went away; I told them there that I'd foot it, if you didn't."

"I'll foot it—I'll foot everything," said Sim deliriously, taking her nonchalance, as well he might, for direct encouragement; "I've got enough to last us well for a good while, Raldy. And so it's all right, isn't it?—isn't it, Raldy?"

He rose to his full height with a sudden dilation of impetuous passion, which compelled the scornful woman's admiration. Then he stretched out his arms to her mutely, and she let them fold her in.

She had been starved for love. "Now," she said to herself, laying aside all of her coldness and her asperity—"now I will love him as other women love. I will marry him. He has proved his love to me. He is going to be a different man, and I am his motive. I will believe in him; I will be a true wife to him, and a mother to his little children." And she did not chide Sim Peebles as he rained kisses upon her fair hair and her smooth, broad forehead.

"To-morrow—to-morrow, Raldy," pleaded her intoxicated lover; "marry me to-morrow!"

"No," Raldy said thoughtfully, becoming herself again suddenly, and tearing herself away from him—"no; one week from to-day I'll marry you, Sim. And if I put this trust in you, Sim"—with a sudden quiver in the clear voice, which thrilled all through Sim Peebles's poor shivering soul—"you won't disappoint me, Sim, you'll never disappoint me?"

"Never, Raldy, never," he said, with an almost manly tenderness, and he drew her unresisting face to him and kissed her once again before she passed through the door to her home.

Raldy's preparations for her wedding were few and very private. She did not tell even Mart. "If I choose to throw myself away," she said to herself—for Raldy Scott knew well that from the head of the Wisconsin to the Mississippi there wasn't a woman to equal her—"if I choose to throw myself away on Sim Peebles, it's nobody's business but my own. They'll talk enough afterward—and they may."

At last came the morning of the day which Raldy had set for her wedding; and Sim went about with a look of bliss upon his face which would have told the story to the whole neighborhood, in spite of his solemn promise to Raldy not to reveal it, if she had not studiously kept him busy upon the place in making up the garden.

They were to be married at noon. Eleven o'clock was near at hand, and Raldy called out softly to Sim to see to the children. She was going over to Mart's to put on her best dress, and was hurrying out of the gate, when she encountered Mrs. Jenks.

"Good-morning," said that lady beamingly.

Instead of pushing past her contemptuously, as she would usually have done, something made Raldy stop civilly.

"Glad to see Sim's getting ahead a little," said Mrs. Jenks, with a smirk.

Raldy stared at her mutely, and did not stir.

"Sorry he's come by his money just as he has, though," went on Mrs. Jenks, sending her shaft well home.

The color left Raldy's steady face, and her mind flew back to the momentary suspicion with which she had first received the news of Sim's good fortune.

"How is that?" she said imperiously.

"Oh, don't you know?" rejoined Mrs. Jenks innocently. "All Dearborn's talkin' about it. You know Sim ain't oversmart about coverin' up his tracks."

"Well?" said Raldy breathlessly, as her tormentor paused.

"You know old Jake Torrey died up in the pines six weeks ago?"

"Yes, yes," impatiently.

"And maybe you know he died all alone with Sim Peebles?"

Raldy did not know it, but she bowed her head.

"At least," said Mrs. Jenks spitefully, "Sim thought he was alone, but my Sam happened to be within hearing, just out of sight, and he heard old Jake say, 'Take this money, Sim, and send it to my daughter in Varmount,' and he told him where, and Sim writ it down, and," went on Mrs. Jenks, with satisfaction enough to atone for all the innumerable slights and snubs that she had received at Raldy's hands, "and then the old man dropped away; but Sim, mind yer, he never said a word, not he, but he's come all of a sudden by a big pile, so he makes his brag—'extra job,' he says, I hear." And Mrs. Jenks passed on.

Raldy went a few steps further, her proud head bowed a little, and her firm step slow and faltering. Then she turned quickly, and re-entered Sim Peebles's little cabin. The children were playing outside, and she closed and bolted the door behind her as she went in. Then she motioned to Sim to sit down opposite her. Her keen, indignant eyes searched him through and through. He looked back at her for a moment with all the fond joy of an expectant bridegroom. Then the purpose of her gaze seemed to penetrate him. The light went out from his face, his eyelids drooped, his head fell. Then he groaned aloud, and she knew that Mrs. Jenks's story was true.

"Sim," she said softly, "is it true? Tell me as you would tell your Maker"; and there was a ring in her low tone which compelled him to be honest with her. "Did you take that money that Jake Torrey left you for his daughter, and pretend that it was your own?"

"Oh, Raldy," he began weakly, "not all—oh, not nearly all. You can write——"

She interrupted him sternly. "Did you take any of that money, Sim?"

"Just enough," he said pleadingly, "just enough to pay me for doing the business, you know, Raldy—not much, you know. Oh, Raldy, you won't cast me off for that, will you? Oh, not now, Raldy, not now!" and the man, putting his head in her lap, wept bitterly.

She stroked his hair tenderly, but her firm face did not weaken.

"I have thought a great deal of you, Sim," she said in a dry, hard voice, suddenly rising and pushing him from her, "but now that I find that you are a mean and dis-

honest man—that you can cheat the dead, Sim—that's all
over.   I hope you'll get somebody to take care of the
children, Sim, for I must go.   I reckon I'll go down to
Fond du Lac or Milwaukee, and go out to service. Mart's
married, and"—wearily—"I might as well."

She turned before his face, unlatched the humble
door, through which an hour hence she had thought to
walk as a bride, and before he could open his paralyzed
lips to speak, she was gone.   And Sim Peebles never saw
her again.

The Charcoal Burners.

THERE was not a cloud in the sky. The whole long, undulating range of the Green Hills stood out vividly in the light. This made the smoke rising from the top of Sherbury more than usually conspicuous. Sherbury was only a knoll, compared with the loftiest of its neighbors: but it was peculiarly placed, and could be seen as far up and down the valley as old Killington itself. Since Josef Varvin had taken to burning charcoal up there, people called Sherbury "the Volcano." The old Frenchman had built half-a-dozen great kilns on the top of it, and its vast forests were falling in order to feed them. It was said that he was growing rich. He employed now about a hundred hands in felling trees and tending the kilns. There was, therefore, quite a little settlement on the summit of Sherbury, and the roads up and down its sides were almost impassable from the wear and tear of the heavy teams. Most of the families who lived in this new "Smoke City," as it was called, were Canadian French, like Josef Varvin himself. There was no church, but once a month the Catholic priest came up there to preach in the school-house. It was not considered by the inhabitants of the surrounding country that a very high state of civilization prevailed in that part of Sherbury township which was known as "Smoke City."

It had to be admitted by everybody, however, that there was a garden in Smoke City which could not be excelled in the whole State of Vermont. It belonged to Pierre Beaubien, who had learned the florist's business in Montreal, and it had been wrought by him out of the primeval forest in the space of only five years. I have said, "by him:" but Marie, his wife, and Pierrette, his daughter, had done as much in the matter, perhaps, as had he himself. To be sure, they kept a houseful of boarders during the busy time, and always two or three, so that their domestic cares were not inconsiderable; but then Pierre had his work at the kiln to do also, and sometimes there were whole days when he could not touch his garden from morning to night.

On account of this garden, in which the Beaubiens took a justifiable pride, it was felt among their neighbors that they held themselves as quite the aristocracy of Smoke City. Old Adolph Roney could read, and write both French—Parisian French—and English, and had a shelf of books hanging in his best room, —which was also his dining-room and kitchen, except during the warmest weather. Pierre Beaubien and his wife could not read a line in either tongue, and his eighteen-year-old daughter, Pierrette, had never gone to school until the family had come to Smoke City, five years before.

"These Beaubiens are clean people, and they know how to make a garden," old Adolph would growl, as he sat smoking his pipe beside his kitchen door, and looking over toward the spring beauty bursting forth from every nook and corner of his neighbor's far from extensive inclosure opposite; "but why should his Pierrette snub my Jeanne and my Marceline? Are Beaubiens any better than Roneys? Am I not descended from that famous count who was one of the generals of Louis XI.? Have I not read it all in the book on my shelf yonder?

And who are they? They can scarcely tell the names
of their own grandfathers! Bah!"

And yet old Adolph was nettled by the hauteur of
his neighbors, though there was an inexpressive something about them which exacted deference from everybody. Even Josef Varvin, while he would not have
owned it for the world, felt it; but he was far enough
above his laborers to feel rather proud of the Beaubiens
and their airs, for which he reasoned they had not in-
sufficient grounds. He liked to see the tall, straight
mother and daughter—the daughter taller by a head—
moving about among their bright blossoms, or training
the peas and hops which filled the ample vegetable
patch behind the flowers.

"At any rate, they don't gossip," Josef Varvin said
to his wife with a grin.

No, they did not gossip. They were too "high and
mighty" for that. Still, even the Beaubiens were interested when one day—that bright day when there were
no clouds, and everything seemed to be at peace—Larle
Pichaud had a strange visitor. Larle Pichaud was on
the very top of a kiln, when the stage which passed
through Smoke City twice a day came along. Suddenly
the vehicle stopped in front of the kiln, and a woman
sprang down from it, shouting angrily the name of the
handsome young charcoal burner, and daring him to come
and meet her. A crowd of the villagers gathered in less
than ten minutes, listening speechlessly while the woman,
pale with rage, stood pouring out a torrent of abuse, in
mingled French and English, upon his head.

Even Marie and Pierrette Beaubien had come
among the others, and with open mouths had
watched Larle Pichaud, who seemed too bewildered to

know just what to do, while he scrambled down from the kiln and stood before the woman, begging her to keep still and to go to his house. His young wife, who was scarcely older than Pierrette herself, and had been her schoolmate, sat, white and scared, on a stump near by, holding her three-months' baby. She was a daughter of one of the charcoal burners, and her father and brothers also were gazing on the scene with fierce, menacing brows. Then everybody had heard Larle say, "I thought you were dead, Aline," upon which the woman had given him the lie and had sprung on him like a wild beast. The men standing by tore her away from him, but it took four of them to hold her and get her to the cell at the back of Josef Varvin's barn, where offenders against the law were usually locked up. Pierrette Beaubien shrieked, as did all the other women, when they saw Larle Pichaud's face bleeding, and traced the marks of the woman's nails on his cheeks and forehead. There had never been such a day as that in Smoke City. Larle, as well as the woman, was finally arrested, but before many weeks he came home to his distracted young wife. The case had been settled somehow. All that the people ever knew was that he had made love to the hot-blooded young creature—who was, however, older than himself—but had grown to hate her because of her violent temper, and had broken off the match, two years or more before. Then he had got married at once to somebody else. It was easy enough; all the women were wild after him. Another story was that the wronged woman was always sweet and gentle until her lover had deserted her, when she had been rendered insane by his heartlessness, and after brooding over her sorrow till she could bear it no longer, she had sought him out, and at-

Framingham State College
Framingham, Massachusetts

tacked him before the very eyes of the innocent girl who
had married him.

Pierrette had her own theories of the matter, and
from that day she hated the sight of the handsome charcoal burner—by far the handsomest man in Smoke City
—though previously she had greatly admired him, always secretly, and never with any glow of love. Pierrette had never been in love in her life, unless with her
ravishing beds of roses and chrysanthemums.

One day she met pretty Fernande Pichaud alone upon
the road, and said scornfully to her, "How could you
keep on loving Larle Pichaud, and let him come back
and live with you? Do you not believe that he used to
love that poor girl who flew at him?"

The young wife replied only by a frightened sob.
Pierrette had spoken very harshly.

"I would die before I would love him again, after
that—for all his fine, black eyes," Pierrette had scoffed
on; "I would rather die than that he should ever kiss
me again."

Fernande had only cried the faster, and hugged closer
the babe in her arms while she hurried away. Pierrette Beaubien looked after her, her strong proud face,
brown and firm-set usually, now flushed and working
with passion. It was clearer in her mind than ever—as
it might have been, and probably was, in the minds of
her neighbors—that there was something radically different in the blood of the Beaubiens from this girl's and
the others'.

"Yes, I would die," repeated Pierrette to herself, as
she watched Fernande scudding off with her child; "I
would be torn limb from limb before I would let him
come back to me. I would take my baby in my arms

and work in the kilns as my father does, before I would
touch a cent of Larle Pichaud's money again.   I would
not care how black my face and hands got!   Ugh!"

That summer the garden was a perfect dream of beauty.
It had never been so fine.   It was perhaps three acres
in extent, and was fenced about rudely but closely with
brush, over which Pierre Beaubien had trained morning-
glories and convolvulus and clematis and honeysuckle,
until it was as fair as the very dawn.   It seemed as though
he had but to tell a vine to grow in a certain way, in
order to make it take the direction he desired.   There was
scarcely an uncovered space on the whole brush-fence.
It was either freshly green or gay with bloom everywhere.

August came, and the Beaubien garden was a tangle
of golden glory.   Most people do not work much in
their gardens in August, but every morning, almost as
faithfully as in May and June, the Beaubiens were astir
by daybreak, weeding, watering, seed-gathering, training.   The other dwellers in Smoke City might call
them "cold" and "stuck up," but there was a passion in
them for this little plot of ground and its products,
which proved that their "coldness" was not a thing of
universal application.   And any one who ever thought
of such subjects must have admitted that their presence
in Smoke City was a distinct source of refinement and
elevation to the place—with its unpainted cabins, its
smutty-faced men, its swearing teamsters, its unfenced
door-yaids, still full of stumps from the recent clearing
of its forests, and its swarms of neglected, jabbering
children.   There would have been almost nothing to re-
deem its sordidness and ugliness, but for that rare, sweet
garden of the proud, unneighborly Beaubiens.

There was a great rush of business as the fall came on. The kilns had never time to cool off. The charcoal had to be taken out almost before it was well burned through. Josef Varvin was even compelled to use again the large old kiln with which he had first begun the business all by himself, and which he had not used now for several years. It had not been very strong, to begin with, and at last it had been patched up with skins and timbers. Into the deep earth-hole beneath it a rude causeway led, roofed over partly with earth and partly with boards. It was closed at the entrance with a clumsy, but tight-fitting, door. One of the hands, who had gone in there to warm himself on a cold day, had pulled to this door and had fallen asleep. He had been suffocated by the fumes of the charcoal. Josef Varvin had found him insensible, and had with his own hands carried him into the open air and tried to resuscitate him, but without success. The old man had never got over the shock. He was kind-hearted, and it had quite unnerved him. The kiln had not been used since then. But now sentiment and superstition were alike laid aside. Josef Varvin must use any means in his power to fill his orders. The old kiln was repaired afresh, and once more the slow smoke came curling out from the round hole in the top.

An influx of new workmen came too. Within the space of a fortnight a dozen were added to the force. The September haze was never so thick. The tourists who climbed Killington and Pico declared that Sherbury Mountain must be on fire, because it was covered with such a cloud of smoke. But all these were only the signs of Josef Varvin's prosperity. The long loft above the three rooms in which the Beaubiens lived had had two pallets laid beside the two beds there in which their regular boarders slept, for two new men who could get no other resting-place in the crowded little city.

One day Adolph Roney came hurrying into the Beaubien garden, where his neighbors were hard at work.

"A new man has come, Pierre," he said, deferentially. "He is a nephew of mine—André Reboul. But I cannot take him, for my house is full. We would like to have him near us, and we all know how well Madame Beaubien would feed him. Cannot you make room for him?"

It was finally decided that another pallet could be laid upon the already well-filled floor of the Beaubien loft, and one was hastily constructed. The Beaubiens were thrifty. They meant to gather in all the pennies that they found in their way. That night André Reboul slept on the new husk pallet, and the next morning he ate an abundant portion of the savory croquettes which Pierrette fried for breakfast.

He was a tall, strong, good-looking fellow—this newcomer. Pierrette was half a head taller than her father, but André Reboul was a head taller than she. He carried himself well. He was not handsome with the picturesque beauty of Larle Pichaud, but he had a firm, well-curved cheek, a flowing black mustache, a masterful dark eye, and a well-set head. His voice was a trifle harsh and thick, and he spoke no English. He watched Pierrette sharply while she served the breakfast. It was a new thing for her to be much noticed by men. Her face was irregular, and her nose had a contemptuous turn to it which was not likely to please a stranger, while her tongue was well supplied with stinging words, which she bestowed freely upon those who did not please her. She liked the appearance of old Adolph's nephew, however, and did not resent his observation. She was even pleased when she fancied that his tone softened in addressing her. Seeing him, it suddenly occurred to her, was like finding a plant in bloom which she had never seen before. There was an interest in it.

When the dishes were washed, the kitchen swept, and the soup set boiling for dinner, Pierrette went out to her garden, but she did not seem to get along very fast. Instead of cutting away dead stalks and collecting the seeds in little papers, as she had been set to do, she found herself leaning against the trellises and holding her shears absently in her hands, while she looked toward the woods in which the old kiln lay. André Reboul was at work there. She imagined him coming along the road to his dinner. Then she was seized with a sudden spasm of fear lest the soup should burn, and she hurried into the house to look after it. When she came out, her mother said, "Why did you go in, child?"

"I wanted to see if the soup was burning."

"How could it?" asked her mother almost angrily. Had not the soup boiled calmly away on the stove every morning, now these many years? Was the girl going crazy?

It seemed a long time to Pierrette before the sun had reached the middle of his course. The table had been laid. (There was no cloth on the Beaubien table except on feast days.) Everything was shining neat. The soup was done to a turn—thick with peas and lentils and garlic. The tall young figure of André Reboul came out from between the trees and into the road, just as Pierrette had pictured it. There were six other men in the family, all of them young and not ill-looking.

Only two of them were married. They were to bring
their families down to Smoke City soon, if Josef Varvin
should decide that he would want them during the winter. Pierrette had seen the others come to their dinners
now for many a day—yet she had not watched for any
one of them to appear in sight upon the road. As she
turned back to place the mustard on the table and get
the tea, a sudden thought came over her. Did that
foolish wife of Larle Pichaud like to see him coming
along the road as she, Pierrette Beaubien, liked now to see
this stranger? Perhaps Fernande Pichaud had liked to see
him as much when she had known him only as long. Perhaps she had kept liking it better and better day by day
through all those months. If she had—a sudden under-
standing of the case came over the mind of the simple,
haughty French girl.

When the twilight drew on, Pierrette strayed, as usual,
out into the garden. Some of the men followed, and
strolled up and down the borders, smoking their pipes
and talking together. There were great bowers of nasturtiums in bloom. The beds of marigolds sent up a
pungent odor. Long lines of brilliant, speared gladiolus
seemed to be marching with banners across the garden.
Bushes of blood-red salvia were just beginning to flower.

"You did not cut away this bed of withered stalks, as
I bade you this morning," grumbled Pierre Beaubien to
his daughter as she came dreamily along the path.

"I worked all the morning," she protested.

"Oh, but so slow! Mon Dieu! I watched you. You
dropped your shears a dozen times. You are getting
too vain. Why is your hair braided so finely this evening?"

Pierrette's brown face flushed like the salvias. She

tossed her head, and drew herself up until she towered far above her shrunken little father.

"You want me like the Roneys and the Bellons, then?" she said, scornfully. "You would like my hair hanging off in little locks all over. That would be very tidy, I think! People might at least keep themselves as well as their gardens."

She tossed her head again and walked away. She was in no mood to be scolded. She had hoped that André Reboul would come out into the garden after supper, like the other men, but, instead, he had gone over to see his cousins. It piqued her very much. The next few days she scarcely spoke to him, and she kept her fine, gray eyes fixed on the ground whenever he drew near.

A week passed by, and André Reboul had not yet walked in the garden with the other men in the twilight. Some evenings he had had to go down and watch the old kiln. Generally he spent the time with the Roneys. Pierrette could hear their gay voices as they talked, though seldom his. He was either very shy or very morose. At any rate, he said little, and he spoke almost always in that harsh, forbidding tone. But Pierrette still fancied that, when he spoke to her, his voice sounded different. She would not care for that, however, she told herself. He did not seem to seek her society, and she was determined that she would be as distant as he was.

On the evening of the tenth day after André Reboul came to live in the Beaubien household he did not go down to the old kiln, nor over to the next house. Two or three of the boarders sat down on the rough door-step and smoked their pipes; the others strolled about aimlessly, as usual. Pierre and Marie were picking late beans, hurrying to get in all that they could before dark.

Pierrette was clattering the dishes in the kitchen. One of the young men came in and asked her for a drink of water from the pump in the sink. She gave it to him, good-humoredly enough, and then he lingered a moment, chaffing her.

The sound of his bantering voice and a brief word or two from her came plainly out at the door. Suddenly Pierrette said, loudly and crossly, "I would thank you to go about your business!" and the young fellow came slinking, with a flushed face, out along the pathway. Shortly afterward Pierrette came out also. Her movements were slow and sulky, but she held herself up as proudly as ever. She made her way to the aster bed and stood there, gazing down at the beautiful flowers, which the two or three light frosts of September had not injured. To-night it was as warm as early August. The flowers seemed to revel in the heat as though they knew it would soon fail them.

Pierrette had not noticed that André Reboul was leaning against the house when she came out. She had been too angry with Nicholas Coigny, who had just tried to kiss her, to pay much attention to her surroundings, and she supposed that André had gone over to see his cousins.

Presently she was aware that there was some one beside her, and she started a little when the voice of André Reboul said softly, in his thick, broad French: "You like these flowers the best?"

"No—no," stammered Pierrette, warm waves of color chasing each other over her strong French face; "I like them all—some at one time, some at another."

"You have been troubled," he went on, looking squarely into her eyes.

"I—I did not say so."

"Oh, no!" The tall stranger spoke a little bitterly. "You tell me nothing. You speak to me as though— as though I were a lump of charcoal. Mon Dieu! I might be a dog!"

"I?" The girl lifted her thick, black eyebrows, incredulously. "I—I did not dare to speak to you. I—I thought that it was you that treated me as though I were a dog."

Then they laughed into each other's eyes.

"I have wanted to come out into the garden every evening," he said, "but I was afraid that you would snub me."

"Oh, you must have known better!" she smiled back to him, reprovingly. "I would have liked to have you come."

"Mon Dieu! Why did you not say so?"

"I am not running after people to come and walk in my garden!"

They both laughed again. It seemed as though a chain had been subtly clasped, joining them together in the twinkling of an eye.

Silently they walked along to the other end of the garden. The dew was as heavy as in midsummer, and the vines shed drops upon them as they passed. Pierrette was almost trembling with a new excitement. She thought, in her dim, unreasoning way, that it was a kind of reaction from her wrath at Nicholas Coigny. They stood still at last behind the trellis covered with nasturtiums. No one could see them. Pierre and Marie had just gone in, treading heavily with their baskets of beans.

"That little idiot of a fellow troubled you just now in

the kitchen?" began André Reboul, recurring to his former topic.

"He tried to kiss me!"

Pierrette threw back her shoulders and tossed her head.

"He was not so much to blame! But all the same, I came near rushing at him and pitching him over the roof." The stalwart young fellow made a significant motion upward with his outstretched arms.

"I would have liked to see you! Why did you not do it?"

"I thought you would probably raise yourself up as you did just now and say, 'André Reboul, leave me to manage my own affairs!'"

"No—I should have thanked you."

"Sacre! How is one to tell what a girl will like! You have said such short words to me!"

"Nicholas Coigny knows well that most of the girls in Smoke City like that sort of thing. Oh, I have seen them! But I am not of that kind. No man has ever kissed me—and I have made every man's ears burn who has tried it. But," she added under her breath, "I am not pretty like Estelle Bellon and Fernande Pichaud."

"You are the prettiest girl I ever saw," he said, slowly.

"Oh!" she laughed, coquettishly, "I have heard that men talk in that way just to flatter. I know how I look. I am brown. I do not wear a veil like Estelle, and ——"

"Stop! stop! I will not let you!"

"Yes," she persisted, playfully, "my nose is too big, and my eyes are too big. Oh, I am the homeliest girl in Smoke City!"

"I would rather look at you and hear you talk than all the girls I have ever seen in my life!"

"Oh!" she went on, still laughingly; "it is likely that you talk so to girls very often. I have heard that men do."

The young Frenchman's dark, well-shaped face flushed.

"Before God," he said, in a low, passionate voice which frightened her, "I never said so to any woman before. I thought it when I saw you that first night, but I did not imagine I should ever dare to tell you so. I dreamed of you all night long."

"And yet you did not come into the garden," she murmured, reproachfully.

"I did not dare to, I tell you. You seemed so cold toward me, I thought you despised me. They told me that you did despise everybody."

"I do," cried Pierrette, with a proud little laugh, "everybody but you!"

"I think you must despise me when I come in all black from the kiln. You are very neat. I never saw a girl so neat."

Pierrette blushed with pleasure. She was neat, and she knew it.

"I would not despise my good father," she retorted. "He has to get all black, like the rest. I think I like you best with the charcoal all over your face and hands. Somehow you look bigger and stronger then!"

They walked slowly toward the house, in response to a sharp summons from Marie. The damp chills of the September night were beginning to make themselves felt through the heat. Killington and Pico stood out from among the shadows opposite, side by side, straight, steep, towering up, as though with their needle-like points they would pierce the very mysteries of the heavens. The

man went directly to his pallet in the loft above, whither
all of his companions had repaired before him, while
Pierrette assisted her mother in some final household
labor. Her father was already asleep in the little bedroom opening off from one end of the kitchen, and Pierrette entered presently her own tiny closet at the other
end; but when they were all quiet, she stole out under the
stars to look at the mountains again. She had always
loved to see them, but now she felt a deeper interest in
them than ever.

"They must love each other—like people," she mused,
in her childish way. "How many, many years they must
have stood side by side!"

As she gazed, the same inexplicable feeling filled her
which she experienced when she looked at her garden
in its splendor, in the first exulting flush of some fortunate morning.

"It must be beautiful to stand so—always beside the
one you love—as they do," she murmured. Then sleep-
iness overcame her unwonted sentimentalism, and she
crept off to her poor little bedroom; but she tossed uneasily, instead of falling into her usual sound, dreamless
slumber.

The chief events of her meagre little life seemed to
pass in review before her. The principal one was the
affair of Larle Pichaud. She had never until lately been
able to consider the conduct of his silly little wife without
a curl of the lip. Now that conduct seemed no longer
contemptible. It might be possible to cling to a man
through everything—and very sweet. Things had never
looked to her as they looked to-night.

The next two weeks were like a dream to Pierrette.
The cold weather hung off. It was nearly the first of

October, yet still the hard frosts delayed, and the warm, bewitching evenings continued. There had been no farther misunderstanding between Pierrette and André Reboul. The two shy, proud souls, unlearned as they were in the world's wisdom, had studied and comprehended each other, once for all. Kisses had passed between them now, and they had told each other of their love. but no word had been uttered regarding marriage. It was all too sacred and too new for that.

"I am not like these girls around here," Pierrette Beaubien said to herself. "Now there was Fernande. She had not known Larle Pichaud a month before they were married. They know nothing of such heavenly joy as mine—any more than they can make or understand a garden like ours. And André is different. Mon Dieu! How glad I am that we are different from these rude creatures. He has never kissed any one but me, I have never kissed any one but him—yet I am eighteen and he is twenty. What is a kiss to these people? It is nothing!"

October came in cold and crisp, at last. The wonderful garden was all ready for winter. The outside doors were shut, and the warm mists from the kitchen filled the little cabin.

One afternoon the work was done early, and Pierrette was sitting by the window sewing. It was a gray, chilly day, and the indefinable sadness of autumn was heavy in the air. The happy young girl felt it, in spite of her joy. Every one knew now that André Reboul was her lover. Pierre and Marie were not pleased. They did not see how they were going to get along without Pierrette, and they felt a certain fear of the still, harsh-voiced young fellow who had come among them so recently. The mother muttered fretfully when Pierrette went into

the little shed for wood and André followed after her,
ostensibly to help her, but really, as Marie knew, to
snatch a kiss from her proud daughter.

"Who knows what he thinks, or what he has been doing all his life?" she flung out crossly to her daughter.

"He is Adolph Roney's sister's son," returned Pierrette, calmly, but with a bright red spot burning in each
cheek.

"Oh, how he mumbled when he told your father that
he wanted you!" sniffed the older woman. "And who
are the Roneys? What kind of a kitchen does Marie
Roney keep? And such soup! And the beds! Adolph
Roney! Faugh!"

Pierrette's face flamed angrily, but still she said nothing. She thought of the silent mountains. Like Killington and Pico, her lover and she were to stand side by
side forever.

As she sat this afternoon, looking out at the ugly,
deep-rutted road, and glancing now and then to where
the smoke was curling up from the woods in the direction of the old kiln, she saw the Sherbury stage coming.
It stopped in front of Adolph Roney's—a most uncommon proceeding—and a woman was helped out of it.
She was a young woman, though apparently some years
older than Pierrette, and was very smartly dressed.
Through her flimsy dotted veil her face shone red and
white. Pierrette gazed fixedly at this strange vision.
Her work fell from her hands. The little school-house
near by began to belch forth a tumultuous stream of
girls and boys. These also saw the new-comer picking
her way daintily up the path which led from the street
to Adolph Roney's door. The white-haired old Frenchman happened to be at home, and he stood staring at

the woman, who was evidently an unexpected guest. The children stood still in a body, and contemplated the scene with undisguised interest. When Pierrette saw them, she resumed her work. She was not going to stare like them.

Some time elapsed—long enough for the children to disperse to their homes—and then Adolph Roney came out of his door with the stranger. They turned toward the cabin of the Beaubiens. Pierrette felt a strange sinking at her heart as she saw them. Perhaps they would go past. No—they stopped, and came up to the door. They knocked, and Pierrette went to let them in. Her strong young frame trembled when she saw that Adolph Roney's kind old face looked troubled. The face of the young woman with him looked saucy—even insolent.

"This is Miss Delia Redmond, Pierrette," he said, briefly. Pierrette nodded her head stiffly, and glared at the gaudily-arrayed creature before her.

"I suppose André is down at the old kiln?" went on Adolph Roney. Pierrette nodded again, speechlessly.

"You can come in and wait for him, madame," he said courteously to his companion.

"I guess I won't," snapped the young woman, with a viciousness which completed Pierrette's horrible dismay. "He'll be surprised enough to see me. I'll come over after supper. I want the fun of walking right in on him."

There was a disagreeable tang to her words.

"Don't say anything about my coming, please," she concluded, as she turned away. She made a supercilious gesture toward the French girl, and gave her a brilliant, ugly smile as a parting salute.

Delia Redmond was fair-skinned and blue-eyed—an Irish girl, as Pierrette could tell by her talk, though she had used French words as though she could talk French if she chose. She had an experienced, self-confident air. She evidently knew what she was about. In her fierce, undisciplined young soul Pierrette Beaubien hated her.

It was six o'clock, and the blackened troop of charcoal burners came straggling along the road to their suppers. Among them was André Reboul. Pierrette hardly knew what she was doing as she put the victuals upon the table. The men ate heartily, but she could not taste of the porridge which her mother had seasoned so carefully. Every moment she kept imagining that she heard footsteps at the door and that Delia Redmond was coming. But the men finished eating, and yet she had not come.

Pierrette now could only long for a chance to tell André of the expected visitor. He ought to be warned against this wicked creature, who, Pierrette felt sure, meant no good to him.

As she passed the window, the moon—a glorious hunter's moon—was just rising. She would ask him to come and see it.

"Look, André," she whispered, pointing up at it; "come out on the doorstep with me, and watch the moon rise."

As the door closed behind them, she caught his hand eagerly.

"Some one is coming to see you right away, André," she stammered, incoherently. "She will be here before you know it. She has some grudge against you, I think. She says her name is Delia Redmond. Who is she, André?"

"What do you say, Pierrette?" he asked, staring at her, and his thick French sounding thicker than usual.

"Delia—Delia Redmond. She is coming. Mon Dieu!

I fancy I hear her this minute! She seems angry with you. She says she wants to surprise you."

"D——n her!" he muttered. He looked around, as though with a sudden impulse to escape. There had been such a look on Larle Pichaud's face when the woman had come—a woman whom the stage brought, just as it had brought Delia Redmond—to accuse him. An awful fear, which had been gathering in Pierrette's innocent heart for the past hour, began to put on a definite, blood-curdling shape.

"What will she do to you, André?" she whispered, weeping and winding her strong young arms around him. "Run away and hide, André! Quick! I will see her. Oh, I will tear her eyes out! I will kill her!"

"No, no!" he muttered; "I will see her, and I will make it right with her. I can't now, but I can soon— very soon—and then I will tell you all about it, Pierrette. I should not have done it, but——"

He stopped abruptly and shook himself from Pierrette's trembling embrace. There was a patter of footsteps on the path. Adolph Roney had come, and with him was Delia Redmond.

André braced his broad back against the door and faced the new-comers, looking straight into the woman's smirking countenance. The moon shone full upon him.

"Good evening, Mr. Reboul," she said in French, and with an affectation of great deference. "I suppose you thought you had hidden yourself pretty well, but I have found you at last. Where is that letter that you promised I should have a month ago?"

"I have found you at last!" Those were the exact words of the woman who had attacked Larle Pichaud. Pierrette heard nothing more. She slunk to one side among the shadows, and leaned fainting against a lilac bush which grew there. Then a sudden flare of light appeared, as some one from within opened the door. When she came to herself, she saw André walking off with Adolph and the woman in the direction of the Roneys'. She was completely chilled through, but she felt as though she could not face the scrutiny of her father and mother. Where could she go to get warm? Oh, there was the old kiln! There was a great fire going there, she knew, and the passage-way dug in the earth was dark and shut away from all peering eyes.

"A man was killed there once, I know," she murmured dully to herself, "but I am not afraid. I should not care if I were killed, too. At least, I should be warm there —and what have I to live for, anyway? People will despise me after this, if I cling to André—just as I despised Fernande Pichaud. Everybody will know about this woman by to-morrow, and how they will hoot at me in their homes. They will say, 'That proud girl of Pierre Beaubien's was deceived, as if she had been any common, empty-headed thing.' For that Delia Redmond must have loved André, just as that poor woman had loved Larle Pichaud—and he might have—yes—he might have told her that he loved her and have kissed her as he kissed me. Oh, if I had only died last night! Then I should never have known this! Yet I love him so! I would give anything to have him fold me in his arms just once more!"

Growing wilder and wilder as she stumbled on, she reached the old kiln. The great, rough door at the end of the passage-way fell toward her as she pulled at it, and bruised her, but she lifted it easily and put it in place behind her. As she had mused, the fire within her had burned. When she had made the place all dark and close, she threw herself on the earth—warm and grateful from the fire so near—and sobbed despairingly.

"Mother of God!" she prayed, over and over. "My heart is broken! Help me! Help me!"

*   *   *   *

The next morning André Reboul came down to his kiln. He was in a daze of unhappiness between his experiences of the previous evening and the disappearance of Pierrette, for whom he and several others had spent a large part of the night in searching. André knew nothing of the story of Larle Pichaud, or else he might have conducted himself differently during the scenes of the last evening. He was coming down to see if the fires in his kiln were going, and then he was prepared to resume the search for Pierrette. Suddenly he saw the fresh footprints leading toward the old kiln, and with an ominous sinking at his heart, he followed them down to the long-used door. With shaking hands he pulled at the old timbers, and in a moment the white light was shining upon the prostrate form of Pierrette.

With a groan of horror he dropped upon his knees beside her. He had heard the story of the chilled workman's death, if he had not heard the scandal regarding Larle Pichaud. The place was full of gases from the burning charcoal. In a wild hope that the fresh air might revive her, he lifted her and bore her out into the sunshine. He chafed her hands and bathed her face with water from a spring close by, but when she still gave no sign of life, he threw himself down in an agony of despair, and grovelled among the dried leaves that were heaped about her.

"Oh, Pierrette!" he cried, bending above her again,

in a last vain hope of making her hear him; "don't you
see how it was? It was nothing—nothing! I owed Delia
Redmond some money for ten weeks' board. I spent the
money in a lottery, and I lost it all. Wake up! It will be all
right, Pierrette—I am earning so much now! I was
ashamed to have you know that I had been so thriftless!
I would not have had your father know it for anything. I should have been afraid he would not have
let me have you. They said she liked me, Pierrette,
but I never liked her. I never kissed her, mignonne!
It was as I said—I never loved any one but you! Oh,
wake up, wake up!"

But all his endearments were powerless to arouse
her, and, still murmuring fond, formless words into her
deaf ears, he struggled up to her father's house, carrying
her in his arms. The doctor was summoned from Sherbury at once, but Pierrette never breathed again.

*   *   *   *

From that day André Reboul was seen no more
among the charcoal burners. Whither he went was
never known, but, though many years have passed since
then, on the top of Sherbury Mountain the smoke still as-
cends to the sky from the kilns of Smoke City. Dropped
in among them is a lovely garden—as though a star had
fallen from heaven into its rough streets. It is tended
by a bent little old Frenchman and his wrinkled wife.
If you pause to praise it, the tears will gather in their
eyes and they will say, "Oh, you should have seen it
when our daughter—our own Pierrette!—took care of it.
She was strong as a man, and so beautiful! Every one
turned to look at her when she went by! The flowers
would bloom if she but told them to. Alas! our garden
will never look the same again. You have heard the

story, monsieur? No? Ah! It will break your heart. You would like to hear it?"

And you will forget the smoke and the shouts of the charcoal burners in listening to the broken words of the old couple as they tell you of the tragedy of their sad and simple lives.

Cupid and Minerva.

A TALE WHICH ILLUSTRATES THE EMPTI-
NESS OF THE OLD LINES:

"The safest shield against the darts
Of Cupid, is Minerva's Thimble."

"IT is a most gratifying letter," exclaimed Mr. Michael
Penrose, warmly.

"It is just splendid!" cried his young and pretty
sister Amy. "I am quite in love with that Mr. Menninger."

"You in love with him!" rejoined her brother, in playful disdain. "Why, puss, he is the very cleverest and
most distinguished literary critic in New York. My
impression is that he is old and gray and very rheumatic. At any rate, he wouldn't look at a dear little
goose like you."

"I don't know why," pouted Miss Amy. "If he can
praise my brother's books so highly, he mightn't scorn
me. I am thought to resemble my brother—and maybe
I know more than some people think I do."

Mr. Michael Penrose murmured some reassuring
words to his sister and kissed her tenderly. Then he
proceeded to read the letter over again, Miss Amy peering at it from behind him.

"You needn't tell me," she insisted, "that anybody
with the rheumatism wrote that."

The hand in which the "gratifying letter" was in-
dited was, indeed, a bold and handsome one.

"I send you herewith," it ran, "a copy of the current issue of 'The Age of Intellect,' containing my review of your masterly work upon Anemophilous Monocotyledons. Three years ago I had the honor to commend highly your first production (as you stated in your preface) upon Entomostraca and Larvæ—evidently the result of years of study. I have read since then with great pleasure every article from your pen which has come under my notice. It is my hope, as it is that of every lover of science in America, that you may long be spared to make the profound researches of which your works bear evidence.

"I am, sir, with the deepest respect,
      "Yours faithfully,
           "Laurence Menninger."

"I wonder if he is German," suggested little Miss Amy.

"I have asked ever so many people about him," responded her brother, "but nobody seems to know him personally. He has written the scientific reviews four or five years for the 'Age' now, and has made them the most important part of the magazine. It is said that he is averse to society—a perfect recluse—and never goes to the office. Probably he is old and rich—dabbling in scientific experiments all the time. I am thinking that he might possibly help me to get a place as an instructor in some sort of a scientific institution. I would like such work ever so much better than reading weak MSS. for 'The Brain of the West.' Oh, if I could only give all my time to original study!"

"It is a shame that you can't!" declared little Miss Amy, severely, as she stroked the bowed head of her gifted brother. "There ought to be a fund for geniuses like you, Mike, dear, so that you could compose wonderful deep books all the time, and not bother to earn money."

"Oh, you precious little goose!" laughed her brother, regaining his courage under her adoring sympathy; and then he rose and went up to his own room.

It was a long apartment, with a curtained alcove at one end, where he slept and dressed. At the other end were herbariums, cases of defunct bugs mounted on long, slender insect pins, horrid snakes in alcohol jars, perches covered with stuffed birds, minerals, vases of dried grasses and similar memorabilia, until one could scarcely make one's way around. The young man himself, thirty-two or three years old, robust, "well-looking," as the English say, and full of zest and energy, seemed out of place among these dusty treasures.

He took up a freshly prepared case of stuffed birds and looked at them critically.

"I believe I'll send these to Mr. Laurence Menninger," he mused. "They have considerable value, and he has been so awfully good to me that I wish I could do something for him. I fancy the old fellow would appreciate them."

There was no address upon Mr. Laurence Menninger's note beyond the letter head of "The Age of Intellect." Mr. Michael Penrose accordingly wrote and asked him where he should send a package for him, partially defining its nature.

"I hesitate about giving my address," began the letter which the young author received in reply, "but your kind desire to send me a valuable gift, of the fragile nature which you suggest, is too warmly expressed to allow me to decline, especially as you reside in the Far

West. I beg you, however, as for special reasons I shut myself away from general society, to regard the number which I send you as given in strict confidence. I thank you most sincerely for the favor which you intend to do me.

"Faithfully yours,

"Laurence Menninger.

"27 Hamilton Square, New York."

The birds reached their destination in safety, and brought a brief but delightful acknowledgment from the great reviewer. Several of the specimens were quite new to him. Mr. Michael Penrose had captured them during a trip which he had taken to Mexico, in order to prepare a series of articles on that region for "The Brain of the West."

A few months after this occurrence, Mr. Michael Penrose came home one day with an excited look upon his face.

"Amy, dear," he said, trying to speak calmly. "I have come to an important crisis in my studies for my new book on 'The Bats and Seals of the Oceanic Islands,' and have got leave of absence from the office for three weeks. I feel as though I must go to New York for awhile, and get into that Genobel Collection. It isn't large, you know, but it is choice and just what I need. They say it is almost impossible to get into it, but I shall bring all the influence I can to bear in the matter, my publishers may be able to help, and there's that old Mr. Menninger. He might manage it, if the others couldn't."

"And now I shall know just how he looks!" exclaimed sentimental little Miss Amy. "I imagine him, dear, as

just forty-five—that's such a sweet age for a man, you
know—and with dark, flashing eyes, and a perfectly
awful manner—like a king, you know—and a fierce mustache. As for the snuffy, rheumatic old duffer you fancy
him—I don't take any stock in him at all."

"Well, I may not succeed in getting into his presence,"
laughed her brother, as he began to make preparations
for his journey, "but if I ever do, I'll photograph him
for you just as I find him."

In New York, Mr. Michael Penrose paused at his
hotel only long enough to perform a hurried toilet before making his first attempt to enter the wonderful collection, on which he felt the success of his new book
so greatly to depend. He found that his publishers and
the eccentric owner of the museum were at swords' points
over some book of his which they had refused to bring
out. There seemed nothing left for him but to throw
himself upon the good offices of Mr. Laurence Menninger, which he accordingly proceeded to do.

The house proved to be a grand mansion on a quiet,
old-fashioned, open square. Half-a-dozen of the same
stately sort of residences stood near it—all that were left
in the down-town whirlpool when the world of fashion
had taken its flight twenty years before toward the Park.

"I know I'm a wretch to come, after what he wrote,"
guiltily mused the young man, as he mounted the queer,
old marble steps, "but when he finds out my errand,
I somehow feel as though he would forgive me."

He rang the bell, and, card in hand, awaited the opening of the door.

Suddenly a carriage drew up in front of the house, and
simultaneously the door in front of him opened, emitting
a tall young woman with such force and rapidity that

she almost dislodged the muscular assistant editor of "The Brain of the West."

"I beg your pardon," she began, drawing herself up haughtily, just in time to preserve both their lives. "I was hastening to meet my friends in the carriage, and I did not know that any one was here. Did you wish to see my uncle?"

"Just my conception of him, precisely," flashed over Mr. Michael Penrose's mind. "An elderly uncle—the term just fits him."

The young woman was shapely as well as tall, and her head was fine and finely set upon a pair of noble shoulders. The assistant editor of "The Brain of the West" thought that he had never seen a more interesting specimen of womanhood, as this rather stern young person stood before him, a slight color tinging her grave, handsome face. She glanced beyond him toward her friends who were alighting from the carriage, though she politely awaited his reply to her question.

He simply handed her his card, stammering—for he had not retained his self-possession as well as she had, "I came—to see—if I might—Mr. Laurence Menninger."

"Mr. Penrose," she said, in a voice not calculated to displease her visitor. "I have heard of you, but I cannot say whether Mr. Menninger will see you or not. He does not often see people, but he might consent to receive you. Will you wait a few moments?"

"Wait a few moments!" He only wished that she had asked him to do something long and difficult, such was the delicate flattery of the deference which this enchanting young woman had infused into her manner toward him. Was it possible that this radiant being had read his stupid books—or was it only because she had heard her uncle speak well of him that she seemed disposed so favorably toward him?

Mr. Michael Penrose had never cared for society and knew little about it. Women he had gauged, therefore, as all such men do, by those of his own family—his mother, a calm, busy, practical housekeeper, with decided views concerning woman's sphere; and his pretty little sister—bright, superficial and inconsequent. This brilliant-faced, perfectly dressed New York woman, who might have been either twenty or thirty, so fresh, yet sedate, was her beauty, gave him the impression of a new and intensely interesting species. "No wonder," he mused, "that old Mr. Menninger does not need any other society, with such a charming niece in the house. How lucky that I happened to encounter her! It might have chanced, I suppose, that I might have been here a dozen times in the ordinary course of things without once seeing her."

Presently the young woman herself came back to him. Her visitors had gone, and all traces had disappeared of the slight embarrassment which she had shown after her providential escape from a violent assault upon our peaceable young scientist.

"I neglected to state to you before, Mr. Penrose," she began, pleasantly, "that I am Miss Helen Laurence. Now please tell me what was your errand with Mr. Menninger. I am sure that he would not object, for I transact nearly all his business for him."

"Your uncle is not well, then?"

"I am sorry to say that he is a great sufferer from the gout."

"Ah!" thought her visitor. "Gout and rheumatism are not so very dissimilar. I am a fair prophet, after all."

Then aloud he replied to her question, and proceeded to state his case with as much grace as he could muster.

When he concluded, Miss Laurence gave him a re-assuring smile. "I am happy to tell you," she said, "that we know the Genobels very well, and are on the best of terms with them. If this is the urgent cause of your wish to see my uncle to-day, you might as well postpone it, for he is particularly unwell just now, and if you will accept of my poor services, I shall be glad to go with you at once to examine the Collection. I am an indifferent scholar beside my learned uncle"—she smiled deprecatingly, and always with that subtle defer-ence so flattering to her hearer—"but I am still somewhat familiar with scientific matters. I have read your books, and I know how highly my uncle regards them."

Ecstasy! To be actually within reach of the Genobel Collection, and to visit it in company with this lovely creature—who had read his books! It was too much!

He had supposed that a woman acquainted with science must be a sort of monstrosity, but here was one, blonde, supple, elegant, beautiful.

Under the circumstances, he could not help distrust-ing somewhat the accuracy of her knowledge, until they were fairly within the walls of the famous collector, when it was impossible not to gather, during the hour which they spent there, that Miss Helen Laurence, however modestly she might value herself, was no sciolist, but an honest and thorough gleaner in his favorite fields. He reflected again what a companion she must be for that gouty old uncle of hers, with his elevated tastes, but most probably irritable temper. Mr. Michael Penrose could readily imagine what an angel she was to him.

There was not time to examine half of the things he

6

wanted to see that afternoon, so the next day he went again—still under the guidance of Miss Helen Laurence. She was allowed by the ugly, suspicious Herr Genobel, who dogged their steps everywhere, to unlock drawers and cabinets as she **chose,** and to handle everything at pleasure.

After this second visit he was invited to stay to luncheon with Miss Laurence, where he met her brother, who, though not so accomplished a naturalist as his sister, and also a rather taciturn and plain-looking young man, was still a not unacceptable addition to their party.

As there was going to be a lecture on the following evening by a friend of Mr. Penrose, upon the "Modern Cromlech Builders," and in a hall not far away, he invited Miss Laurence and her brother to accompany· him thither. They accepted the invitation.

A day later the brother called to drive him to the home of a queer old electrician, who, Miss Laurence had reported, had read Mr. Penrose's books, and was anxious to meet him. Of course Miss Laurence was to go too.

Ten days of Mr. Michael Penrose's vacation passed away, and upon looking back over them he found that he had every day seen Miss Helen Laurence, yet had never once been able to gain access to the chamber of her eccentric uncle.

"Still, they have been the happiest days of my life," he murmured hotly to himself as, after an evening at a delightful reception to which he had been carried by Miss Laurence and her brother, he returned to his hotel. "Every day shows me more and more how noble and sweet and wise she is!"

                        "A thousand fantasies
              Begin to throng"

into his mind as he thinks of her and of the future. He has always looked forward in a vague way to having some time a home of his own, which, of course, will be full of his beloved seaweeds and corals, strange bugs on insect pins, birds on perches, gneiss and asbestos, but to-night over and under and through them all—let no scientist dare to dispute the fact!—shines the apotheosis of Miss Helen Laurence, dignified and learned, yet fair-browed and beautiful. And does his image haunt her also? He can scarcely dare to hope so, but he cannot help knowing that during his stay in New York, Miss Laurence, once or twice in the face of her brother's remonstrances, has put off engagement after engagement in order that she might show him some curio, the sight of which he has long coveted, or attend some lecture with him. And has she not declared within his hearing— he blushes to think of it—that he is bound to become one of the foremost scientific authorities of America? She has been shocked to find that his studies are prosecuted during such hours as he can snatch from his exacting duties as assistant editor of "The Brain of the West." She had supposed that all his days and his nights were given to science. She had also confided to him, now that they are so well acquainted—indeed, it seems as though they had always known one another—that she had pictured him as a thin, elderly gentleman, with spectacles, of course, and with a vast brow, cavernous eyes, and a soul entirely above the delights of lunching and gadding about, even for scientific purposes, with a young person like herself.

When this disclosure was made to Mr. Michael Penrose, he had, as was natural, laughed immoderately, and had responded, with sparkling eyes and a beating heart,

that an eremite might well renounce his vows for such
a privilege; upon which, Miss Laurence, though necessarily accustomed to compliments, had blushed a brilliant
carmine, and had asked him abruptly to restate his views
regarding the ears of saurians, in which she was pro-
foundly interested.

The final evening of his leave of absence had come, and
he strayed over to the handsome old house in Hamilton
Square to say his good-byes. The omnipresent brother
for once was away, but he would certainly be in about
nine, Miss Laurence assured him; and he promised, most
willingly, as may be surmised, to wait.

They sat down together in the pretty reception room
where she had introduced herself to him, and then began
to talk enthusiastically, as they always did. They had,
somehow, an infinity of interests in common, and the
young man had never found anybody's conversation so
suggestive and stimulating as hers.

They had been discussing a wonderful kind of dragon
fly, of which they had recently seen the only specimen
in this country, when the clock on the mantel struck half-
past eight. Its silvery chime seemed to send a cold chill
to Mr. Michael Penrose's heart, and to dry up the foun-
tain of his words. Miss Laurence, after several ineffect-
ual attempts to lead him to talk on as before, rallied him
upon his abstraction.

"Ah," she said, "your thoughts are not with me; they
are far over the sea, following that dragon fly to his
native haunts, and extracting from the formation of his
wings some curious theories for your new book. Indeed,
I will not urge you to wait. I will convey your good-
byes to my brother."

"Oh—I— you do not understand," protested the

young man, in confusion. "I—I prefer to wait. I was only thinking——" He paused.

"It is of no consequence—none at all," she protested, in her turn, unheeding that she was hardly polite in her haste.

"But, oh, it is of consequence!" he declared, impulsively, a sudden wave of feeling passing over him. "I was thinking—I was thinking that I—I might never see you again."

"Oh, yes, you will!" she laughed, constrainedly. "We are all so well—and you will soon come to New York again."

Her cool words served to partially restore him to himself.

"I—I have been so sorry not to see Mr. Menninger," he went on, saying over again what he had already said sufficiently often. "I had so much to say to him, and now I have even more. Do you not suppose that he will ever see me?"

A little shadow fell over her face as she looked steadily into his eyes without answering him. "Mr. Penrose," she began, at last, with some agitation in her manner, "I have a confession to make to you; but first promise that you will forgive me."

He bent forward a little to hear what she had to say, eagerly promising what she desired. It was a critical moment.

"Mr. Penrose," she began again, "I have deceived you. But it seemed to happen so that I could deceive you without really meaning to, and I could not bear to tell you the truth. I thought you would be disappointed. My uncle, though he has always been a student, has never written anything beyond his ordinary correspondence.

His mind is now very feeble, and may fail entirely any day. His name is James William Menninger. There is no Laurence Menninger; or—rather—I—am Laurence Menninger."

She put her hands to her face in genuine shame and distress. It was the final touch to upset his balance entirely. He sprang to her side, tore her hands from her face and kissed them passionately.

"Oh, how good you have been to me!" he whispered to her—"you, rich, beautiful, accomplished—to me, a poor, obscure editor——"

And then she hushed his self-depreciations with such decided yet agreeable words that for the next fifteen minutes saurians and trilobites, microbes and bacteria, polypoid excrescences and musical orthoptera, were forgotten.

It was but a few days after this that the mysterious uncle died, and a few months later Miss Helen Laurence went to visit Mr. Michael Penrose's mother by special invitation. This brought the rumor into circulation that Mr. Michael Penrose was about to be married, and as nobody took the trouble to dispute the rumor, it was accepted everywhere as true.

But nobody, not even the inquisitive Miss Amy, knew of the identity of Laurence Menninger with her prospective sister-in-law, until she came on, about a year after Mr. Michael Penrose's introduction to the distinguished critic, to attend her brother's wedding in New York, and to bid him good-bye as he sailed with his bride for a distant shore, where he had been appointed to conduct some great archæological explorations. "The Brain of the West" would have to work out its own destiny henceforward without the aid of Mr. Michael Penrose.

The moment of Miss Amy's entrance into the hall of the old house on Hamilton Square was chosen as the proper time for initiating her into the great secret.

"I engaged," said her brother, leading forward his promised bride, "to introduce you to-night to Mr. Laurence Menninger, whose kindness to me has so much endeared him to you. Here he is. Behold his 'dark, flashing eyes,' his 'perfectly awful manner,' his 'fierce mustache'; and does he not bear his 'forty-five years' with great grace?"

"At any rate," pouted Miss Amy, relieving herself of her surprise by enthusiastically embracing her prospective relative, while the taciturn brother gazed admiringly upon her from a distance—"at any rate, I didn't say that she was 'old and gray and very rheumatic!'"

But the beautiful bride seemed to be only flattered by the bridegroom's preconceived notions of her as thus described, and they all fell to talking merrily—apropos of a fine flower show just then in progress in New York—of the segregation of the homogeneous fluid in the cells of drosera, which greatly affected, so the bride remarked, to the deep interest of the bridegroom, the nervous matter in the plant, and the continuity of protoplasm.

The Case of Parson Hewlett.

A TRUE STORY.

THE impression which Parson Hewlett first made upon his Birchmont parish was very favorable. It is said that all of the people, including Deacon Aaron Rice, a famous judge of pulpit eloquence, thought him "a most uncommon preacher"; Goodsir Giles, the chief stickler for orthodoxy in the parish, declared the new parson to be "as sound on the doctrines as Jeremy Taylor himself"; and he offered a prayer long enough to satisfy even Dr. Hartshorn, who is said to have considered it a piece of irreverence in a clergyman to consume less than an hour in making his "long prayer"; while the women agreed in pronouncing him "the comeliest minister in all the country round." Even old Mistress Betty Weddell, who lived alone in her little cottage among the pines on Birchmont Hill, said that the new parson "knew how to speak to a body."

Mistress Betty has come down in history as a very cross old woman. It turned out that the new parson did not much care to speak to her, well as he knew how, when he became better acquainted with her.

These remarks were all made upon the tenth day of August, 1767. The new pastor's full name was the Reverend Jonathan Hewlett, late of the college at New Haven, and later of Walpole, N. H. He wore "a great white wig and a cocked-up hat, and made a dignified appearance." One of his ministerial friends said of him to another: "He could do more execution with one nod of his wig than you or I could in talking half an hour."

Yes, a man of power was the Reverend Jonathan Hewlett, and the mark which he left upon the town of Birchmont, and, indeed, upon the whole county, has remained to this day.

The story of his calling is thus told in the old town records of Birchmont: "The vote was put whether the Town was ready to make choice of a gentleman to settle with them at present, and it past in the affirmative. Then, according to the advice of the neighboring ministers, the Town proceeded to Chuse and Call the Rev'd Mr. Jonathan Hewlett to the work of the ministry among us. Agreed and voted to give the said Mr. Jonathan Hewlett, provided he Accepts and Settles among us, one hundred pounds settlement; to be paid as followes, viz., sixty pounds the first year and fourty pounds the second year. As also an annual salary, to begin as followes; viz., fifty pounds to be paid the first year, and to rise two pounds a year for five years, and there to remain, and likewise to find him his wood."

Shortly after Parson Hewlett's coming among them, the people voted to make a new meeting-house for him "forty-five feet long and thirty-five feet wide and twenty foot post." Later, it was voted that when sixty families were settled in the town, the salary should "rise one pound upon each family that shall be added above sixty, till it comes to be eighty pounds a year, and there to remain during his continuance with us in the work of the ministry. It was likewise agreed upon and voted that the selectmen shall lay out the minister's right in publick land where the minister shall chuse." Then "a commity was appointed to provide for the Rev'd Jonathan Hewlett's

installation" and "to build him a house."   All of which
looks as though Dr. Hartshorn and Deacon Rice and
Goodsir Giles and the rest had meant to be fair and
square, and even generous with the pastor they so much
admired, when they "settled" him; still, his subsequent
history leads us to believe that the preparations for his
reception and maintenance were very closely supervised
by the thrifty parson himself.   He certainly found the
people ready and willing to do his bidding, however, and
if his life had but been in accordance with his prayers and
his profession, it is reasonable to believe that his parish-
ioners would have supported and loved him to the end.
But, like many another, Parson Hewlett had a nature
which grace failed to subdue, and, though his side of the
story has not come down to us so fully as has that of the
town, it is plain to see that he showed himself very soon to
be "an hard man, reaping where he had not sowed, and
gathering where he had not strown."   His sound and doc-
trinal sermons, however, his grand looks and courtly
manners, and, above all, the innate respect for his office
which was a part of provincial human nature in those
days, kept Parson Hewlett in good and regular standing
among his people for several years.   Then the mutterings
of discontent which had been making themselves heard
distantly here and there began to grow louder.   Mistress
Betty Weddell was one of the first to "speak out."

"What's fair words," scolded the poor old woman, from
whom the parson had wrenched her share of the "minister-tax," at his own convenience, instead of hers.
"What's fair words, when the Evil One is behind them?
Oh, I wish," tradition says that she confided to her neighbors, "I wish that Parson Hewlett would go by my woods
some dark night on his high-stepping horse!   How I

would love to jump out of the bushes and 'Boh!' at him!"
But poor old Mistress Betty never had the chance she
coveted.

Goodsir Giles, too, had hard luck, and was not able to
pay his minister-tax any better than Mistress Betty; but
this did not deter Parson Hewlett from insisting upon his
rights in the matter. One morning he came around to
see the old Goodsir, and urged upon him with prayer
(very likely an hour long), the wickedness of putting off
the payment of his tax.

"But I tell you I can't pay a penny this year, parson,"
explained Goodsir Giles, for the dozenth time; "I said so,
and I mean it. My wife has been sick this twelvemonth,
my hogs have died, my horse broke his neck in the pasture, and I can't even pay my score at the mill."

"Tut, tut!" reproved the parson, "I can't believe that
you are so badly off as all that! Come now, and let us see
what you have."

Shrewdly exploring the premises, he discovered a fine
milch cow, which he proceeded to lead off for himself,
under the very eyes of its indignant owner. The poor
old Goodsir pleaded that this cow was all that stood between his family and starvation, but even this availed him
nothing.

"Ha, sirrah!" scolded the pompous parson, "pay your
debts before you lay up for the future. Read your Bible,
and learn from that, that the Lord will provide. If you
are needy, call upon the town."

Goodsir Giles had a better chance than Mistress Betty
to avenge himself upon the insolent parson. One day in
early spring, when the ice was still pretty firm in the
Birchmont River, Parson Hewlett crossed it in the morning to attend a "Conference" upon the other side. The

sun was very warm at noon, and upon his return his sleigh broke through the ice in the very middle of the stream. Goodsir Giles, whose house was on the bank close by, heard loud cries for help, and hurried out to see what was the matter. His heart, which had been moved by the piteous cries, hardened when he saw who was in trouble.

"Help, help, Goodsir Giles, for God's sake!" roared the haughty parson, now humble enough.

But the Goodsir was ready for him. He made a trumpet of his two hands and bawled through it: "Keep up your courage, parson! The Lord will provide! Call upon the town!" Then he went back to his house.

It was a long, cold half-hour, tradition tells us, before a chance passer-by rescued the doughty parson from his perilous and uncomfortable position. He and his horse were half dead from fright and exposure, but naughty Goodsir Giles felt no compunctions.

Parson Hewlett raised a large family, and, though he was a very serious man, he had one humorous conundrum which he always asked of strangers to whom he wished to make himself agreeable.

"How many children have I?" he would inquire jocularly. "I have eleven sons, and every one of them has a sister."

If the hearer, after scratching his head for a while over the matter, worked out at last that there were twelve children in the family, the parson would shake his hand heartily and regard him as a man of great acumen.

One of these eleven sons, who ventured once too often to remonstrate with his father upon the severities which he practised upon the poor in collecting his salary, was never forgiven by the stiff old man for his presumption;

as a punishment the lad was apprenticed to a blacksmith, and a blacksmith he remained to the end of his days, having been granted far fewer privileges than fell to the lot of his more discreet brothers.

In those days, the clergy all liked their toddy, and there was not one in the county but was a discriminating judge of rum and brandy; but, in spite of this fact, and that Parson Hewlett himself liked only the choicest liquors, his brethren well knew that the prudent old fellow would serve them the cheapest brands when they gathered with him for conference. Perhaps the parson was afraid they would take more than was good for them, if too tempting an article was supplied.

In spite of his hardness and closeness, however, even this severe old theologian laughed when good old Deacon Hastings, in a time of drought, prayed in meeting, in all good faith: "O Lord, thou knowest how much we stand in need of rain! We pray Thee that Thou wouldst send it to us. We ask not that it should come in copious confusion, O Lord; but we pray that Thou wouldst send it to us in a gentle sizzle-sozzle."

And he laughed again when the same old man, noted for his extraordinary petitions, prayed: "Remember also our good neighbors, Brother Crane and Brother Felch, O Lord,—both of 'em living in the same house, and both of 'em living with their second wives,—singular circumstance, O Lord!"

The Revolutionary times came on. Parson Hewlett was a Tory of the Tories, and tried his best to keep his people with him; but the tide of patriotism grew gradually higher and higher in the town, until at last it culminated in an outspoken declaration against the injustice of Great Britain. As this declaration marks the first general and public outbreak against the authority of Parson Hewlett, and widened more than anything else the breach between them, it is reproduced here in full. It ran as follows:

"At a meeting of the freeholders and other inhabitants of the town of Birchmont on Monday, the fourth day of October, 1773. to take into Consideration the Melancholly state of the province of Massachusetts Bay, occasioned by the unnatural oppression of the parent State of this province, after seriously debating the matter [they] made choice of a committy to prepair a draft of resolutions for the Town to Come into and then adjourned the meeting to Monday the 25th inst. The Committee having Met and Considered the matter do report that the Inhabitants of this Town are possessed of the warmest sentiments of Loyalty to and the highest respect for the sacred person, Crown, and dignity of our Right and Lawful Sovereign, King George the Third and the Illustrious House of Hanover, that this Town are fair from once harbering a thought of Disuniting from the parent State. But with the greatest Sorrow and Concern would we His Majesties Most Dutiful and Loyall subjects the Inhabitants of this Town say that the Humiliating and Violent oppressive Mesurs of the parent State fill our Loyall minds with the most fearful apprehensions of the Consequences; That the Ilegall and unconstitutional strech of power put into the hands of the Courts of Admiralty is a very Great Greevance and renders precarious and uncertain the lives and property of the Honest Inhabitants of this province; that the parlement of Great Briton assuming to themselves a power of making Laws Binding on us in all cases is a very alarming curcomstance and threatens our ruin; That the leavying taxes on us without our consent either in person or by Reprisentative and establishing a board of Comitions in the province to Collect the same, with all their expensive attendants, Importing them by a fleet and Army to Aw us into a complyance is a very grate greevance; that the taking the payment of our governor out of [our] hands is a very grate greevance. But the rendering Independent of the people and altogether Dependent on the Crown the Judges of our Supe-

rior Courts seems calculated to Compleat the Cystim of our
slavery and ruin; That the inhabitants of this town hould
sacred our excellent Constitution, so dearly purchased by our
forefathers; that we also hould Dear our possessions so **Dearly**
purchased by ourselves, where to settle this Town and Make it
more advantgeous to his Majesty and profitable to ourselves
and posterity we have been alarmed by the Yells of Saviges
about our ears, been shocked with seens of our Dearest Friends
and Nearest relations Butchered, Scalped and Captivated before
our Eyes, we, our wives and children forced to fly to garison
for safety. Therefore we must hold the man in the greatest
Scorn and Contempt who shall Endeavior to Rob us either of
Liberty or property; That certian Letters signed Thomas Hutch-
inson, Andrew Clive, Charles Paxton &c. which letters were
layde before the Honorable house of Representatives of this
province in their last session were wrote and sent to the gentlemen to whom they were with a desire to overthrow our excellent Constitution and Consequently Rob us of our Liberty and
Prosperity; That we look upon it as a Very Grate Frown of
Almighty God to permit a man to govern us that seems so much
Bent to Ruin the people he is set to protect and the place that
gave him Berth and Education; and it shall be our Constant
prayer that God would give us and the whole people of this
province Repentance for all our sins and especially those that
pulls down such a heavy judgement as an oppressive Governor;
that He would Continue our invaluable priviledges to us and
neaver suffer us to be Robed of them by Crafty, Designing
men, and that they may be transmitted down to the Latest pos-
teraty.

"The above Report being Repeatedly Read in Town meeting,
it was unanimously voted in the affirmative, and ordered that it
be recorded in the Town Book, and that a true copy of the same
be transmitted to the Comitee of Corisnondence of the town
of Boston." [1]

---

[1] This is a literal copy of the "Declaration of Rights," of the
town called in this story "Birchmont," as recorded in the "Town
Book."

"And a fig for the Tory sentiments of the Parson!" was implied in every line of this fiery statement of "Grate Greevances." The town fathers of Birchmont were not infallible spellers; they were not even consistent in their orthography, such as it was, but they knew enough to spell "Liberty" with a capital letter, and they would no more brook the petty tyranny of Parson Hewlett than the encroachments of "Grate Briton."

At the very time when the grasping old man was clamoring at the loudest for his "back pay,"—for the collection of his salary, originally much too large for the then young and poor town to offer, had been hopelessly delayed by the war,—at this time imagine his wrath when he learned of the following correspondence, now carefully preserved among the archives of Birchmont:

To the Overseers of the Poor of Boston:

JULY 9th, 1774.

SIRS,—The Inhabitants of Birchmont have considered the deplorable condition of your town, and, like the poor widow, cast in their mite. They committed to me two barrels of flour to be sent to you for the relief [of] the poor, which I have sent by the bearer, desiring you would receive it for that purpose, and please signify that you have received it, and you will oblige,

Your friend and servant,

AARON RICE.

Great pleasure was expressed throughout the poor but generous little town (excepting, it may be safely asserted, in the home of the Tory parson), when it was "signified" as follows, that the flour had been received,—

BOSTON, July 20, 1774.

SIR,—I received your favor of the 9th instant, advising that you had sent two barrels of flour for the relief of such poor

people as do suffer by the shutting up of this port, which flour
I have received, and it shall be appropriated accordingly. The
distresses of this Town begin to come on, and I do expect them
to be great, but we are not intimidated, nor shall we give up
any of our liberties, although we are surrounded by fleets and
armies. Our Committee to employ the Poor are not together,
of which I am one, as well as one of the Overseers of the Poor,
so do in the name of both, return you thanks for your kind
donation and am, Gentlemen,

Your very humble servant,

SAM PARTRIDGE.

To Mr. Aaron Rice, Birchmont.

It must have been o'er exasperating to the Tory parson
that his town, in large arrears to himself, should be giving
away its substance to "rebels,"—whom he regarded as
much worthier of halters than of good flour; but he could
not help himself.

Finding that the money to pay him could not possibly
be raised, as the war continued, he devised a method of
punishment for the delinquents, of which we learn from
the following spirited entry in the Town Book,—

"Agreed and voted that whereas the Rev. Mr. Hewlett
hath Desired the Town to come into some method by
which he may have his salary at the Time it becomes due
or the interest till it is paid: as for any methods being
come into other than is provided, [it is] impractable.
As for his having Interest, we acknowledge it is his just
rite. But it is an unusual thing for a minister to have
Interest for his salary, and we think it hard that Mr.
Hewlett should ask it of us, especially at such a time as
this, when the publick burthens are so great, and humbly
beseech the Rev. Mr. Hewlett to consider us in this
Difficult time, not only with regard to having interest,
but to make some further abatement in his salary. for we

7

judge ourselves unable to fulfill our contract with him without bringing ourselves and children into bondage."

But Parson Hewlett had no sympathy with the war which was draining the resources of his people, and he would not desist from his persecutions. He even insisted upon having everything which was donated towards his salary, such as beef, butter, wood, etc., valued upon a specie basis. No depreciated continental currency, nor its equivalents, for him!

The trouble between pastor and parish naturally grew deeper and deeper, until, at a stormy town-meeting held on the 26th of April, 1779, he was formally declared dismissed, and Birchmont—guileless little town!—fancied itself rid of its arch-tormentor. The parson, however, insisted that no dismission was possible, under the circumstances, without the verdict of an ecclesiastical council. One was accordingly called, which advised that the parson remain for six months longer, and see if matters could not be composed.

Then a warrant was issued by the town, bidding the constable to warn every man in Birchmont to assemble at the meeting-house on the 29th of August, 1781, to see "wheather they would dismiss and discharge the said Mr. Hewlett from the work and business of dispencing the word of God to the inhabitants of the said town."

The meeting voted unanimously to have nothing more to do with the redoubtable parson; but still he stuck like a burr, and though the doors of the meeting-house were closed against him, he still preached every Sunday in his own house, and a few faithful adherents came to hear him, who, with his own family, must have constituted quite an audience; and still he kept presenting his bills to the town, refusing to depart till they were paid, and instituting lawsuits to bring his debtors to terms.

To the simple and law-abiding people of Birchmont, to whom the great wig and grand presence of Parson Hewlett were a "holy terror," it must have seemed hopeless that they should ever get rid of this specious nightmare. They had tried every means known to them, and he had met and baffled all their attempts to displace him. Whither should they turn?

About this time the northeastern portion of Birchmont began to petition to be made into a separate township. The measure had encountered serious opposition, but one day when the selectmen were assembled to consider the matter, a happy thought struck Deacon Aaron Rice.

"It might do, brethren, to make a new town," he suggested jocosely, "if we could only pack away Parson Hewlett and his farm into it."

"It would be a stroke of generalship!" cried Dr. Hartshorn.

"Why can't we do it?" echoed George Cannon.

"But it would make the shape of our town as kitty-cornered as one of Mistress Weddell's Spanish-galleon quilts," objected Deacon Rice, upon second thought.

"And the meeting-house would have to go," mused Dr. Hartshorn.

"My brethren!" cried good George Cannon, "we never can get rid of that old reprobate unless we do something radical. I tell you, it would be cheap if we could foist him on another town by paying so small a price as the meeting-house and the shapeliness of our town!"

So it came about that when the petition went in final form to the Great and General Court of Massachusetts, for the laying off of the northeast corner of the town of

Birchmont into the new town of Leith, it was specified
that the separation was desired only upon the condition
that the house and farm of Parson Hewlett should be in-
cluded in the new township.

It must surely have been worth while to see the stately
parson when he learned of this checkmate move upon
the part of the people whom he had no doubt believed
to be completely in his power. Napoleon at Waterloo
could scarcely have felt more crestfallen. The old fellow
was fairly outwitted; and he could not circumvent the
will of the majority, though he still continued to harass
Birchmont for his unpaid salary, and in various other
ways to keep wagging tongues busy. Strong in doctrine
and lengthy in prayer as ever, he preached on for many
years in the old church, now restored to his use. He was
never able, however, to make so strong and advantageous
a contract with the town of Leith as he had made with
Birchmont, and he lived, during his latter years, chiefly
upon the produce of his farm.

It had almost seemed to the people among whom he
had dwelt for so long that his indomitable spirit would
never yield to the King of Terrors; but, in 1802, Parson
Hewlett's time came, as it must come to us all.

He was buried upon a burning summer's day, and his
coffin was carried from his house to the graveyard,
according to the custom of the period, by four "bearers,"
chosen from among the most prominent men in the vicinity. It is related of them that, the road being long and
mostly up hill, they were compelled when half the distance had been accomplished to lay down their burden
until they could recover their breath. As they waited,
good Deacon Rice, who, having never come to an open

rupture with the parson, had been chosen as one of them, mopped his dripping brow and remarked:

"The parson was a heavier man than he looked, my brethren."

"Aye, aye," rejoined worthy George Cannon, with a twinkle of unsanctified mirth in his eye, "it is a heavy load that we have to carry; but I bear it cheerfully, my breth-ren,—I bear it cheerfully!"

"*For Looly.*"

"WELL, Tom, here's your month's wages."

Old Tom Wicks's wrinkled and tobacco-stained visage put on a grin of intense delight as he took the gold piece that the distillery paymaster, young Jim Baskins, handed him.

"And look here," pursued that young man, whose flashy attire indicated the would-be exquisite, "why don't you use this money, Tom, to fix yourself up a little? Here you've been working for us six months, and every time you come around to get your pay you look poorer than you did before. Now," continued Mr. Jim Baskins, out of the kindness of a heart which really liked and pitied the quiet, ragged old teamster, "take this money and get yourself a suit of clothes."

The old man did not look displeased, but he shook his head decidedly.

"I like ye fustrate, Jim," he said, "but I cayn't."

"Why not?"

"Why, Merce, my gal—Mercy—— I do' know's you knew I had a gal."

The old man stopped, and looked as though he wondered if he could quite trust Jim Baskins. Then he went on, as though the recollection of that young person's kind offices, which had been as numerous toward Tom Wicks as their circumstances had permitted, had reassured him.

"Merce, you see, she ain't had no chance. An' thar's Looly; she's the little 'un; she's goin' on 'leven now, ye know?"

The young man laughed at his interrogative tone. "No, I didn't know; but I do know now."

"Wa'al, she's right peart, Looly is; an' Merce she says, says she, 'Looly's got to have a chance.' She jest sots by Looly more'n anything else in the world. An', Lord! what'd she do when I got this chance to team it but, says she, 'Now, paw, we've got this er money,' says she, 'an' when thar's a lot saved, why, we'll take it, an' Looly shall go to school, an' Looly shall have good clo'es,' says she. 'I'm too old,' says she—goin' on twenty, Merce is. 'But,' says she, 'I'll fix things so 't Looly kin go, 'f ye'll give me over the money,' says she."

"Most girls would have wanted it for themselves," commented Mr. Jim Baskins, getting interested in old Tom Wicks's strange daughter.

The old man shook his head. "Merce ain't that kyind. She's most twice's old's the little 'un; named her herself outen a book she read. Merce is a powerful hand to read—kin read anything an' everything; hez read all the neighbors' books; reckon she'd 'a come down to Marlinsburg to git books, on'y she ain't been down yer f'r two 'r three years now; says she's 'shamed to come yer, 'count of her clo'es; powerful proud, Merce is. 'But,' says she, 'Looly'll grow up harnsum an' smart,' says she, 'an' Looly'll have a chance, an' good clo'es; an' Looly shall go to Marlinsburg an' everywhar, an' hold up her head with anybody.' 'But,' says I"—old Tom Wicks warmed to his subject, as he saw the eager attention paid him by his absorbed listener—"says I, 'thar's the boys. Ye cayn't keep them boys from the money,' says I—them boys—they's two on 'em, eighteen an' sixteen y'rs old they be, an' a powerful hard lot, Jake an' Lewt—up ter everything. 'They'll git holt of it, Merce,' says I; 'they'll steal it outen my pockets, or outen the teapot, or outen any place ye chuse ter put it,' says I. An' Merce, she says, says she, 'They will, will they? That money'll go fer Looly,' says she. 'I'll hide it whar nobody cayn't git it, boys nor nobody else,' she says; an' 'pon that she—— Now ye won't never tell what I'm goin' ter say?" queried the old man, pulling himself up short, and suddenly recollecting that he was on the verge of disclosing a state secret of stupendous proportions. The painfully curious look he gave into the vain but honest face of Jim Baskins, added to the bluff assurance of the latter that "he never would, so help him!" delivered in the most convincing manner, restored the old man's confidence, and he went on: "She started"—Tom Wicks lowered his voice impressively—"the fust night I drawed my pay, an' up she skips it onto the mountain; an' she's got a iron box up thar, an' she's dug a hole, an' thar she puts it, an' them boys hain't no conceit o' whar the money goes ter. They thinks I banks it 'r sutl.in' down yer. That's why I wants it in gold," said the old man, apologetically. "Merce says, 'It mought be ten years afore we'll get it all spent,' says she, 'an' it'd better be gold.'"

"You do pretty much as 'Merce' says, don't you?" remarked the young man, with something of a sneer in his tone.

Tom Wicks bristled. "Ye—don't—know—Mercy Wicks," he said, straightening up and looking at young Baskins with warning in his eyes. "She's a prime 'un, Merce is. Got a head—lord, what a deep 'un she is! Talks jes' like a book—read so many novels. The old woman she dips mostly; an' thar's Bet to hum—she's goin' on fifteen. Then thar was some more, but they died when they was babies. But Bet she's sorter wooden-

"For Looly."

headed, an' it's Merce 't keeps 'em all a-goin'. Merce ain't had no chance, but she's a powerful smart gal."

"You haven't ever asked me up to your house, Tom," said the young man, insinuatingly.

Tom Wicks understood him, but he hesitated.

"Do you have to ask 'Merce,' as you call her, before you can invite anybody to tea?"

Young Baskins laughed good-humoredly, but his words had a sarcastic sting in them for the fond father.

" 'Tain't much of a place to ask folks to," he said at length.

"Well, I'd like to meet your family," persisted Jim Baskins. "I've been a good deal interested in your account of them, and I'd like to see them."

"Merce, she says," suggested the old man, floundering about in his attempt to avoid doing something which he knew would displease his daughter—"she says we're too dog-on low an' poor to have respectable company, an' she ain't a-goin' to have no other kind."

"She must be a very proud-spirited girl." Mr. Jim Baskins ignored any inferences that might have been drawn by a more captious person from Mr. Wicks's remonstrance.

"Wa'al, the old woman she ain't no great hand fer cookin', an' Merce ain't never had nobody to tell her how. She does the best she knows, but, lord—wa'al, I s'pose ye can come, 'f ye'll excuse the looks"—the old man's naturally hospitable disposition inclined him to yield to Mr. Baskins's importunity—"an' 'f Merce is kinder cross, ye mustn't mind."

Mr. Jim Baskins smiled a complacent smile as he glanced down at the tawdry plaids and checks of his spring suit and the glittering chains and rings which bedecked his comfortable person. It must be a very hard-hearted maiden, he thought, who could long be angry with such as he.

"I'm not so terribly afraid of 'Merce' as you are," he said.

The old man gave his head a significant twist, as much as to say, "Wait until you see her," and turning his gaunt horses away from the low distillery in front of which they had been talking, they jolted away up the mountain side and toward the lonely gulch, or hollow, in which stood the small homestead of the Wicks family. It was a weary ride, and the long spring day had vanished into a starry night when Tom Wicks drew up with a startling "Whoa!" in front of the squalid and unsavory-looking abode where they were to alight.

Mr. Jim Baskins could not help giving a little gasp of dismay when he saw it. He hadn't expected anything quite so bad as that.

The old man vaguely felt his visitor's disappointment.

"I told you so," he said, half angrily, half sorrowfully. "Ye needn't 'a come. I didn't urge ye."

"Who said anything?" began the young man, in confused apology for his unspoken offence, when his speech was cut short by the apparition of a young woman who had opened the door at the sound of Tom Wicks's "Whoa!" and was hurrying towards him. "Have you got it, pa?" she asked, eagerly, and she had approached quite close to him before she observed the young man sitting on the other side.

"Here's Mr. Baskins—Jim Baskins, of Marlinsburg —Merce," he said, trying feebly to smile as he announced his unwelcome guest. "He thought he'd kinder like ter

see the country hereabouts, and I brought him up to
supper with us."

Mercy Wicks's fine face darkened, and she looked
down instinctively upon her soiled and ragged dress and
her bare feet. Old Wicks could not have told what
there was in her motion that affected him—this sudden
mortification on the part of a girl who had scarcely ever
in her life worn a better garb than the tattered and unsightly one in which she was clad at that moment; but
he felt just then as though he would rather have died
than have brought young Baskins up from Marlinsburg.
He rejoiced inwardly that he had had the courage to
suggest to that individual during their ride up the
mountain that, in case there wasn't any place for him
to sleep in the Wicks cottage, there was a man a mile
further on who would keep him for a slight consideration.

"There isn't much for supper," said Mercy, deliberately
regarding the interloper with wide blue eyes, and holding
herself erect with an air of dignity quite out of keeping
with her surroundings, "but what we've got, Mr. Baskins
can have too, I suppose. Supper is all ready."

Her voice was pleasant, in spite of the disapproba-
tion which deepened it, and her manner was that of a
person accustomed to authority; and although the light
braids of hair which hung far down her back bore visible
signs of neglect, and the details of her whole appearance
were far from prepossessing, there was something about
her which made the young man feel that her father's
eulogies upon her were not misplaced, and that she was a
girl capable of much heroism, albeit Mr. Jim Baskins was
not particularly susceptible to impressions, and his fibre
was coarse. He wondered whether, if she were attired

after the fashion of the "set" of young ladies with whom he associated in Marlinsburg, she would be "pretty." This, however, was rather too much for Mr. Baskins's imagination, and he did not long dwell upon it.

The supper consisted of a hoe-cake, a pitcher of molasses, some cold sliced bacon, and a pot of tea, and though served in a style which was not particularly appetizing, young Mr. Baskins was able to disregard that, and to eat a hearty meal. The two "boys" were not present, but their absence did not seem to be anything unusual, and nobody appeared to sorrow because they were not there.

They were scarcely seated around the rickety table when Mercy exclaimed, "Bet, where's ma?"

A tallow-faced girl, to whom Mr. Wicks had not thought it necessary to introduce their visitor, rose from the table, and turning herself slowly about, peered into the recesses of the one room which formed the lower story of the little cabin.

"I dun know," she answered, stupidly.

"Go out doors, Looly," said Mercy to the bright-faced little creature who was sitting close beside her; "maybe she's out there—fell asleep, perhaps, under the big tree."

The child started obediently, and soon returned, saying that her mother was indeed "out under the big tree," but that she could not wake her up nor make her understand that supper was ready. Her sister made no comment upon this information, nor did anyone else, and the meal went on in silence.

"Been having a big revival in Marlinsburg," began Mr. Baskins, at last, in an attempt to promote sociability.

"Ye don't say," responded Tom Wicks.

"Oh, yes; they're all getting religion down our way. Moonshining'll have to go under, I reckon."

The old man looked half alarmed. He could not bear to think for an instant that the great industry upon which he was a pensioner could possibly "go under."

"Oh, not so bad as that," continued Mr. Baskins, with a short laugh, observing his host's startled expression, "but it does seem as if half Marlinsburg was going to the meetings and getting converted. Old Sparhawk, that railroad man down there, lives in that splendid house, richest man in Marlinsburg, he's been converted; and his son—just come of age, I believe—he's going to be a parson, they say. Oh, there's no end of a fuss down there. I don't take much stock in it myself."

Mercy was looking at him now, with wide-open, interested eyes.

"I went to a meeting once, she said, with a simplicity that disarmed all his previous criticism.

"Well, you didn't think much of it, did you?" he asked, jokingly.

"Yes," she answered, gravely. "I liked it very much. The man that preached—it was up here on the camp-ground—he gave me a Testament. I've read it through a great many times."

"Understand it all?" inquired the young man, cynically.

"No," she said, relaxing nothing of her seriousness. "But I can understand some of it," she added, a moment later.

"Pretty good hunting hereabouts?" asked Mr. Baskins, abruptly. He wanted to change the subject of the conversation. He had not counted upon the girl's taking it so much in earnest.

"Ask Merce," said the old man; "she an' the boys
mostly 'tends to the shootin'."

"So you can shoot?" interrogated Mr. Baskins, turning patronizingly to Mercy Wicks.

"Yes," said Mercy, pleasantly.

"Can you hit 'em on the wing?" inquired the young
man, jocularly.

"Every time," she returned, as good-humoredly. A
little scowl that had hitherto rested upon her face was
disappearing, and this unwonted social relaxation lent
her a look of interest and vivacity. Mr. Baskins began
to decide that, properly accoutred, she might, after all,
be "pretty."

He sat next her, and now he moved his chair a little
nearer to hers.

"Why don't you sometimes drive down with your
father to Marlinsburg?" he said.

"I don't get much time to drive around," replied
Mercy, shrinking into herself a little as she felt, rather
than observed, the slight change in his manner.

"I should be pleased to take you around the town,"
he continued, with attempted gallantry.

"I can't go." Mercy turned abruptly to her father:
"You'd better go out and fetch in ma. She'll catch
her death out there in the damp."

The old man rose slowly and walked away.

"Are you going back to Marlinsburg to-night?" inquired Mr. Baskins's peculiar young hostess. She had
been perplexed upon this subject ever since he had
come, and her straightforward and untaught soul was
determined to discover his intentions.

"I don't know," replied her guest, in some embarrassment. "Your father said something about a house not far away where they sometimes took lodgers."

"You see, we haven't any room in this house to keep anybody," said Mercy, with frank seriousness. "I didn't know but you came up to see somebody else."

"No," said the young man, looking intently into her face. "I came up here expressly to see you."

"To see me?" she repeated, incredulously.

"Your father has told me a good deal about you, and I thought I should like to get acquainted with you. He warned me that you didn't like company very well."

"I wish pa would keep still," said Mercy, angrily.

At that moment the old man appeared at the door, leading his wife by the hand. She was a flabby, stout old creature, and even more untidy and unkempt-looking than her daughters.

There was a fire burning on the ashy hearth, for it was still early in May, and the evenings were chilly. The old woman, after a staring survey of the newcomer, and a word of welcome upon her introduction to him, dropped into a large rocking chair in the chimney corner, and, while Mr. Wicks and Jim Baskins engaged in a mono-syllabic conversation, Mercy and her two sisters cleared the supper table, and in a lame and perfunctory manner washed the dishes. During the progress of her work, Mr. Baskins had ventured to address several remarks to Mercy, but she had answered him very briefly. It did not suit that independent young person to have her father bringing home with him young men tricked out as this one was, and avowing that they had come "expressly to see her." In truth, it was chiefly pondering upon this strange avowal that had kept her so silent. The young men in the neighborhood of "Wicks's Hollow" were all utterly disagreeable to her, and as she took no pains to disguise her feelings, she was naturally not popular among them. She had long ago given up all thought of life as holding any especial sweetness or glory for herself. Love was something that she had read a good deal about, but she had long felt that there was nothing of that sort in store for her. Therefore the idea of having a young man come to see her aroused but faintly her long-subdued desire for affection, and she felt only a vague and unpleasant self-consciousness whenever she looked in Mr. Baskins's direction.

When her work, over which she had busied herself an unusually long time, offered no further excuse for her to move about the room, she beckoned her father to come to her, and held a whispered conversation with him in a distant corner of the room.

"Not to-night," Mr. Baskins heard the old man say, after a little.

"Oh, yes," pleaded the girl. "The boys may come home any time now."

"But he's here," objected Tom Wicks, in a loud whisper.

"I don't care," returned Mercy; "I don't want to see him."

Mr. Baskins winced a little. He was used to being made a great deal of among his "set" in Marlinsburg, and though he cared little enough for this untaught daughter of the backwoods, he did not enjoy such absolute indifference on her part. It was rather interesting to see her blue eyes open wide, to hear her voice, and to watch her stately figure as she moved around the room. On the whole, he did not fancy the idea of her willingness to be gone all the evening any more than her father seemed to, and he understood very well, from what Tom Wicks had told him, that she was asking for his month's pay, in order to secrete it up on the mountain, and that her father was protesting against such an uncourteous proceeding. On the whole, Mr. Jim Baskins concluded that he had better be going.

"I wonder if I can find that place where they keep people over night?" he remarked, interrogatively, as Mr. Wicks, having evidently been worsted in his argument with Mercy, prepared to resume his seat beside his guest.

"Sho, now," said the old man, looking appealingly toward his daughter; "cayn't we fix him up——"

"Now, pa, you know," interrupted Mercy, fiercely, "there isn't a decent bed in the house."

"They ain't made o' down, I know," admitted her father, meekly; "but sho, now, Merce, cayn't we git him up——"

"No, we can't," declared Mercy, peremptorily. And here Jim Baskins, who could not help noticing that her face had assumed a color and her eye a fire during this discussion which made her positively handsome, interrupted the discussion to decline any further effort to arrange quarters for him in the Wicks mansion.

"I wouldn't inconvenience you for anything, Miss Mercy," he said, politely; "and although I appreciate your kindness, Mr. Wicks, it is much better that I should go elsewhere."

The genuine courtesy of his manner wakened Mercy's sense of propriety, and she spoke repentantly and eagerly.

"I'll show you the way," she said. "It isn't much further for me to go past there. It is a pretty good place—much better than our house."

8

"I'll go with him if he's got to go," said Tom Wicks, sullenly.

"No, you needn't," returned Mercy, the violence of her manner all gone; and quietly taking down an old straw hat and a worn shawl from a peg beside the door, she put them on, and they walked out into the clear starlight of the May night.

Everything was very still, and they hurried on some distance without speaking.

"I should think you would be afraid to go upon the mountain alone at night," said the young man at last.

She raised her shawl and showed a belt beneath it, in which was thrust a shining revolver. Then she folded her shawl together again, and drew herself up proudly.

"I'm not afraid when I have that on," she said. "There's wildcats on the mountain," she added, "and some foxes, but I don't mind them. I don't mind anything"—her voice dropped almost to a whisper—"when it's for Looly."

"You do it for Looly, then?" said Jim Baskins, pretending ignorance.

"I don't know as I ought to tell you," she said, simply, and looking at him hard in the dim light, "but father says you're honest as the day is long, and so I don't mind telling you. You see, the boys would get father's money if it was left anywhere around the house, so I hide it up on the mountain, and I'm going to spend it for Looly one of these days."

"I should think you would have your father put it in a bank."

"The boys think that is where he puts it, but pa brings me up a newspaper now and then, and I'm always reading how somebody has run off with the bank's money; so when pa said, 'Put it in a bank,' I said, 'No; I'll hide it where it will be safe'; and I do. You'll surely not tell?"

"Oh, no," he said, soberly. "I'm your friend, and I think it's very nice that you are saving up your money for your pretty little sister. Most girls would spend it for themselves."

Mercy's fine face softened. "I'd rather have Looly have things," she exclaimed, passionately, "than anything else in the world."

"She is a very pretty little girl," said Jim Baskins, patronizingly.

"She's very much nicer than Bet," Mercy continued more quietly. "She can read and write and cipher some; but Bet's dull enough."

"Who taught Looly all these things?"

"I did," said the girl. "I don't know who taught me. I reckon pa began it. He can read, and so could ma years ago, but she's forgotten how. Bet's hateful, too," pursued Mercy, with a philosophical calmness of analysis, "while Looly never is. I don't let Looly run around as Bet does. I've seen lots of wickedness in this neighborhood," she went on, with an air of experience, which was amusing even to Mr. Jim Baskins's somewhat obtuse perceptions, "but Looly shan't see any of it. I'm going to give Looly a chance. But here's your place. Good-night."

She turned from him abruptly, the flutter of her garments swept past him in the starlight, and he found himself standing alone beside a faintly illumined house, while a dark figure creeping up a hillside several rods away showed him that the daring girl was already well started on her errand of love.

Then he went in. He found that everything was as his young conductor had described it, and he was soon asleep, and dreaming of young girls who walked like empresses, abjured ceremony altogether, wore revolvers in their belts, and climbed lonely mountains at dead of night.

In the meantime Mercy was resolutely pursuing her way up the mountain side, and it was a full hour after she left Mr. Jim Baskins before she paused at all. Then she threw herself down underneath a great pine tree which had been struck by lightning, and which, standing by itself upon a little knoll, was easily discernible from the valley below.

Beneath its bare and blasted limbs was a large brown stone, as large as Mercy could lift, but she managed to insert her hand beneath it, and to draw out therefrom an iron box. This she unlocked, depositing her treasure in it, and then she returned it to its hiding place.

"It's very strange," she soliloquized, "that that young man should have come up from Marlinsburg to see me. Any of the young fellows around Wicks's Hollow could have told him that I didn't treat the young men very well. Now there's Sally." "Sally" was Mercy's older sister. "Ever since Sally married Bill, what a life she's led! Sally was better than Bet too, but now it's drinking and quarrelling and quarrelling and drinking every minute. I wouldn't marry one of 'em—not for anything; and I wouldn't let Looly. Perhaps Looly'll grow up and be like the ladies that ride by once in a while in their carriages. Perhaps she will marry one of those fine men—such as we read about. I'd like that for me, too, but not one of these men around here, nor like this Mr. Baskins; but of course I can't; I haven't had any

chance. Looly shall be different. I won't have Looly
feel ashamed of herself as I do, not if I die for it."

There was a rustling in the bushes, and the girl sprang
up a trifle nervously, and peered into the darkness,
clutching her weapon more closely. Then she pulled her
shawl around her, and taking a different path from that
by which she had come, she was not long in reaching her
father's cabin. "The boys" had not come even yet, and
all the rest were asleep, excepting Bet, who sat beside
the sputtering candle, nodding in a stupid doze. The
foul air of the squalid interior struck with a new force
upon the girl's quickened sense.

"I wish it was different," she sighed aloud. "It isn't
as it ought to be; but dear me! dear me! I can't seem
to fix it"; and she wearily climbed the ladder that led
to the loft, and was soon asleep beside her little sister.

It was less than a week from the time that Mr. Baskins had made his first visit to Wicks's Hollow that he
found his way thither again. This time he came on
horseback by himself, and early in the afternoon. Somehow the thought of the proud girl whom he had seen
had haunted him. He wished, with a sort of unreason-
able persistence, to see her again, and as Jim Baskins,
though by no means refined, and not what would be
called a cultivated fellow, was clean, and had been
brought up by a neat and methodical mother, he thought
with real pity of Mercy's ignorance of the first principles
of tidiness and good housekeeping.

"I wonder," reflected Mr. Baskins—"I wonder if she
couldn't learn a good deal out of one of these books that
they have about such things?"

He decided that probably she could, and he therefore
bought a work of that character; and as he happened that

very day to come across a little book of the nature of a tract, entitled "Cleanliness is Next to Godliness," he determined to make up a package of books for Mercy, and to inclose surreptitiously within it the two volumes which he intended for her personal improvement. This package he finally concluded to take up to her himself.

He found her as indifferent to him as before. The influences of the starlight, and of her repentance for her rudeness to him, had made her very gentle and communicative during their evening walk together, but Mercy had thought matters over thoroughly since then, and she had made up her mind that, in case Jim Baskins should ever come to Wicks's Hollow again— something which she thought very unlikely to happen —she would not be any more agreeable to him than was absolutely necessary to insure the safe-keeping of the secret which, not knowing of her father's previous confidences, she felt that she had rather unwisely confided to him.

But Mercy's indifference was not proof against a package of beautiful new books.

"For me?" she cried, when he had handed them to her, and she had opened the bundle. "And Looly and I can read them? See here, Looly! Isn't it splendid?"

Mercy's face grew rosy with pleasure, and her eyes glowed. The young man forgot her tangled braids and her tattered gown. She was positively beautiful.

She opened one book after another in bewildered ecstasy, and could hardly wait until her visitor had gone, to examine their contents. Mr. Baskins did not stay very long. He saw her impatience, and it pleased, while at the same time it piqued, him. When he rode away, he mentally registered a vow to come soon again up to

Wicks's Hollow, and to observe what effect the works, upon whose selection he had expended so much care, had had upon the young girl whom he so much desired to cultivate.

That night, when Mercy went to bed, she thought more favorably than before of Mr. Jim Baskins.

"How good it was of him to bring us so many books!" she reflected, gratefully. "I shouldn't blame him—nor anybody else—for despising us; but he has been very kind to us, and the next time he comes, I'm going to treat him better."

On the following morning Mercy was up betimes, and as soon as her father and his horses disappeared behind the brow of the hill that overhung Wicks's Hollow, she sat down, with Looly beside her, to the pile of books. "The boys" were off on a fishing expedition, Bet was idling under the shade of a tree outside, and Mrs. Wicks rocked and dipped in placid stupidity by the fire, all oblivious of the breakfast table still standing, and of the general disorder of the little cabin.

The cover of the volume on "Cleanliness is Next to Godliness" was of an enticing blue, and Mercy hastened to open it and to inspect its contents. The subject was treated plainly and practically, and Mercy read on absorbedly after she had once begun. No such work had ever before come under her notice, and Mr. Jim Baskins had builded even better than he knew in enclosing it in his friendly package.

"That's the way people live," she said, raising her head after a while, and looking sadly out of the window; "nice people don't live as we do. That's the way I want you to live, Looly—dear little Looly!" She caught the delicate child up in her arms and kissed her. "And yet how we live! How lazy, how very lazy, we are!"

She sat there for a moment, rocking and kissing the child passionately, when a shadow fell across the doorway, and Mercy saw that a young man was standing there, and that a beautiful horse, from which he had evidently just alighted, was tied to a tree outside.

She sprang up and looked at him in curious surprise. He was a gentleman—this Mercy felt, without any definite thought on the subject, in every fibre of her being. Then she looked down at herself, as she had looked when her father had brought Jim Baskins up to see them, only with a keener mortification, and from herself she looked around upon the untidy room. If she had felt its meanness and foulness a moment before, in the light shed upon it by the illuminating little volume which she had just been reading, how much more did she feel it in the presence of this man, whose elegance and refinement struck the girl with a sense of romance—as if he had just stepped out of one of the novels that she had read. His glance rested, as he bowed to her in kindly greeting, upon the disordered room, and Mercy herself almost felt the little shudder which he gave as he took it all in.

"I know," she cried, without waiting for him to speak, intuitively fathoming his thought, and as intuitively imploring his leniency—"I know I oughtn't to have let things go so, but Mr. Baskins brought me up some books to read, and so I sat right down to read them. It wasn't nice; it wasn't right."

She spoke with an eagerness that, knowing nothing of the experience through which she had been passing, her visitor could not understand.

He murmured some formal words, politely disclaiming

the need of apology, but was interrupted by the drawling tones of Mrs. Wicks, who had temporarily roused herself to gaze upon the distinguished stranger.

"Law, Merce," she said, tugging at her chair so as to bring it around where she could get a better view of their visitor, "what ye goin' on so, fer? Cayn't ye give the gentleman a chair?"

"Excuse me," said the young man, who seemed little more than a boy, with his fresh face, slight mustache, and crisp dark hair; "my name is Wesley Sparhawk, and I live in Marlinsburg. I was about to take a ride across the mountain, and my father suggested that I should carry with me some Bibles and tracts, and distribute them along the way. I'm not much used to such work," he said, smiling into Mercy's eager face, "but I'm more than willing to try and do a little good—and I will leave some with you, if you like."

Looly took a book that the stranger held out to her, and gazed up into his handsome eyes with winning sweetness. He had spoken rapidly, and Mrs. Wicks had not been able to rouse herself enough to follow him.

"What?" she said, stupidly.

The sound of her crackling voice checked the answering smile with which Wesley Sparhawk was looking back into the child's face, and just then Bet came sauntering in at the door, adding another unpicturesque element to the already far from pleasant scene.

"Some Bibles and tracts," repeated the young man.

"Ye don't mean it!" rejoined Mrs. Wicks, having finally grasped his meaning. "Law! I've seen—men with sech things—colporteurs, ain't it?"—extricating the word from the confusion of her memory with a ludicrous effort—"but ye don't look like that kind—ye don't reely."

In response to this remark, which she evidently intended to be highly complimentary, the young man looked down at his clothes, as if with a sudden sense of their unfitness, and blushed slightly.

"I'm not, exactly," he stammered, approaching her with a tract in his hand, "but I trust that you will like the books that I leave with you just as well."

Mercy had caught at the Testament which he had given Looly, and was looking at it intently.

"I've one just like it," she said, proudly. "See here," and she hastened to get the well-thumbed volume from a shelf near by and to exhibit it.

"That's good," said Mr. Wesley Sparhawk, approvingly, and noting the girl's glowing face and noble carriage with surprised interest. "Please accept this Bible;" and he held out to her the most elegantly bound among the half-dozen books that he carried.

Her hand trembled with pleasure as she took it. "Thank you," she said, simply; "I love dearly to read."

The difference between the girl's language and her mother's struck the young man with astonishment. This slovenly, good-looking, majestic young daughter of the backwoods interested him.

"I see you have a good many books," he said, pointing to the pile beside the chair where she had been sitting.

"Yes," she said—"some new ones that Mr. Baskins sent us. Some of them tell about housekeeping and such things. I've learned a great deal from them, and I mean to read every word in them. It's for Looly more than for the rest of us," she went on, in obedience to the look of inquiry in his face. "It doesn't make much difference about Bet and me—we're older—but I mean to give

Looly a chance to learn and have things, and I mean
to bring her up right. This is Looly." She gathered the
child to her affectionately. "I want her to grow up to be
a lady."

The terrible discrepancy between her desires and the
realistic squalor of the room seemed to strike the poor
girl with crushing force. Her self-command failed her
in her excitement; she put her apron to her face, and he
could see that she was crying quietly, while Mrs. Wicks
began a drawling remonstrance. The whole thing was
a total mystery to her.

The young man flushed with pity. The situation lay
revealed before him, and he felt an instinctive desire to
help this groping soul.

"I'm very sorry," he said. "I'm going to be away
several days, but when I come back, I shall stop again,
and leave you some more books." He handed some
tracts to Bet as he spoke, and bidding them all a courteous good-morning, flung himself upon his horse and
rode away.

Mercy rose and wiped her eyes, and as she looked
after Mr. Wesley Sparhawk, riding up the mountain side,
her heart gave a quick, determined throb. "It shall be
different when he comes again," she resolved, and turning back into the unsightly room, she began, with a firm-
ness of touch and an energy of spirit not unlike that
which must have characterized the great reformers, to in-
augurate in her own small sphere an era of reform.

An hour later she sat over her little sister, curling
her long, light hair—Mercy's pride, but hitherto only
occasionally reduced to order. Then Bet received what
that young woman described to her brothers later as a
"goin's-over," and afterward Mercy herself underwent

a species of transformation. Then, thoroughly wearied, but with a glow of pride more fervent than any that she had ever known before, she sat down to gaze about her, and to enjoy the result of her laboriously worked-out resolution. Then she fell to reading.

That night she lay long awake, pondering on what she had read, on the ways which she might use to bring about certain needed reforms, and on the strange happenings of the day. The thought of resentment toward Mr. Jim Baskins had not occurred to Mercy. Instead, her soul, which had scarcely ever known a small or a selfish consideration, was filled with gratitude to him. She understood now how it had been something more than shame of their poverty which had made her so averse to going anywhere or to having company, and why the better class of their neighbors upon the mountain had seemed to slight and shun them. She felt that now she had found the key to better times for Wicks's Hollow, and her soul rejoiced in that consciousness as she fell asleep.

A few days later Mr. Jim Baskins paid another visit to the locality which had come to hold such a fascination for him, and he was filled with an honest pleasure when he saw signs of revolutionary tendencies among the residents in the Wicks cottage as he drew rein before the door. Beside the window, and showing unmistakable signs of careful attention to her toilet, sat Mercy herself, awkwardly, but with feverish haste, sewing away upon a piece of new calico.

"I'm making a dress for Looly," she announced, smilingly, looking up at him with a tired and heated face as he entered, but not deigning to rise. "I've enjoyed

those books so much! Looly and I have read nearly all
of them, haven't we, Looly?"

The child nodded, and crept close to her sister.

"I'm very glad," commented Mr. Baskins, with a beam-
ing face. "I thought you'd like them. And how nice
you look here! You must be expecting a beau, I guess."

Bet, who was lying on a settee in the corner, giggled
at this, and sat up, as though the conversation for once
began to assume an interesting complexion; and Mrs.
Wicks, who was stationed by the door in the inevitable
rocking chair, and engaged in her usual absorbing oc-
cupation of dipping snuff, cackled forth a feeble expression of mirth.

"Sal used ter have lots o' beaus," she remarked,
proudly, and smiling a weak but approving smile upon
Mr. Jim Baskins, as she thus endeavored to cover what
she considered to be one of Mercy's most important deficiencies. "An' Bet seems ter please the young fellers
more'n Merce does," she continued. "Merce she cayn't
abide 'em, she says. I do' know—I sh'd think——" And
here Mrs. Wicks's discourse relapsed into a mumble,
which neither Mr. Jim Baskins nor any of the others
present could very well understand.

"I liked this book best," said Mercy, ignoring the
recent turn of the conversation. Her heightened color
and uplifted head were the only indications that she
had heard what had just been said. She took up one of
the books as she spoke, and opened its leaves caress-
ingly, and though Mr. Jim Baskins could not understand her fondness for it, nor for any other book, not
being a man much addicted to reading, he sat down and
devoted his energies to making himself agreeable to this
obdurate young woman. She was handsome enough to

excite his profoundest admiration this afternoon, and in her gratitude to him was uncommonly complaisant. Her subdued laugh rang out pleasantly several times, and Mr. Jim Baskins had to acknowledge to himself that he had never heard a more melodious voice than hers. It was not until the shackly wagon and lean horses of old Tom Wicks came rattling down into the Hollow that Mercy's visitor took any thought of the flight of time. She politely invited him to stop to supper again, but she did not urge him. She had been civil, and even very pleasant, to Mr. Jim Baskins, but she did not like him very well, after all, and she was not sorry when he declined her invitation with thanks, remounted his horse, and rode slowly away. To tell the truth, Mr. Jim Baskins was getting to be somewhat in love, and, as the Marlinsburg belles of that young gentleman's "circle" would have expressed it, "with one of those"—or the belles might have said "them"—"low-down Wickses upon the mountain."

It was two or three days after this that another young man flung himself from his horse and entered the Wicks cabin. It was Mr. Wesley Sparhawk, who had been playing, in a rather awkward but quite honest fashion, the part of a missionary toward the benighted mountaineers in the region adjacent to his home. Young Sparhawk had not found this improvised sort of "circuit-riding" altogether productive of pleasure, and his face was somewhat paler and his air more subdued than when he had called before in Wicks's Hollow. Still, as Mr. Wesley Sparhawk had a good deal of "bottom," he was not disheartened. He was only a young man, accustomed to no harder labor than such as pertained to the care of his toilet and to the acquisition of his lessons at

school and at college, and he had found his long ride and
the numerous calls that he had made in his new capacity
excessively exhausting. He had rather dreaded appear-
ing again at the Wicks cottage, for scarcely in all his tour
had he encountered one so uninviting. But he remembered the tall, fine-faced girl whom he had met there, and
he felt a strong desire to see her again, and to learn
whether the protestations that she had made so earnestly
had amounted to anything.

Mercy saw him coming, for, though she would not
have admitted it even to herself, she had been watching
for him for several days, and she looked around her home
at the various metamorphoses which she had accomplished, with a flutter of pride and delight. It was true
that Bet had hardly been able to keep up with the march
of civilization in Wicks's Hollow, and that Mrs. Wicks,
long since past regeneration, had absolutely refused to
submit to many of Mercy's regulations. She had even
roused herself to a more violent exertion than for several
years past, to denounce in unqualified terms the revolutionary measures which undoubtedly contributed more
to her immediate discomfort than to her pleasure. Therefore she still remained a blot of no small proportions upon
the landscape; but Mercy herself was fresh and neat,
Looly was as sweet as a daisy, and the cabin was as clean
as Mercy's strong young arms could make it.

Mr. Wesley Sparhawk paused upon the threshold, and
surveyed Mercy's rejuvenated domains with a smile of
surprised approval.

"I declare you've kept your word," he said, and as he
took her hand and looked into her proud eyes, the blood
flowed faster in his veins. She felt a thousand-fold re-

paid for the labor she had given, and also a new impulse to continue the good work.

He came into the cabin and sat down, laying beside her chair a pile of books and papers which he had brought. A book which she had been reading lay on the window sill; it was the book of which she had spoken in such admiring terms to Mr. Baskins. He picked it up and turned the leaves.

"This is a nice story," he said; "the only trouble with it is that it ends in such an improbable way."

The girl looked at him inquiringly. This was icono-clastic.

"I mean," he explained, "that it was a pity the hero should have married that girl. Not but that she was noble and all that, but they had been brought up so differently, of course, they could never be happy to-gether. It isn't in reason," continued Mr. Wesley Spar-hawk, marking the intense concern which the girl man-ifested, and glad to be able to enlighten her ignorance. "He had been brought up in the midst of elegance, and her advantages——" He checked himself. He had for-gotten for a moment the circumstances under which he was speaking. "It was different with her," he concluded, lamely.

"Yes," said Mercy, in a low voice, "she had been poor always, and hadn't had any chance."

"It made a nice story, only it couldn't ever have hap-pened and turned out well in real life, you see. The general test to apply to a painting or a story or almost anything is, Is it natural? Is it practical? If it isn't, it isn't good."

"Yes," said Mercy, gravely, "I understand." She drew herself up a little. Her pride had been touched, how deeply she did not know until long afterward. Her large, toil-stained hands, especially disfigured by recent unwonted exertions, opened and closed convulsively. Was there, then, no chance that Looly should ever grow up to marry a different sort of man from Sally's Bill and the young men around Wicks's Hollow? And a dim little hope which, in spite of her efforts to crush it, had dared to bloom for herself in her innermost heart, seemed to be trodden down in a moment.

The young man sat talking longer than he had meant to. He felt, without formulating his feelings, that he had hurt the girl's self-respect a little, and he tried to make her forget it, by taking up book after book and commenting laughingly upon them all. And Mercy forgot everything else in listening to him, until she too began to impart her impressions of what she had been reading; and her ideas were so unsophisticated, so daring, so original, her face was so fair, and her eyes so luminous while she told of them, that, unawares, the young man was more charmed by her than he would have cared to own.

"I wish you would go down to Marlinsburg to some of the meetings," he said at last. "You would like them."

Mercy shook her head. "I wouldn't go down there for anything," she said. Her figure dilated a little, and she held her head a trifle higher. "The Marlinsburg people look at me so," she added, "I can't stand it. I've only a sun-bonnet to wear and a calico dress, and I'm never going anywhere again until we get enough money saved to educate Looly. It's too late to do much for me, but I mean to give her a good chance."

The young man asked some questions about this matter, and Mercy told him what she was doing, though not so fully as she had told Mr. Jim Baskins.

"And your father is saving this money for Looly?"

"He lets me save it," she said, smilingly.

The young man, accustomed as he had always been to the luxuries of great wealth, glanced pitifully around the bare little dwelling. To put away money, needed, it seemed to him, to supply the daily wants of life, for such a purpose as that for which this girl was hoarding it, struck him as rather fine—rather grand. He began to admire from the bottom of his heart this strange exotic among the regulation "poor white" growths of Wicks's Hollow.

The clock struck six.

"I must go," said the young man, rising reluctantly: "I've a fancy that you will go to the meetings some time, if I'll come and get you," he added, as he rode away.

She shook her head, but she smiled. She would rather do even that than not to see him again.

"I reckon you will," he laughed back to her, and her heart thrilled with intense regret as she watched him disappear behind the hill. How handsome, how distinguished he was! How inferior to him Mr. Jim Baskins appeared, as she mentally compared them! Yet perhaps she should never see him again, and her heart gave a great throb of pain as she thought, but she did not stop to account for it.

It was now nearly time for her father to come home, and Mercy hastened to kindle a fire, and to get everything in readiness for his arrival. She had been very watchful of him and attentive to his wants lately, and no one had appreciated more warmly, or at least more demonstratively, than he the efforts which she had been making for the elevation of the Wicks family.

"Now ye don't, Merce!" he had exclaimed, when the reforms had first begun in earnest. "Law, now, chile, ye've had all the work to do for years, now, an' I allers thought ye more'n done yer juty; but now—— Law, Merce, I'm right smart proud o' ye; I reely be!"

Mercy loved her father next to Looly of all the family, and his praise was very sweet to her; and so when the hour drew on for him to appear—earlier than usual on this night, as it was Saturday, the day on which Mr. Jim Baskins had made his first visit to Wicks's Hollow —she saw to it that her father should be well received. A stern something within the girl, something which must have descended to her from some far-back Puritan ancestor, was constantly warning her against retrogression.

"I'm going to keep it up," she had said to herself through shut teeth, when her mother and Bet had stood like roaring lions, so to speak, in the way of her projects —"I'm going to keep it up, if it kills me." But it was not going to kill her. Her plans once matured and system once inaugurated, she had an executive ability and a natural love of method which were gradually developing, and which made things easy for her.

Young Sparhawk remembered his parting words to her. Indeed, they and Mercy Wicks's face had been in his mind a great deal since he had made such an unexpectedly long call at Wicks's Hollow, and he had wanted to go and see her again even before he could invent a reasonable excuse. But he learned that a camp meeting was to be held in a grove half-way between Marlinsburg and Wicks's Hollow, and he decided to

invite Mercy to attend it on a certain afternoon with him.
As he mounted his buggy and took an early start for the
mountain, he could not conceal from himself that the
camp meeting would offer a pleasanter way of keeping
his promise to Mercy than bringing her down to Marlinsburg, where he was well known, and where he understood that no amount of deference to his acknowledged desire to do good would mitigate the fact that he
was, in a small way, "waiting upon" a young woman in
just the social position of Miss Mercy Wicks.

Mercy, in the meantime, had passed through a rather
harrowing experience. Mr. Jim Baskins had made her
another visit, and his manner had been such that Mercy
had felt it incumbent upon her to treat him in a very
cavalier, not to say forbidding, way. In fact, so very
caustic had she been upon his departure that Mr. Jim
Baskins had left in high dudgeon, and she knew very
well that he would never come back. He had not "made
love" to Mercy, but her quick sense had detected strong
indications that he was about to do so, and she had felt
that that was something she could not and would not
allow. She had thought of it since with some misgivings.
How kind Jim Baskins had been to give her those books!
What a blessing they had proved to her! Perhaps she
had been too rude to him; and then perhaps—she had
gleaned this impression from the stories that she had
read—perhaps she ought to give Mr. Baskins back the
books he had brought her. This was much against
Mercy's inclinations, and she did not propose to do it
unless some new revelation of her duty should be made
to her.

When young Sparhawk drove up to the door, therefore, Mercy was sitting in a deep, brown study by the

window, with her sewing lying unheeded in her lap; but when his eyes met hers, a tell-tale glow overspread her face, and she sprang up to welcome him. A voice within him chided him a little as he saw her brightening face. Were these quite the circumstances under which to do missionary work to the best advantage?

But it was a beautiful day, and he felt young and happy, and he acknowledged to himself a very strong desire to listen again to this frank girl's pleasant voice, and to watch her as she made her odd comments upon life and books.

But Mercy steadfastly refused to go to the meeting with him. And when he found there was really no use in urging her, he asked her suddenly if she wouldn't drive a little way with him.

Her face flushed with pleasure, and her heart beat so fast that she could scarcely answer him.

"To drive with you?" she repeated, wonderingly. This was like the books that she had read. It was like a beautiful dream. But she preserved outwardly her usual calm dignity of demeanor as she made her preparations, and amid the wide-mouthed but fortunately indistinct comments of her mother and of Bet, she kissed Looly, and drove away with Wesley Sparhawk. Their road lay through piney, shady woods. The girl threw off her ugly sun-bonnet, and her fair hair curled about her glowing face as she talked gayly with him of the books which she had read and of the scenes through which they had been passing.

It was a delightful experience to him, and like a fairy hour to her, and when he left her at the door of the little cabin, he promised to come again soon, and to bring her some books of which he had been telling her.

Before many days he kept his word, and appeared, bearing the parcel of books that he had promised. A week later he came again, and another visit succeeded. By this time the young man owned to himself that he was the victim of a violent passion for the beautiful backwoods girl, and Mercy knew in her secret heart that she was living but for her lover's smile, and that the days were dark when he did not come. Still, the young man said nothing. So beautiful a dream should not be disturbed, he reasoned in his blindness.

One evening, after he had left her, Mercy watched him out of sight, and Looly, who had come quietly up beside her as she stood looking after him, twined her arms around her sister, and they walked gravely in together. Then Mercy moved silently about the room preparing supper. Her mother had grown almost afraid of her, and very respectful, since this fine young man had begun to come to Wicks's Hollow, and, indeed, Mercy's manner, always dignified, had become almost majestic during these glorified weeks which had seen the growth of this love in her heart—a love such as the common souls by which she was surrounded could neither appreciate nor understand. They had all felt a subtle change in her, even to "the boys," but they had dared to say very little to her, though at Bet, who was constantly indulging in flirtations with the neighboring farmers' sons, they were always flinging taunts and innuendoes. To-night, however, when "Jake" came, he had been drinking a little, and he had met Wesley Sparhawk as he had been going home.

"Fine beau ye have thar, Merce," he said, sulkily, as he came in at the door. "Wonder 'f he'll be too stuck up ter speak to his gal's relations after the weddin'?"

Mercy turned on him with flaming eyes, and seemed to grow perceptibly taller as she looked at him.

"He's not my 'beau!' " she cried, passionately. "Don't you ever say such a thing as that again"; and the boy, excited though he was with drink, did not dare to re-open his lips.

That night Mercy went early to bed, but her brother's words rang in her ears, and she kept thinking, over and over again, of the story about which Wesley Sparhawk had talked with her weeks before.

"He had been brought up in luxury, and she—so differently." "They could never have been happy." "It could never have happened in real life."

As she thought, she sobbed and cried until, with the violence of her grief, although the night had worn then into the small hours, she even wakened Looly, who begged piteously to know why she was weeping. The morning was growing red in the east before she finally fell asleep.

The next day she read the story over again. Somehow lately she had not thought much about it. After she finished reading it, she laid the book down and thought out a sequel to it. Her quickened imagination devised a multitude of things which a girl like the one in the story might do to shock and offend a fastidious husband. No; such a thing could not happen in real life, as Wesley Sparhawk had said. It ought not to happen. People should marry people something like themselves; and as she worked out the problem more and more clearly and convincingly in her mind, a little poem which she had read somewhere, and which had for its refrain,

"I have dreamed my dream,
I have wakened at last,"

flitted through her mind again and again as she went sternly about her work.

In the afternoon she had usually sat down of late to a long, happy time of sewing, or of reading with Looly, but to-day Mercy could not work. She could only sit and hold her little sister and cry silently as she kissed and kissed the wondering child's face. It was only two or three nights before, that she had made the long, lonely journey up the mountain side to deposit some more money for Looly. The boys were getting very impatient lately because so little of their father's earnings found its way into their hands, and Mercy was inwardly fretted lest Jim Baskins in his pique had managed to let them know her secret. She had, therefore, removed the box in which she kept the money to an altogether different part of the mountain, and had hidden it anew.

"Whatever happens to me, my pet, your future shall be sure," she murmured in the child's ear. "Mercy will see to it that her little Looly has a chance. She shall have everything that Mercy can get for her."

Then she looked up and started, for a horse was cantering swiftly down the hill, and she knew that Wesley Sparhawk had come again.

He alighted, fastened his horse, and came toward her. She looked very grave and stately, and very cold, though her lashes were wet, and she was holding her little sister to her with desperate closeness. When he had left her on the evening before, she had been all smiles and warmth. He could not understand this sudden change. He took a seat beside her underneath the great tree where she had been sitting, and then she released Looly, whispering in her ear, and the child silently disappeared, leaving them alone together.

Young Sparhawk's face was very pale, and his lips trembled, and as soon as the little girl had left them, he began, impetuously: "I have come back because—because I have thought it over a good many times, and I want—I want, as you say, Mercy—I want to 'give you a chance.' You are young yet, Mercy; don't you want to go to school?"

She looked at him in vague bewilderment. "I couldn't," she gasped. "Oh, no; it's out of the question. There's Looly, and father, and Bet, and all of them, and I couldn't. I'm twenty now, and oh, I couldn't that way, anyway."

She stopped, for her voice began to choke. Her sleeplessness of the night before, and the long strain which she had been unconsciously enduring for the last few weeks, and which had culminated in her terrible mental struggle of the past twenty-four hours, had left her very weak. She knew what he was going to say, and a voice within her kept repeating: "It can never be; it can never be."

"I've come, Mercy," he said, huskily, "to think everything of you, and I believe you love me. Now the only thing you need to make you all that—all that—is necessary is an—an education. I've plenty of money, Mercy, and two or three years at a good boarding school would be all that you would need, and then, then——" And in spite of the fact that he knew Bet to be furtively watching him from a convenient window, he seized Mercy's hand and drew closer beside her.

"Don't you know," she said, with a great effort, and in a strangely altered voice—"don't you know in the story—he had been brought up in luxury, and she—it had been so different with her?"

"That was another case altogether," said Wesley Spar-hawk, impatiently. "She had not been educated."

"Oh, yes, she had," corrected Mercy, growing more fluent as her convictions became more intense. "She had, as you say, 'seen a great deal of the world,'" and she went on to describe some of the details of the story which had apparently escaped his mind, until he stopped her, imperiously.

"Well, they were not we, Mercy," he said. "I can't be happy without you, and if you want me to have any peace of mind, you must marry me. You're a good girl; you're a perfect queen, Mercy; you're the noblest girl I ever saw. Just think what you've done up here in the woods without any help—in fact, with everything against you! It's wonderful! How different your life is now from what it was only six short months ago when I first saw you, and——"

She stopped him with a gesture of despair.

"But I could never learn——"

"Yes, yes——"

"No, I could never learn to be what your wife ought to be. I should always feel that you had stooped to marry me. I could never bear the scorn of your friends, nor your scorn of mine. Oh, it would kill me!"

Her hands hid her face from him, and she began to sob.

"Now listen to me, Mercy," he commenced, again per-emptorily, but again she stopped him.

"I cannot tell you how plain it is to me," she said, growing calm and dispassionate once more; "it is as if an angel had shown me what was going to happen. I seem to see our life just as it would be, even if I should try to learn how to be different, and should marry you.

I seem to see such suffering for you, such misery for me——"

"The picture is not true!" he cried, despairingly. "I shall do by you just what is right, as nearly as I can find it out, and it would bring happiness to us both. I have always had my way, Mercy, and I am not a bad man, am I? I should not scorn you, nor let you be scorned. I would kill any one——"

She checked him again.

"It is of no use," she said. "I have made up my mind that it is best that you should go, and not come back. You will find somebody——" Her eyes filled with tears, her voice failed her, and she left her sentence unfinished. "I commenced," she said, a moment later, while he watched her in a silence half mournful, half angry—"I commenced by working for Looly, and I am sure that that is my work that God has given me to do—to help Looly on—and that that's why He never gave me any chance for myself. I think you are good—oh, I do respect you very much—but I think I can stand it, and be happy—after a while—working for Looly. You had better go now. Good-bye."

She walked away from him, slowly, sorrowfully, but with an air that forbade him from following her. He turned once when he had nearly reached his horse, but she was nowhere to be seen, so he mounted and rode away. A few days later he came again, but she had seen him coming, and in evident expectation that he would return, had prepared a note, which, running away herself, she had left with Looly to be given him. It said, in Mercy's cramped and unaccustomed hand, "You must not come; I shall always be gone." And after that he came no more.

It was a raw and gusty day in the following March, when Mr. Wesley Sparhawk, sitting in his father's elegant library in Marlinsburg, was told that a visitor wished to see him, and a moment later Mercy Wicks was shown into the room. At first he did not know her, but she quietly removed her woolen hood, and then, in spite of a great change which had come over her face, he recognized it.

"My God!" he cried, springing up and leading her tenderly to a seat. "What is it, Mercy? What ails you? Have you been ill?"

She nodded mutely. Tears were trickling down her face, and she coughed again and again.

"Ah, you have come to tell me," he cried, "that you have changed your mind?"

"No, no," she said, unsteadily; "I was right; I see it now more plainly than I saw it before; but, oh! it was very sweet to have you—love—me!"

Her tears began to flow again, and the young man, overcome by the pathos of her looks and of her words, laid his head in his hands upon the table and sobbed aloud.

When she grew calmer, she drew a small but heavy bag from underneath her shawl.

"I came to bring you this," she said. "It's Looly's money, you know, that I used to keep on the mountain. I went up there, two or three weeks ago, and got it. I was growing so weak that I knew I couldn't go again, and I've brought it to you. You'll see that it is spent for Looly—you'll see that she has everything done for her that this money can buy, won't you?—for the love that you said you had for me."

He bowed assent, and took the money in his hands.

He could not speak, but she had grown quite calm, and went on to tell him about herself.

"I've been running down ever since you saw me,' she said. "They say it's quick consumption, or something like that, and the doctor said that it would kill me to go out to-day; but I felt able, and I wanted you to see to this. I felt as if I could trust you, and you would know just what kind of a lady I wanted Looly to be. If I'm to die before she is grown up, of course it might as well be soon as a little later. I think Looly'd better go away somewhere before long. I've told pa, and he has promised to do just as you say. I rode down with him, and I know he's in a hurry to go back, so I reckon I hadn't better stay any longer, for you understand."

She rose weakly, and though he begged to be allowed to take her home, she would only let him go with her to the place where she was to join her father.

"I declare!" said one street idler to another, as he saw them going by together, "who's that Wesley Sparhawk's helping along with such care? Looks like somebody out of the backwoods, and I reckon it is. By the way, I've heard he was just smitten with a daughter of that old Wicks that lives up on the mountain in what they call 'Wicks's Hollow.' Heard that he offered himself to her, and she wouldn't have him; but of course, that couldn't possibly be so."

"Of course," rejoined his companion, with an incredulous sneer, as they watched the strange pair out of sight.

A month later Mercy Wicks died.

Tomlin Dresser's
Disappearance.

THE stage started from Vine Lake every morning at seven. It reached Doremus about half-past nine. If more housewives than usual stopped Gale Truax, the handsome and accommodating driver, to hand him a letter, or to ask him to buy a spool of silk or a package of bird food for them in Doremus—why, then it was ten o'clock, instead of half-past nine, when the stage drew up before the door of the Doremus post-office. Ten o'clock was early enough, so that Gale Truax did not usually have to hurry the housewives.

Tomlin Dresser's house was ten miles from Vine Lake, on the road to Doremus. The neighborhood in which he lived was in the latter town, but it was called Bashan. It was in New England, and not many miles from a famous college, though you might not have thought it. There was more need of missionaries in Bashan than there is in some parts of Ceylon or of Uruguay.

The Vine Lake stage usually reached Tomlin Dresser's about a quarter before nine. It often stopped there. This was not wholly because there were so many passengers or packages to be left there, but was partly because Tomlin Dresser's young wife Rose had come from Vine Lake, and had known Gale Truax for years, as well as many others who resided there. Gale Truax often had messages for Rose from these various friends and acquaintances. Besides, Rose was much tied at home with the care of her housekeeping and of her pretty baby, and she had often to send to Doremus for little things which she wanted, and which Gale Truax brought back with him when the stage returned, about two in the afternoon.

It seemed to Tomlin Dresser one April morning, as he was ploughing on the slope about twenty rods back of his house, that Gale Truax stopped too long to talk with Rose.

"He seems to have more nonsense to talk to my wife, confound him!" muttered Tomlin Dresser, "than he talks to all the girls in Doremus."

Tomlin had been ploughing for more than two hours. It occurred to him now that he was tired. He would sit down and rest, and then he could think.

Every one must have noticed that the same thing can happen, day after day, for months, perhaps for years, without attracting attention, until suddenly, without special reason, one begins to think about it as if it were very new. This was the way in which Tomlin Dresser began to think about the Vine Lake stage stopping in front of his door.

As he sat on his plough chewing a blade of grass— the worst thing that Tomlin ever chewed—the sound of Rose's fresh, young laugh came floating up to him.

"—— that good-looking Gale Truax!" thought Tomlin Dresser, with unwonted profanity. "What's he saying to my wife?"

Presently he heard Gale Truax chirrup to his horse, and Rose's voice crying after him:

"Now, Gale, don't you forget—two yards."

What a sweet voice it was! Tomlin Dresser had courted Rose for two years, and he had been married to her for two years more, but the sound of her voice

thrilled hi n through and through to this day. He was
a sluggish man, too—square-built, slow-motioned, slow-
spoken. He was of medium height, with straight black
hair, which was not often cut. There was only one
barber in Doremus, and he was generally busy when
Tomlin could get time to go to him. Tomlin hated to
wait, so he seldom went. Consequently now and usually
his hair was long in his neck and behind his ears. His
young beard was soft and black around his face, yet
growing already well up into his cheeks; his eyebrows
were black and straight; his eyes were black, and there
was a defect in one of them, which sometimes made him
look cross-eyed, though the general effect one commonly got from looking at them was that they were
steady and level. They were very sombre—almost too
intense.

Tomlin was very strong. There was probably not a
stronger farmer than he in all the country around Doremus village.

"I ought to be strong," he said to himself now, as he
looked down on his brawny arms and passed his left
hand over the hard muscles of his right forearm. "I'm
strong, and I ought to be. I've worked like a dog, and
it's all been for her. First I thought she never was going
to look at me. Then I pitched in and earned my horse,
so that she would sorter notice me. Then when I could
see she was beginning to think of me, and thinking I
might maybe amount to something sometime, I worked
harder yet, and earned a patch o' land. Then she said
she'd have me, and I put in and got money enough to
build my house and barn, and since we got married and
moved in, Lord, how I've worked! And now there's
the young one. I'd work myself to death for them.

and I'll bet I'm a fool for doing it! The neighbors must have noticed that confounded fool stopping here so every day or two," pursued Tomlin Dresser, in his slow, sullen way, the smouldering fire within him eating deeper and deeper into his soul. "Likely as not they're laughing in their sleeves at me for letting my wife flirt with that good-looking Gale Truax. I've kinder seen it for weeks, now, but I ain't thought about it as I'd oughter."

The sweat poured from him as he reflected. His head drooped. He took off his hat, and rubbed his forehead and neck hard with his clean, red handkerchief.

Suddenly a voice spoke just beside him. Rose had come up so softly that he had not heard her, and was standing there with the baby—a beautiful baby—perhaps nine or ten months old, fair and blue-eyed like its mother, whose golden hair, smoothed carefully when she had twisted it into a generous knot that morning, was now in little rings and curls all over her shining head. Her face was rosy, her eyes laughing and sunny. She looked as pretty and girlish and wilful, as she stood gazing into her young husband's face, in her loose calico gown, with her plump baby on her arm, as any ballroom belle that was ever seen.

Her eyes grew clouded and anxious as she gazed into his.

"What are you sitting down for, Lin?" she asked him. "You sick?"

"I was—well—sorter tired like," stammered Tomlin Dresser.

"I saw you out of the window, and I didn't know but you'd got hurt or something. Says I to myself, 'Maybe the horse has kicked him.' "

"No," returned Tomlin Dresser, shaking her off as

10

she took hold of his arm with her free hand, and looked searchingly into his face. "I'm all right. You'd better go in."

The baby crowed at him, and stretched out his little arms, but his father did not respond as he usually did.

"You'd better go in," he repeated, as Rose held the baby out toward him, expecting him to take the child. Tomlin only nodded to him, and turned away.

" 'Twouldn't hurt you to hold him a minute," hinted Rose, pouting.

"I ain't got time. Take him in. Get along."

Tomlin turned and took hold of his plough.

"Why, Lin Dresser!" cried Rose, half in jest and half in earnest. "I shouldn't think you liked us a bit—should we, Dick?"

She kissed the child, and pressed him close.

"Well, good-bye, crosspatch! I've got a good mind to let your dinner burn."

She made up a playful face at her husband, and walked with a leisurely step toward the house.

"What ails him?" she thought. "It can't be money matters. He said he wasn't sick. What is it? Maybe —maybe—" and Rose remembered, with a blush, Gale Truax, and what a jolly talk they had had together at the gate. Rose's father and mother had died in Vine Lake when she was a little girl. She had never had brothers nor sisters; but she had cousins still living there, and one of them was going to be married soon. Gale Truax had been telling her all about it. "Very well, if Tomlin Dresser is going to act that way," thought his spirited little wife, "I'll—I'll—well—I'll teach him that he needn't be so cross to baby and me."

She kissed the baby, and sat down to rock him to sleep.

There were tears in her eyes. Her husband had never looked at her before just as he had looked at her that morning. The recollection of it made her hot and angry. Then the defect in his eye—it had never seemed so glaring to her as it had that morning; it made him look fierce and ugly, somehow. A sort of a foreboding of evil shadowed the girl's bright young spirit. She had never rocked her baby to sleep before without singing to him, but to-day she could not warble so much as a note.

In spite of her defiant feelings, Rose did not burn her husband's dinner. Instead, she cooked it even more carefully than usual. The baby had a long nap, and while he was asleep, Rose tidied her house up to the last point of neatness.

When the stage came along after dinner, Gale Truax stopped and held out Rose's parcel. Rose had wavered between thinking that she would talk with him a good while, and that she would just thank him coolly and let him go right on. What she finally did was to run out and get the parcel, take it merrily, and talk until she heard pretty much all of the Doremus news. She laughed a great deal, and she knew that she was looking very flushed and pretty, for Gale Truax regarded her with unmistakable admiration. When she turned at last to go into the house, she found that she had been talking out at the gate for quite half an hour. There had been no passengers, as was often the case, and Gale could easily make up lost time.

"I don't care," thought pretty Rose Dresser, tossing her head; "he needn't be so cross." But in her heart she yearned over the dark-browed young fellow following his horse through the toilsome furrows. In her secret soul she believed that no other woman had ever been

loved as she was loved by her husband. Rose was modest
enough about it. It was not, she had hundreds of times
said to herself, because she was so much more charming than other girls, but because no other man whom
she had ever seen or imagined was capable of loving so
ardently and so evenly and so long as Tomlin Dresser.
The sustained, unfaltering power of his will, the awful
self-obliterating humility of his love—though poor Rose,
who had little enough education, could not have analyzed
it—frightened her whenever she thought of it soberly.
Now she could not help a tremulous fear within her.
If Tomlin Dresser really were jealous, what might he
not do?

Supper time came. The baby was very gleeful, and
Rose played with him, with a good deal of noise and
demonstration, but Tomlin paid little heed to it all. Not
once did the dark look on his brow lighten. His eyes
were duller and smaller and more sullen than Rose
had ever seen them before. But she sang about the
house as though everything were as usual, got the baby
to sleep, and then sat down beside the lamp and sewed.

Tomlin Dresser took up a newspaper and read it for
a while. Then he dropped it and looked into the fire;
for the evening had come on chilly, and they were glad to
gather around the kitchen stove, through the open grate
of which the coals showed cheerily.

After a little he rose and began to pace slowly about
the room. His wife was humming some rattling revival
melody. At last she said:

"Lin, you make me as nervous as a fish, walking
around so. You're awfully poky to-night. Why don't
you sit down and keep still?"

"I'll go out if I disturb you," he said, huskily, and taking up his hat, he strolled out into the night.

There was a bright moon, almost full, and he roamed around in its light for an hour or more, first out into the barn, where the horse and the cow were naturally surprised to see their master at such an hour, and then into the field where he had been ploughing during the day. It has often been remarked that things put on a very different look in the moonlight from that which they assume in any other. Now, as Tomlin Dresser wandered aimlessly about, his whole life looked to him very different from what it had ever looked before.

When at last he went in and sought his bed, he found Rose and the baby fast asleep. He locked the doors softly, and lay down quietly in his place. The moonlight made the room almost as light as day. He could plainly see Rose's pretty face as she slept.

For hours he lay there wide awake. The moon sank low, and still he could not sleep. The slow devouring fire within him was burning more and more fiercely.

"She's sick of me," he was saying over to himself, in his sure, deliberate way. "She's sick of me. At first she was contented with a hard-working man, who didn't care for any other women, and never had. She was satisfied with me and Dick; but she's getting sick of me, I can see. She'd rather have that Gale Truax, with his curly mustache, and his 'Excuse me,' and all his palaver."

Tomlin Dresser anathematized the handsome stage-driver, with hot, reiterated imprecations.

"Well," he went on once more, in the same train of simple reasoning over which he was going again and again— "well, if she wants him, I want her to have him; I want

her to have what she likes. If I was out of the way,
maybe she'd have him."

It did not occur to Tomlin Dresser, in the anguish of
his soul, that the course ·of reasoning which he had
adopted might do his wife an injustice. He did not
think of the lack of character, of stability of purpose,
which he was unconsciously attributing to her.

In his simple, unsophisticated mind she had always
stood unquestioned, like a goddess. Now she stood
unquestioned still. She had talked with Gale Truax in a
way which showed plainly to her husband that she loved
the handsome stage-driver—the Adonis both of Vine
Lake and Doremus. He was glad enough to have her
smile upon him, of course. Any man would be, thought
Tomlin, bitterly.

She was not to blame, as he saw the matter now; at
least he did not blame her, though he heaped fresh
maledictions every hour upon the head of the dapper
youth who had stepped between them.

When Tomlin rose in the morning, he was unrefreshed.
He ate his breakfast in silence, and went out again to his
work. He had planned to go off to a distant lot to-day,
for he had ploughed as far as he meant to this year on the
hillside. When he was ready, however, he could not
bear to leave the vicinity of the house. He had a horrible
desire to see whether the stage stopped again. There
was a little more planting that he might do in the garden.
He would do it to-day.

The stage came along early. It stopped. Rose went
out to the gate with the baby on her arm. Again there
was a merry dialogue between her and Gale Truax, and
again she gave him an errand to do for her in the
village.

Tomlin Dresser ate his dinner as if he were in a dream. He did not speak. Rose was saucy and indifferent. The stage stopped again at two o'clock, and Gale Truax gave her a parcel.

When Tomlin came in to supper, Rose showed him a little fancy bon-bon basket.

"See here," she said, with a fresh desire to torment him; "Gale brought this to Dick from Doremus. He said that I could have some of the candy if I wanted to. Of course, he knew I wouldn't let Dick eat it. Wasn't he good? My husband, maybe, doesn't care to speak to me; but luckily everybody doesn't dislike me so much."

She tossed her head, ate some of the candy, and threw a piece of it toward Tomlin. He let it fall to the floor. Then he picked it up—it would save her trouble for him to pick it up—and threw it into the fire. His sombre eyes were more lightless and wretched than she had ever seen them. Besides, he looked very cross-eyed.

Rose went on mechanically with a song which she had begun. Now and then she stopped in a conspicuous way to enjoy her candy.

About nine o'clock she yawned, and remarked that the baby- was "a good deal better company than somebody else that she might mention." Then she went off to bed, and was soon asleep. Tomlin Dresser sat moodily before the fire, or paced up and down the clean and pleasant kitchen. He was filled with only one thought now. He wanted to get away—to get away from Rose and Gale Truax and Doremus, and all the people whom he had ever seen. Everything seemed warped and unnatural to him. He felt as though he were crazy. Perhaps he was.

At last he took ink and a pen from a shelf, and found a

sheet of paper in a table drawer. Tomlin was not a ready
writer, but he had composed before long a legible if not
an elegant letter. It said:

"Dear Rose: I am going away.   I shall probably
never come back.   There is money in the bank.   The
book is in my desk in the parlor.   Use it all you want.
There is a little more ploughing and planting to do.   You
will have to get somebody to do it.   I can't.   Good-bye.
I want you to have a good time.   Lin."

Not a word about the baby.   What did he care about
the baby?   His heart, his mind, his whole being, were
full of Rose, only Rose.   He went into the bedroom, and
looked at her asleep in the moonlight.   Her baby lay
upon her breast.   Tomlin Dresser's powerful frame was
shaking like a cluster of green hop blooms in the August
breeze.   His heart hammered, hammered against his
ribs with a force which seemed to him greater than the
force of his strong right arm, but he managed to creep
out again into the kitchen.   Then he looked into his
pocketbook to see if he had money enough; brought a
valise, and tumbled a few things into it; got his hat, put
out the light, and stole softly away from the house
through the woodshed.

He had calculated to catch the midnight train to Boston, and he reached the Dorcmus station just as it was
coming into view around a curve half a mile away.   The
next morning he was in Boston.

In the morning paper he read that a number of men
were wanted to ship ice to New York from some place in
Maine.   He went up there, was employed, and worked
hard all summer.   Other men were discharged, but Tom-

lin was kept. He did the work of two men, the "boss" said. When the ice job was finished, he was put to work on lumber.

The winter came on, and Tomlin went up into the woods chopping. He seldom spoke, and he acquired the nickname of "Tomfool" among his mates, with whom he would not drink and carouse. He had a long pipe, which, when work was over, every day, he smoked, smoked, smoked, until he went to bed. All through the summer and winter he was in a dazed and bewildered frame of mind. He worked unceasingly, so that each night he was utterly exhausted. He felt as though he had turned into a machine.

April came around again. It found Tomlin Dresser up at the headwaters of a great Maine river, sending off rafts of logs.

One day it was soft and balmy, and he began to feel as he had not felt for months. It seemed to him as though his head had been sealed up with sealing-wax, and that suddenly the sealing-wax had been broken and his head was free. Pictures presented themselves before him incessantly of his distant home upon the hillside. He seemed to see his wife moving about the plain rooms which he had taken such pleasure in planning conveniently and comfortably for her. He had had no clear vision of her in his mind before since he had left Doremus. Oh, how pretty she was! How red her lips were! How merry her eyes! Instinctively he put out his arms to gather her into them, and he groaned aloud when they closed upon the empty air. He seemed to hear the baby crowing and laughing. What a bright baby it was! Oh, what an interminable age it had been since he had seen them! How could he have staid away so long!

"Oh, yes!" he told himself, bewildered. "It 'is because Rose does not love me any longer. She loves somebody else, and perhaps she has gone to live with him."

"What!" cried an awakened voice within him! "Rose live with somebody else! You insult her. Rose is a good girl. She is married to you, and she will stick to you."

"Why," he asked of this voice, "do you think that she loves me now?"

"Of course she does," answered the awakened voice. "She is true and good. She promised to love, honor and obey. Rose isn't the girl to go back on her promise. She isn't like some of those creatures who live on the edge of Bashan, and who have the finger of scorn pointed at them by every honest man and woman. You wrong her cruelly."

"But she did not laugh and talk with me for many a long day as she laughed and talked with Gale Truax at the gate; ay, and she laughed and talked with him for weeks nearly every day."

"Oh, she is young and light-hearted," admitted the awakened voice. "Perhaps you were not quite tender enough toward her, and perhaps she liked to see how jealous she could make you. Perhaps you were really morose and ugly to her. Didn't she keep your little house beautifully neat for you? Wasn't she a dutiful wife to you? Couldn't you have overlooked a little folly on her part, and wouldn't she have come around all right if you had only shown her that you trusted her fully? What a brute you were to go off and leave her to shift for herself!"

This involuntary interview had the effect upon Tomlin

Dresser of a vivid, awful dream. He had come to himself at last. It is said that overweening love unhinges a man; Tomlin Dresser had perhaps loved his wife too intensely. At any rate, he felt now as though he were just regaining his common sense, after having been without it for a long time. In a tremor of agitation, he rushed at once to throw up his place, and two days later he reached Doremus by an evening train.

He skulked off from his car on the side opposite the station, leaped a fence, and was almost out of sight before the train passed on. A little way from his home he overtook two men in a wagon—old neighbors of his. Their talk sounded loud in the calm moonlit night. Tomlin hurried to come nearer, though he kept close in the shade of the bushes by the roadside.

"I never could understand Tomlin Dresser's going off so," remarked one of them, an elderly man. "Some think he was crazy."

"I don't know," replied the other, a young fellow, shaking his head. "Some think there was foul play there."

"Oh, but he wrote his wife a letter!"

"Do you know that he wrote his wife a letter?"

"Know? I know I've heard it all around."

"I don't believe he ever wrote her any letter. She's that proud she won't tell anything, and nobody knows anything for sure. I've heard that she thinks he was a little mite off his head."

"Maybe. Anyhow she's showed pluck, if ever a woman did."

"Well, she had to. It was pretty mean in Tomlin Dresser to go off so, if he did know what he was about. She didn't have any home to go to, as some women

have, so she just made up her mind to keep this one.
They say she is out in all weathers, raking and hoeing
and planting, and what not; takes care of the horse and
cow pretty much herself; nobody to help her most of the
time but that great hulking boy, that cousin of hers from
Vine Lake, and he's no good—a simpleton if ever there
was one. She does all of the head-work, and a good share
of the hand-work. Rose is clever, but it's hard on her.
She looks a sight older than she did a year ago. They
say she's running down all the time. The doctor says,
I've heard, that she's going into a decline if something
doesn't happen pretty quick. They say she expects him
home again some time."

"Sho! Just like a woman. If Tomlin Dresser'd been
a-coming, he'd have come long before this time. I don't
believe he'll ever show his face in this part of the country,
nor anywhere else. I believe he's dead."

The other man began to rake up remarkable instances
of which he had heard of men who had returned after
mysterious disappearances, and Tomlin gradually fell
away behind them. About half a mile from his home he
left the main road for a short cut which he knew well.
In a few moments he was beside the little house.

It was about half-past eight. The curtain of the kitchen
window was up, and Tomlin looked in.

The "hulking boy" was mending a farm tool on one
side of the table, and Rose, with her lap full of sewing,
was sitting on the other side. She had dropped her work,
and her head was resting upon her arms on the table.
With a little stamp and shuffle upon the mat opposite the
door, such as he always used to give, he lifted the latch
and walked unsteadily in. Rose started up with a little
shriek, and her work fell in a heap to the floor.

"Oh, Lin!" she cried, and then she threw herself into the strong arms which he opened to receive her.

He raised her from her feet as though she had been a child. His heart smote him afresh when he felt her weight to be so light. He bore her into the little bedroom, laid her gently on the bed, and covered her face with kisses.

"Oh, Lin!" she began, fast and pleadingly; "I want to tell you that I am ashamed. I just talked with Gale Truax, first, because I didn't think, and then to tease you. I ought to have known better. I wouldn't do such a thing now. I'm older, you see, and wiser than I used to be. I haven't spoken to him since you went away. I couldn't bear to see him any more. Oh, Lin, wasn't it that that made you go off so? I haven't used all the money. I tried to make it go as far as I could. I was afraid you would not come back. Oh, Lin, it has nearly killed me!"

"I guess I was sorter crazy-like," answered Tomlin Dresser, swallowing hard. "I thought you didn't like me any more, and it made me feel—queer. Don't say any more about it, Rose. We'll act as if it hadn't ever happened."

"Yes, we will," she agreed, still clinging to him fondly, repentantly.

Tomlin Dresser went to the closet, hung up his coat there, and took down an old one which he used to wear. It was hanging in its old place. He put it on. He seemed to hang away the ice and the lumber of Maine with his coat.

"I see," he said, speaking to Rose, who was stooping over the boy, pink and beautiful as ever, in his old place on the bed—"I see that hill patch ain't ploughed yet. I'll go right to work on it in the morning."

Daffodils.

THE STORY OF AN EASTER SUNDAY.

"ARE there always just two daffodil buds in that bunch under the east window, Aunt Justinia?"

Miss Romaine Goddard stood pensively looking down in the yellow glow of the soft March weather at two daffodil buds, which had just revealed themselves above the warm, brown earth among a cluster of tiny, barren leaves.

"Oh, no," responded Miss Justinia Goddard, a little argumentatively, as though her daffodils had been maligned. "Sometimes there are a good many. Then again there aren't any, and I think the plant may die; but it doesn't. It always comes up somehow."

"There were just two buds on it when I was here before."

Miss Romaine looked dreamily off into the distance.

"How you do remember, Romaine!" exclaimed her aunt, staring at her. "It is fifteen years this month since you were here before. Why, I can't even remember how many buds there were under this window last year. It is my sewing window, too."

"The buds were blasted that year, I recollect. They never came to anything," her niece added, a little under her breath. "But what is that noise?" she exclaimed, in a different tone. "Poor little Le Roy! Something has happened to him."

A boy of perhaps eight or nine came slowly around the

corner of the old house as she spoke. He was weeping profusely, and shrieking at the top of his voice.

"I presume he has had some trouble about a postage-stamp," suggested Miss Justinia, not unkindly, but with perfect composure.

"I've—lost—my—new—Guatemala—stamp," sobbed Le Roy.

"There! I told you so!" ejaculated Miss Justinia. "If Le Roy Goddard cries, or if he laughs, there's always a postage-stamp at the bottom of it."

Le Roy went on to detail, in the pauses between his heart-broken wails, exactly how he had lost the stamp. He ended by implying that the only way of quieting him was a financial one, as his special friend, Guy Rice, "down by the village," had a Guatemala stamp at his disposal, but charged an exorbitant price for it, refusing to "trade."

"I cannot give you any more money to buy stamps with," said his aunt, severely. "You must learn to be more careful."

Le Roy began to wail more fiercely than ever, but he relaxed a little as his cousin Romaine put her hand into her pocket.

"Here, dear," she said, indulgently, "run along and buy your stamp."

"You will spoil him, Romaine," protested Miss Justinia.

"That is just what you used to say of Justin," retorted her niece, good-humoredly; "but I didn't."

"You beat all to remember," said her aunt again. Justin had been the only son of her favorite brother. He had been named for her, and brought up by her. He was in business in the city, and as his wife had died when their only child was very young, Le Roy had been put under the care of his aunt, as his father had been before him.

Miss Justinia and her niece, who had come from New York only the day before, had been standing, throughout all of the interview with Le Roy, beside the daffodils; but now they began to move away over the brown turf toward the large old-fashioned garden.

"Fifteen years!" mused Romaine Goddard aloud. "I can't believe that it has been even one year. Everything seems just about the same. Lent had just begun then, and it is not half gone now. I was twenty then, but I don't feel so very much older now. Justin was capering about here then, and now we have Le Roy. Justin used to be devoted to me. Do you remember, Aunt Justina?"

"I remember how he used to carry your letters to the post-office," remarked her aunt, with some sternness. "Well, thank fortune, that affair never amounted to anything."

A delicate color crept up Romaine Goddard's refined but strongly marked face.

"Why do you say that, Aunt Justinia?" she demanded. with unexpected emphasis.

"Why—why—because it wasn't a suitable thing," stammered her aunt, taken by surprise.

"But what was there about George Ober that was unsuitable?" continued Romaine, her gray eyes flashing a little. "He was not rich, and so my father did not like him; for my poor father was determined that I should marry a millionaire. Why do you suppose he felt so, Aunt Justinia, when he knew that I should have enough anyway? And was there anything else against George Ober? You knew his family when they lived here. I don't suppose you ever saw George after his boyhood?"

"Yes, I did. I saw him just once. It was in this very garden, that very spring. You had not been gone a week."

"That spring!" said Romaine Goddard, slowly. "What do you mean, Aunt Justinia? You saw him—here? And you never told me?"

There was an old stone bench under an apple tree, just on the edge of the garden. Romaine sank down upon this bench, and nervously pulled her aunt down beside her.

"Tell me about it," she demanded.

"Why, child," remonstrated Miss Justinia, bristling a little at her niece's tone, 'there isn't any more to tell; that is, much. He just came—came right out here into the garden, where I was puttering about just as I am to-day, and asked for you."

"For me! And I never knew his ship had come in at all!"

There was a hint of tears in the dignified Miss Goddard's voice. Her aunt looked at her in dismay.

"Your father and mother didn't want you to know Your father told me so himself, when you went home; and he said, too, that there was a prospect of a great match for you there. I supposed that you had fallen in with that. Girls generally do."

"Oh, that was such a spindling, silly fellow!" exclaimed Romaine Goddard, in disgust. "I never thought of it for a moment. I don't know how father and mother could——"

The hint of tears became more pronounced. Her aunt looked at her sharply and disapprovingly.

"Romaine Goddard! At your age, and your father not dead a year yet, and your mother gone long ago! How can you go on so?"

11

"I'm not blaming them," declared the younger woman, the tears rolling down her cheeks in good earnest now. "But tell me what he said, every word."

"Every word! Why, child, that was fifteen years ago."

"But sometimes we remember what happened twenty years ago better than we do what happened last week. Can't you think?"

Think! Miss Justinia could not forget it if she should try. She had hoped and supposed, in her blind devotion to Romaine's father, that her niece had forgotten her old lover long ago. It had not occurred to this good woman until this moment that perhaps Romaine had lived single all these years because of that handsome young lieutenant.

"Well," proceeded Miss Justinia, gazing disapprovingly into her niece's eager face, "this young fellow, as I was saying, all rigged up in his uniform, came striding around the corner of the house there, lifting his hat, and asking, in the most breathless way, for you. Then he went on to inquire about the young man you were going to marry. You see, your father had written him just what he had written me, and had told him that his daughter, under the circumstances, desired to close the correspondence with Lieutenant Ober."

"Oh, Aunt Justinia! Well?"

"And the young man's face was rather—well—pale, and I felt sorry for him. I fancied he couldn't quite see when he went away, and I thought you oughtn't to have flirted with him so hard."

"Flirted!" breathed the younger woman. "You ought to have known me better, Aunt Justinia. And why didn't you tell me this fifteen years ago?"

"I didn't like to write it," explained Miss Justinia, with

some dignity; "and I didn't see you again—not till your mother died—was it three years afterward? And I haven't seen you since, have I? You know, Romaine, that I'm odd; I don't pretend I'm not; I just live right here in the old homestead, and I don't go out of the gate once a month, except to the little gray chapel yonder. I don't journey unless I have to. It's a hard day's ride from here to New York, and I don't go unless there's a funeral or something uncommon. But I've asked you to come here again and again."

"Yes; and now perhaps you can guess why I haven't come," confessed the younger woman, the despairing tone in which she had spoken hitherto changing to one of rebellion. "I felt as though my life had been spoiled, and it happened here. I always loved the old place itself, and I always loved you, Aunt Justinia, but I might as well tell you the whole story, at our age. George Ober was the only man I ever wanted to marry. Father couldn't understand it; but I have always measured my feeling for other men by the feeling I had for George Ober, and I never cared half so much for any one else as I did for him. Maybe you know how it is from experience, Aunt Justinia. We are two old maids together" —a pitiful look came into Romaine's gray eyes—"but you are so strong and self-contained that you never would pour it all out so foolishly as I do."

She ceased, for an acute shadow passed over her aunt's thin face, though she said nothing. No, Miss Justinia could not "pour it all out so." She wished devoutly that she could.

"I wonder how he had happened to come up here?" Romaine began again, abruptly.

"Oh, there are some Obers down in the village here—

cousins of his. I never see them." Miss Justinia's tone was full of scorn.

"Why? Aren't they respectable people?"

"Mercy! yes, child! Don't speak so cross. The Obers," proceeded Miss Justinia, bent upon giving to the case of her dead brother as good a showing as she could—"the Obers are all well enough; but they are an open-handed, shiftless kind of folks—the whole tribe. Your father never liked them. And 'Ober' is such a name! I always disliked it."

"It is just as good as Goddard," insisted Romaine, amused in spite of herself at the turn of her aunt's argument. "And George's father, though he was only a poor clerk, was just as noble as he could be. I suppose George was about as old as Le Roy here when they went to live in the city. After that Bessie, the sister, went to school with me for years. They denied themselves everything to educate her. I was at their house every day almost, and I can't remember the time that George and I didn't love each other. We never were really engaged, but we always understood each other. He went to the Naval Academy, and then he started on that long cruise. He must have just come back when he was here. I suppose my father's letter was waiting for him when he reached port—very likely before Lent began—so he did not answer my letters. I was proud, and would not write until he wrote, and—well, we have said enough for to-day. I'm sure I never thought of our getting off on this subject when we stood over the daffodils. Those two blasted buds have followed me all my life—but it is absurd. His life hasn't been blasted, I suppose. He was just a year older than I. Now he is thirty-six—a staid, middle-aged man, probably with a wife and half-a-dozen children. Bessie died when we were sixteen, and the Obers moved ever so far out West; but, though I've no means of knowing, it is probably just as I say. He is domestic and contented, and I—I am 'the rich Miss Goddard, with everything on earth to make her happy,' as I overheard myself described at a party one evening."

She laughed bitterly and rose to walk further, when Le Roy came bounding across the leafless beds.

"It's dinner-time," he shouted to Aunt Justinia's dismay; "and here's the Guatemala stamp, like the one I lost, and here's an Egyptian pyramid stamp, and here's the Ionian Islands, and Finland. Aren't they pretty? And I've got a lot more to trade."

He smiled broadly, put his treasures into an envelope in his pocket, and confidingly clasped his cousin's hand in his own, as they proceeded toward the dining-room.

"I'm going down to the hotel with Guy Rice," he rambled on between portentous mouthfuls, after the noon dinner had been served.

Miss Justinia and her niece had been talking about the garden, and she had not paid much attention to Le Roy's occasional remarks, but the word "hotel" now caught her ear.

"I can't have you running to the hotel," she began, sharply. "You have been to the village once to-day to see Guy. It's two miles there. You have walked enough."

Le Roy dropped his knife and fork and began to howl dismally. Miss Justinia twisted his chair a little away from the table.

"Go," she said, peremptorily, to the child—"go, and don't come back till you can stop crying. A great boy like you! What will Cousin Romaine think? After giving you that money, too."

"I can get some splendid stamps without any money down at the hotel," blubbered Le Roy, making no motion to obey orders. "Guy's got a lot there."

"Oh!" said Miss Justinia, weakening a little, for, like John Gilpin's wife, she had a frugal mind. "I didn't understand. How do you get stamps for nothing down there? I supposed you just wanted to tramp."

Le Roy's pudgy little face began to clear. "If you'd 'a' waited, I'd 'a' told you before," he commenced, reproachfully; "but you just told me to 'go.'"

"I was hasty," admitted his aunt, with a sufficient show of penitence. "Well?"

"There's a man at the hotel—he's a Frenchman, or a Russian, or a Kodak, or something," said Le Roy, vaguely. "Anyhow, he likes little boys, and he's been everywhere, and he gets sights of stamps, and he used to know Guy's father, and he gave Guy some stamps, and Guy says he knows he'll give me some. We won't stay but just a minute."

"Well," Miss Justinia conceded after a pause, "you may go if you will be back by four o'clock."

Le Roy finished his dessert in very short order, and was soon on his way to "the hotel." He had left his cousin convulsed with laughter. Whatever turn the conversation at table had chanced to take, Le Roy always brought it up plump against postage-stamps. Romaine had remarked that the number of a certain house in the city was 695, whereupon Le Roy had chirruped that he had exactly 695 stamps in his album. She had descanted upon the poetry of the Queen of Roumania, which elicited the remark from Le Roy that he wished she would send him some Roumanian stamps. A small boy who was mentioned as convalescing, but suffering from too little to do, was gravely recommended by Le Roy to turn his attention to stamps.

After he had gone, Miss Justinia retired for a nap, but Romaine, taking a book, strolled out again into the rare March sunshine. She seated herself upon the old stone bench, and fell to dreaming. Her book slipped down upon the warm turf, and the years slipped as easily away from her mind. Again she was the ardent girl of twenty, writing letters on this very spot to her sailor lover; again she felt the old dumb heartache which had come when he did not answer them any more; again she went through with the dull perplexity which had seized her when she tried to account for it all. To think that Aunt Justinia—what close-mouthed creatures the Goddards were!—had held the key to the mystery for all these years!

"Oh, if I had only known!" sighed Romaine Goddard to herself. "He was poor, and so proud!"

And Aunt Justinia had said that he had been "pale," that she thought he "could not quite see" as he walked away. Oh, how he must have suffered! And Romaine had fancied that he had, perhaps, flung the thought of her lightly away from him. How strange that she had scarcely heard his name mentioned in all these years! Yet she felt sure that, if he had died, she should somehow have heard of it. Suppose he should come back to the city again? Suppose it should all be explained? He could easily find her if he chose, and he could learn all about her from others—how she was free to do as she liked now. But, nonsense! Men of thirty-six did not fancy women of their own age. They liked fresh, young

beauty. "And I was never beautiful," thought Romaine
Goddard, with a pang. She wondered if she looked now
anything as she used to in those old days. Of course,
she must appear older; but still, people were often surprised to learn that she was not in her twenties. Her
figure was as slender and graceful as ever. She wondered how she should look in a bright, flamboyant hat,
such as she had long since eschewed. If he should ever
come—. Here she broke herself off, and laughed harshly.

"I think I had better read," she said, half aloud.

There was a sound of a horse's hoofs in the road. The
horse stopped, but Romaine did not look up. Her tem-
porary exaltation had been followed by the reaction which
usually succeeds such a vision. She felt old and lonely,
and though she was mechanically following the words
upon the page before her, still, in her far inner consciousness, she was pondering whether she had not better sell
the great house in New York and come to live in the
old place with Aunt Justinia and Le Roy.

Suddenly a shadow fell across her book. It startled her,
and she gave a little cry.

"I beg your pardon," said a voice which she knew.
"I had no business to intrude upon you without first an-
nouncing myself, but——"

"Why, George—Lieutenant Ober," she began, feeling
as though the world must have passed away from her,
and she must have entered the realm of spirits.
"This is—why—where—Aunt Justinia was speaking of
you to-day—but—— oh, what does it all mean?"

She laughed feebly. Then she covered her face with
her hands. She felt that she was making herself unutterably ridiculous.

"I am no ghost," he said, gravely, seating himself on

the old stone bench beside her. As he did this, she took her hands down, and he looked keenly into her face.

"Oh, I am altered!" her heart cried within her, with a passionate wish for the youth which she had lost, and for which she had never grieved before. It shook the calm which she had gained after the first surprise, but his quiet voice brought her back to herself.

"I am very glad to see you again," he began.

The commonplace remark was well timed.

"Thank you. It is very pleasant," she replied, with an assumption of gayety. "But I miss your uniform. Are you no longer in the navy?"

"I threw up my commission years ago. I have had a consulate over-seas, Romaine. My life has been passed in foreign lands. I have not been very happy."

"I am sorry," she said, simply.

It seemed hopeless to her to try ever to untangle the twisted threads of the last fifteen years; but, man-like, George Ober cut the knot at a stroke.

"Yes, Romaine," he continued, dwelling on the old name a little, "I have been very lonely. And you? Your little cousin told me that you never married, after all."

The whole situation was revealed to her as by a glance, and she blessed Le Roy and his mania.

"I never meant to marry!" she cried, indignantly.

"But—but your father wrote me so, and your aunt confirmed it."

"I found that out only to-day. I could not understand your silence. Oh, it—it——" She paused.

"Why, Romaine," he exclaimed, his tone growing buoyant, "I wish—— But first I must tell you that I have not grown rich. I have enough, but I am not rich, like you. If I had been rich"—his voice thickened—"I should not have submitted so tamely as I did fifteen years ago."

"I hate money!" she cried, passionately. "It has been the bane——"

"Mr. Ober," shrilled a boyish voice beside them, "you said you had given us some Turkish stamps, but Guy and I can't find 'em. We've looked the whole lot through, too."

"My boy, I'll get them for you this very afternoon," declared George Ober, springing to his feet. "I'll do anything on earth for you."

Le Roy opened his eyes in blissful amazement at the earnestness of this new and to him most desirable acquaintance; and his expression deepened when his cousin Romaine kissed him warmly, and gave him a whole dollar to spend as he pleased.

"It was by the merest chance that I came here," George Ober went on, as the boy ran off to join his playmate, who was waiting by the gate. "I have not been in America before for years, and I was going to sail for the South Pacific in a fortnight; but my cousins in the village wrote me a pressing invitation to come up here, and so I came. To tell you the truth, I had hoped to hear something of you, even though it should be as the wife of another man. But nobody in the village seems to know anything about your life nowadays."

"No," said Romaine. "I have not made Aunt Justinia a visit for fifteen years, and she does not talk about family affairs. She sees only half-a-dozen people a year, one might say."

"But my young stamp collector bore the name of Goddard. I put a few questions to him, and then I galloped off so fast that I think he can hardly have recovered yet from his astonishment." George Ober laughed.

"There!" said Romaine, "you look now as you used to."

"And you look exactly as you used to."

She flushed with pleasure.

"Let's have everything as we used to, Romaine."

"It has always been the same with me," she said, softly.

Aunt Justinia came out on the veranda, and peered over into the garden.

"We must go and see her," suggested Romaine, rising.

George Ober bent down to give her his arm. How distinguished he had grown!

"George," she laughed up into his face, "I feel like a girl, instead of a prosy, middle-aged old maid."

"You are always a girl to me, Romaine," he whispered.

He lingered a long time on the veranda. After a while Le Roy came back. He looked displeased when he saw that his hero had not departed.

"Your horse is pawing round awfully out there by the post," he hazarded, with some emphasis; "and you know we can't have those Turkish stamps till you get back to the hotel."

Easter Sunday broke beautifully that year. There was a great hubbub in the little country village, for there was to be a wedding—a very simple and quiet one—at the pretty gray chapel near Miss Justinia Goddard's. Her niece, Miss Romaine Goddard, the great New York heiress, was to marry the distinguished Mr. Ober, who had been boarding at the hotel for several weeks. Some hints of their romantic story had crept out, and everybody was determined to witness the ceremony which was at last to unite the long-severed pair. It was almost like

the wedding at the end of "The Children of the Abbey."
I said that everybody was determined to go, but there
was one who was not.

Le Roy, who was forbidden always to touch his stamps
upon the Sabbath, was found, after a frantic search, at the
last moment, in a remote upper chamber of the barn,
surrounded by his treasures, which had recently received
large accessions. At first, with tears, he vehemently refused to leave them; but by a judicious use of that wicked
bribery which even the most conscientious mothers and
aunts are sometimes compelled to employ, Aunt Justinia
lured him to appear at the wedding. His pockets were
bursting with stamps, and the prospects which had been
spread before him had not only dried his tears, but had
lent a glow to his countenance which was a positive inspiration to the whole company. Le Roy had become
the envy of all the young collectors in the neighborhood,
and his secret and perhaps not unjustifiable ambition
was to become the envy of the stamp collectors of two
hemispheres.

Romaine Goddard looked like a young girl, when,
leaning on her lover's arm, she stepped out of her aunt's
door to walk over to the church. As they passed the
sewing window, she noticed the daffodils. She had not
thought of them since the day when she had asked Miss
Justinia if there "were always just two buds in that par-
ticular bunch"; but the two little buds had sweetly grown
and grown under the spring sunshine, until now, as she
looked, two bright dewy blossoms breathed up to her a
fragrant congratulation upon her wedding day.

"See!" she said to her lover; "it is a good omen."

And as they walked across the April greensward, she
told him the story of the daffodils.

"Solly."

THE STORY OF A GENTLEMAN.

"DID you ask 'em for any blue pieces, M'lancy?"

"No, I didn't. I've been workin' too hard to think o' pieces—blue pieces or any other kind."

"Now you knew I'd been a-wantin' blue pieces for a week 'n' more, M'lancy. Seems 'sif you might 'a' thought about 'em."

"If I was a great big man, Solly Shedd, workin' out by the day, an' knowin' consid'able about carpenterin' an' plasterin', an' a little mite o' everythin', seems to me I c'd raise money enough to buy some blue pieces for myself! Beggin' for pieces, an' beggin' for pieces! I'm sick o' hearin' you all the time beggin' for pieces!"

M'lancy Shedd's small, black eyes snapped with a dull, contemptuous fire upon her husband. But Solly did not resent her flings at him.

"I ain't beggin'," he persisted, humbly. "Everybody asks for pieces. I give away jest as many as I git, I know. Mis' Murchison had a lot o' blue pieces left from them comf'tables the sassiety made last week. They'll be all gone fust thing you know. You might 'a' thought on 'em, M'lancy—I swan you might."

But not even the tender reproach conveyed in Solly's "I swan" seemed to move to repentance the hard-hearted M'lancy, and she did not appear inclined to push the contention any further. This was rather remarkable. It was usually M'lancy who had the last word in the mild dis-

173

putes of the Shedd family. But to-night M'lancy was
tired, as she had already informed her husband; besides,
she was out of patience with Solly for enjoying patchwork. There had been a time when she had thought his
ingenuity and industry in this direction admirable, and
when she had boasted of it to everybody; but she had
lately heard people laughing over Solly's peculiarities in
this respect. This had put the matter in a new light before her, and she had begun to upbraid him bitterly for
spending so much time over useless patchwork.

"Seems 'sif you might be more like other men, Solly
Shedd. They ain't another man in Carley that pieces
bedquilts but you. Seems 'sif you acshally hated to git
a job at plantin' in the spring, 'cos you hate to leave the
bedquilts you've been fussin' over all winter. If there
was any gain in 'em, it would be different, but they ain't.
Nobody never wants 'em, an' here we've got as many as
a dozen on 'em. I don't s'pose you'd sell 'em if you
was offered ten dollars apiece for 'em."

Ten dollars was a great sum to M'lancy.

"Yes, I would too," protested Solly, meekly. "I should
kinder hate to, but I would. An' how can you say,
M'lancy, that I don't make no money outen my quilts?
That **risin'** sun o' mine took seventy-five cents premium
to the **cattle** show, an' last year the oak leaf one took
a dollar, an' the log cabin one fifty cents. My rose o'
Texas took a premium onst too. An' then I do' know
what we'd do cold nights in winter 'thout them quilts.
I don't never make 'em, M'lancy, on'y when I hain't
got another blessed thing to do—you know I don't.
When they's ploughin' an' seedin' an choppin', I don't
never sew them times."

To be just, this was true. Solly's own domain, which

he rented of Mr. Murchison, was only a garden, in which
he raised "sass" enough to supply the wants of his own
small family. M'lancy and the only scion of the Shedd
family, known as "Alfid," did a large part of the work in
this garden, and Solly went out by the day at anything for
which he was wanted. He was not especially efficient,
but "hired men" were scarce in Carley, and the farmers
were glad to have a man so faithful and honest as Solly,
even if he was not so quick nor so thorough as some
others; but when the "apple-pickin' " and the last fall
jobs were over, and until the "sleddin' " came on, Solly
was glad enough to settle down in a broken chair in the
tumble-down old farmhouse in which he resided, and
piece his beloved bedquilts till the demand for his services revived.

"It's amazin'," he would say, "how you can git on with
a bedquilt when you give your mind to it."

And it was. Yet here late October had come, Solly's
woodpile was well supplied, there wasn't anything in par-
ticular to do, he was at work upon a ravishing "forget-
me-not" quilt, for which blue pieces were especially
needed, and M'lancy had worked all day at Mrs. Murchison's, where blue pieces abounded even as coals at New-
castle, and she had not brought home one. It was hard,
and naturally Solly found it difficult to be reconciled.
Besides, Solly would never have treated M'lancy so, and
she knew it. Solly adored her, and put up with almost
everything from her, as the neighbors could have testified. Solly could not help being a little lame, for he
had been wounded in the army, and could not bend his
right knee, which made his gait a sort of succession of
peripatetic colons and semicolons, vastly amusing to the
small boys of the village. Neither could poor Solly help

a constitutional state of bewilderment in his brain. There was something wrong there, and Solly would not have denied it. The look in his kindly eyes was not that of a person who is quite sane and sensible; but poor Solly was born so, and nobody laid up his deficiencies against him except M'lancy. She thought, and had frequently remarked in her husband's hearing, that "if Solly would kinder stir round a little livelier, he might be smarter"; but poor Solly in his ordinary every-day mood could not do this, and M'lancy should have been the last one to reproach him with his lack of brilliancy, not only on sentimental grounds, but because she herself was considered to be "a little lackin'," while she did not possess Solly's compensating amiability and unselfishness. In fact, M'lancy had a very cross streak in her nature; but in spite of this streak and of the far from exemplary character which she had borne before she married Solly, to him she always seemed to be a pattern of the domestic virtues, and he would believe no evil concerning her.

On this day, when Solly was reproaching his wife for her failure to think of him and of his wants, there was a reason for M'lancy's comparative moderation and her failure to reply to Solly's heartfelt protest, more potent than her weariness or her impatience with his patchwork. M'lancy had something on her alleged mind. There was not room for more than one idea at a time in that poor thick head, and perhaps the reason why she had forgotten the pieces was because the idea which had taken possession of her was of a different nature altogether.

Mr. Murchison's eldest son Frank was building a new house a little way down the road from the Shedds'. He was going to be married very soon, and M'lancy had heard Frank's affairs talked over a good deal that day while she had been cleaning paint and scrubbing floors at the paternal mansion. It seemed that, young Frank Murchison being a popular sort of fellow, his friends in town had "taken hold," and helped him most efficiently. It had been represented in M'lancy's presence that Frank Murchison's new house—a trim and tidy little domicile —was going to cost him hardly anything compared with what he had expected to pay for it.

"I don't calc'late it's cost him more'n two or three hundred dollars," muttered M'lancy, shortly after Solly ceased excusing himself for doing patchwork.

"What you talkin' about, M'lancy?" inquired Solly, as they walked lumberingly along.

Now he understood why she had been so mild—for M'lancy—in answering his protests, and why she had given him the last word. She was thinking of something else.

"Nothin' much," returned M'lancy, provokingly.

"All right," said Solly.

They trudged on until a turn in the road brought them in sight of the weather-beaten, broken-roofed old house in which they lived. A few rods further on was the spruce new residence of Mr. Reynolds, the best carpenter in the village, who also ran the chief sawmill in the place.

"There!" exclaimed M'lancy, pointing to the Reynolds abode, and then to their own poor lodging. "I'd like to know, Solly Shedd—I'd like to know why we hain't got so good a house as Reynolds there? Say, why hain't we?"

" 'Cos we hain't," answered poor Solly, with no suggestion of humor in his voice, and with the sweat start-

12

ing on his homely face at the sharp insistence in M'lancy's voice. "I do' know no other reason, I'm sure."

"Waal, I do," returned M'lancy, viciously. "It's because Reynolds there works at his bench all winter, an' gits pay for what he does, 'stid o' putterin' round, like any old woman, piecin' bedquilts an' sech, that he don't never git a cent for. Oh, you needn't say 'premiums' to me! All the premiums you ever got, Solly Shedd, wouldn't pay for our carrysene for six months. I tell ye Reynolds built a house 'cos he can do things he gits paid for."

"I can't carpenter so good as he can; you know I can't, M'lancy," protested Solly, miserably.

They entered at the creaking door and M'lancy began to bundle about and get some sort of a supper. Alfid, an overgrown boy of fifteen, came in with a bag slung over his shoulder. He had been nutting, and had had "luck." He said nothing, but passed through the room to a little lean-to, which he had converted into a sort of shop for his own use, and in which he kept a few tools.

"Now, there's Alfid," went on Solly. "Mebbe he can carpenter some time as good as Reynolds, if he learns the trade; but I never learnt the trade."

"I intend he shall learn the trade," said M'lancy, in a high key. "I intend he sha'n't never learn to make bedquilts, whatever he does. An' I don't believe but what you know as much about carpenterin' as Frank Murchison does, an' with you 'n' Alfid together, I don't see any reason why we can't have a new house same as Frank Murchison has."

"Same as Frank Murchison has!" echoed Solly, perfectly dumfounded at M'lancy's temerity.

"Yes, sir; same as Frank Murchison has," repeated M'lancy, mimicking Solly's horrified manner. "I'll bet you Mr. Murchison or Mr. Reynolds would give you, or same as give you, a plot; 'tain't much for 'em to do, workin' for 'em long as you have. An' they's lots o' men would help you, I know, same as they've helped Frank. Oh, dear, if you could only git that pension, Solly!"

"Oh, lord, M'lancy! 'tain't no use. It's a year ago sense I went to Square Mansfield about it, an' I ain't heard nothin' about it sence. I sha'n't never hear no more about it, M'lancy."

By this time M'lancy had some sort of a supper tossed together, and Alfid was summoned from the lean-to. Alfid never spoke unless he was spoken to, and his countenance was not entirely free from the vacant cast which, in different ways, characterized the faces of his parents, but he read many books, was ingenious in a mechanical way, and some people thought he had a good deal of sense. To M'lancy and Solly, of course, Alfid was an intellectual luminary of the first rank.

They ate silently for a few moments; then M'lancy added, as though there had been no turn or pause in the conversation about the house, "An' Alfid'll help you a lot."

Solly groaned. The idea of starting out to build a house seemed to him too colossally preposterous to be entertained for a moment.

"I think you'd orter go to Square Mansfield again, an' see about a pension," went on M'lancy, whose ambition had received an unaccountable stimulus since she had heard the inside history of Frank Murchison's new house.

"Oh, I told him all about it, an' how I'd lost all my

papers 'n' things," said Solly, despairingly. "An' how
the knee that was shot was the same one that was allers
stiff a little mite, you know. I had rheumatiz in it when
I was little, an' it's allers plagued me. It's been a sight
worse sence it was shot, of course, but I do' know as anybody'd believe that. The square said they wa'n't much
chance for me, an' he said he'd tell me if they was any
good news come for me, an' of course he would. 'Tain't
no use, M'lancy."

"But you was in lots o' battles," persisted the sanguine
M'lancy.

"Six on 'em, M'lancy—six big ones, an' ten or a dozen
pretty hot skirmishes—an' I never run away."

"An' didn't you capture a flag or somethin', Solly?"

"Yes. I seen one," said Solly, beginning to tell an
old, old story (which the modest fellow hated to allude
to), on purpose to pacify M'lancy—"I seen a flag, an' all
the men was strugglin' along an' hollerin', 'Git it! git
it!' An' it seemed to be the handiest for me to git it;
so I run right along—I was kinder scart, but I never
stopped for that—an' at last I grabbed it, an' flung it
back among the fellers, for jest then they was a ball
come sizzin' along, an' took me right in my knee. The
men managed to drag me away, but I was in the hospital
for more'n three months afterwards. Why, Robin Carter was there, M'lancy, an' Isr'el Warner; they was lots
o' Carley boys in the regiment. Robin Carter see me hit,
himself."

"An' when you got out o' the hospital, I s'pose. you
went to fightin' ag'in," commented M'lancy, disgustedly.

"Course I did," said Solly, simply. "I wa'n't a-goin'
to have the Union go to pieces, not if I could help it. I
was awful scart lots o' times, but I never run away."

"An' you can't work half so good when your leg's hurt as you could if it hadn't 'a' been," sighed M'lancy. "Oh, dear, Solly, you'd orter have a pension! An' '"—flashing up again in a sudden burst of passion—"if you was half a man, Solly Shedd, you'd fly round an' get one."

"Waal, I guess I ain't," sighed Solly, with an air of uncomfortable resignation, "for I know Square Mansfield thinks I ain't got no chance, an' he orter know."

"They ain't no two shingles on the roof that touch each other," complained M'lancy, attacking from another quarter.

Solly merely gave a long, harassed sigh, but Alfid volunteered the information that he could shingle the roof well enough if he only had some shingles and some nails.

Mr. Murchison charged nothing for the rickety old mansion, excepting the payment of the yearly taxes upon it, and the making of repairs. The latter, whenever they required expense, were generally allowed to remain undone. Solly had hard enough work to feed and clothe his family, even with M'lancy's and Alfid's help, without spending money for boards and nails and door-handles.

"Waal," said M'lancy, pitching her voice again well up toward high C, "I've got a dollar Mis' Murchison paid me to-day, but it sha'n't go toward nails nor shingles nuther! I don't want nothin' done to this old hole—not a thing! Mebbe your pa'll have the gumption to stir round 'n' try 'n' be somebody after the rain's wet him through, drippin' in through the bedroom roof a few nights."

Solly had never seen M'lancy so roused up as she was now. Generally when the fit took her for a new dress for herself, or a new suit of clothes for Alfid, or a melodeon, or some other expensive luxury, she stormed around for a day or two, and then was content to wait, if the sum required was reasonable, until Solly could earn it. If what she wanted was too extravagant to be afforded, some new impression would drive the old one away very soon from her shallow and variable mind; but now the clatter kept up for a week at least, and most of the time, as Solly happened to have no demand outside for his labor, he sat by the fire and amused himself with piecing his bed-quilts while M'lancy scolded. He had finally been up to Mrs. Murchison's himself and procured some blue pieces, so that he was well equipped for his work.

During the last week in October Mr. Murchison went away for a visit, and as his son was very busy in putting the finishing touches upon his new house, Solly was engaged to go up to the Murchison place every night and morning to do the chores. He was just returning from there for his breakfast on a certain Monday morning, when, as he approached his own home, he saw signs of an unusual disturbance.

"I could set down and bawl," whimpered M'lancy, as her husband thrust his head anxiously in at the door. "I'm clean used up! 'Tain't no use tryin' to have nothin'. 'Tain't no use tryin' to be nobody. I ain't never goin' to try no more."

"What's the matter, Alfid?" demanded the perplexed master of the house, finding that M'lancy went right on like a mill, paying no heed to anything he said.

"Sumpin's got in an' e't up a lot o' ma's hens," replied Alfid, succinctly.

"Oh, my!" moaned M'lancy. "Oh, my! I sha'n't have no egg money, nor no chicken money, nor nothin'!"

She threw her apron over her head, like the old woman in "Little Dorrit," and rocked back and forth, letting the salt pork in the spider burn in the abandon of her grief.

"It's too bad, I swan!" said Solly, in heartfelt sympathy, but rushing to rescue his breakfast. "I'm goin' to have a job o' huskin' up to Square Mansfield's to-day, M'lancy. Mebbe he'll give me some hens for you. I'll ask him."

But M'lancy's loss had reminded her of all the privations and sufferings which she had ever been through, and had made her very cross. Solly's gentle consolations seemed to madden rather than soothe her. She sprang out of her rocking chair, and confronted him with a savage look upon her face.

"You'll git me some hens, will you, Solly Shedd? Well, you'd orter do something for me, I think—jest a little! Lettin' me live in this old shanty, when you pretend to think so much o' me! Jest by turnin' over your hand, you might git a nice house for Alfid 'n' me. You might git a pension, same as old Luke Travers got one—he wa'n't in the war near so long as you was, nuther—an' there you set from mornin' till night an' sew your old bedquilts, an' let the rain drip through on to Alfid 'n' me! You'd orter be trounced, Solly Shedd! That's what you'd orter be!"

M'lancy, somewhat relieved, fell back into her rocking chair and burst into a flood of tears. Alfid, apparently quite impassive, ate away industriously at his breakfast, which Solly had "dished up" while his wife was talking, and which he too was now partaking of, as though he did not know what else to do, but with a harried, wretched expression upon his face. The echoes of her own voice were all the reply vouchsafed to M'lancy's impassioned outburst, and presently she too, after a few vague mutterings, drew up her chair beside her husband's, and joined forces with him and Alfid. They were late in getting through their meal, and as Alfid had a long walk to school, he started presently on his way thither, carrying his dinner-pail, filled carefully by his own industrious forethought. Then Solly took his leave for the field of his husking labors, giving his wife a feeble, nerveless good-bye as he passed her; but M'lancy made him no response. She was very "mad." Solly, in his gentle, loving soul, had no idea how very "mad" she was.

There was a train which left Carley at two o'clock. M'lancy had found out this morning what it was when anguish, or very marked ill-temper, "to a Pythian height dilates you, and despair sublimes to power." Something had occurred to her by means of which she might "apply the screws" to Solly. It was indeed a desperate step, and one which under ordinary conditions M'lancy would have been too stupid and too lazy and too timid to undertake. But just now she was roused out of her usual sluggishness of thought and action. She "flew around," and did a generous "bakin';" collected all the available funds of the family—several dollars, part of an accumulation making just now for the purchase of a barrel of flour—put on her best clothes, packed a clumsy old-fashioned satchel with her other belongings, set the table for dinner, and then, almost without a pang, in the intensity of her slow-burning wrath, started for the railroad station in time to catch the two-o'clock train. She chose all of the wood paths and back roads for her route to the station, and succeeded in getting there without seeing anybody who cared to ask her any questions. Nobody took any special notice of her as she bought her ticket, waited a few moments, and presently moved away on the train. M'lancy had gone.

That night, when Solly reached home after his day's husking, he brought with him two fine hens for M'lancy. She might forget him and his blue pieces, but he never forgot her little wants. Her large ones were too large for poor Solly to grasp, but Heaven knew that he would have gratified them if he could. His homely, honest face, half covered with stubbly yellow beard, was all alight now as he came into the yard, thinking of the pleasure which he was going to give M'lancy. The hens were Plymouth Rocks, just the kind that she liked best. He walked through the house. The fire in the kitchen seemed to be freshly kindled, but nobody was visible. There was a pounding in the lean-to. Alfid was there at work.

"See here, Alfid," he said, showing the hens at the door of the boy's "shop"; "ain't them fine? Won't yer ma be tickled, Alfid? Where is she?"

"I do' know," returned Alfid, looking up from a rough bicycle which he was fashioning. "I come home from school 'n' found the table was set, but they wa'n't no fire. I made it up new. I guess likely somebody come for ma to work."

"Likely," said Solly. He was sorry not to be able to show the hens to M'lancy right away, but he put them now into some shackly coops out in the decrepit old barn behind the house, fed them, and went in to await his wife's return. He had learned to cook in the army, and in reality excelled M'lancy in the culinary art, though he would not have admitted it. So he and Alfid got along well enough. As the evening wore on, and still she did not come, they concluded that somebody had been suddenly taken ill, and that she felt obliged to stay all night with the invalid.

The next morning a bright idea struck Alfid. "If ma was goin' off so, I should think she would 'a' left a letter," he said.

This commended itself to Solly, and together he and Alfid searched the kitchen. From the mélange upon the dingy shelf on which the family clock rested, a missive was at last extracted. It said, in M'lancy's own cramped and almost illegible chirography:

"I've gone off to Vermont to visit Cousin Emly's folks. I aint comin back. I'm sick of livin in a leaky house an not havin nothin. When I get tired of visitin Cousin Emly's folks, I'm goin to git a place to work. If you should ster round an git a pension or stop makin bedquilts, an go to earnin, or git a decent house to live in, mebbe I'd come back, but I wont till you do. I'll send for Alfid when I git a place for him, but I dont want to see you."

M'lancy's spelling was strictly phonetic, but Solly and Alfid finally made it out. When they had read the letter through in a fever-heat of impatience, Alfid bowed his head on his hands and cried aloud. Even he could not resist the feelings which were evoked in his stolid breast by this plain announcement of the breaking up of the little home. Solly, white and agitated, leaned against the wall, too weak and excited to speak. Then he took a sudden step forward, and lifted his poor bewildered head as if he would vindicate the sweet, strong manhood within him.

"Alfid," he said, in a decided way which half startled the boy, "we must git her back—we must git her back as quick as we can. We can't do without her. You won't leave me till we git her back, will you, Alfid?"

"No," promised the boy, doggedly, wiping his tear-stained face—"no, papa, I won't leave you, an' I'll help you git her back."

"I'm goin' to stir right round," went on poor Solly, as though the use of M'lancy's phrases might in some way propitiate that offended deity, far away though she were—"I'm goin' to stir right round, Alfid; an' we'll tell everybody your ma has gone off on a visit. She's been kinder nervous lately. I've noticed it. It was a good plan for her to go off visitin' for a while. It'll do her good, Alfid. I'm goin' to stir round an' fix things so 't she'll wanter come back pretty quick."

The two deserted beings looked into each other's eyes with a new love and tenderness between them. It was a solemn compact which they seemed to make, and Solly appeared to drink in strength and will from the feeling of his son's co-operation.

Alfid went off to school until something definite should come up for him to do, and Solly went straight to Squire Mansfield. Everybody who saw him remarked upon his altered appearance. There was a pathetically eager expression in his dull eyes. His halting step seemed quicker and firmer than it had ever been before. He held his head up—almost backward—instead of hanging helplessly forward as usual. His face was pale and resolved, and his lips moved constantly, as though whispering words of cheer, beneath his stubbly beard. If M'lancy had planned to "stir up" her husband, she had accomplished her object.

After Solly had had a little talk with Squire Mansfield, he went to see the two old soldiers who had served with him during the war, and who knew all about his honorable record. Both of them were good-natured fellows who liked Solly. When he asked them if they did not think he ought to have a pension, both of them said yes.

"You oughter had one long ago," said Israel Warner. "Here's Luke Travers, never served outside the State, jest staid in camp, an' caught cold, an' had the rheumatiz, or somethin' like that, an' here he's drawed a big pension these ten years."

"I s'pose I hain't had the cheek," confessed Solly. "I'd lost my papers mostly, an' my knee allers was stiff a little, you know."

"Waal," said the shrewd farmer, "I know all about that knee o' yourn; I seen you in the hospital. Don't harp on its bein' stiff when you was little, any more'n you have to. Some folks git up petitions when they've lost their papers an' things like that. You can take my horse, if you're a mind ter, an' go round. Robin Carter an' I'll stand by you every time."

Solly took the horse gratefully, and went back to the Squire, who drew up a heading for a petition, and also some affidavits for Robin Carter and Israel Warner to sign. By the time that poor Solly laid his head upon his pillow that night, grief-stricken as he was, he was not quite forlorn. A great hope was blossoming in his true, unselfish heart.

Solly was afraid that by the next morning the old distrust of himself would take possession of his soul, and that he should be afraid to follow out the lines of conduct which he had laid out for himself; but, no! his heart was still full of courage and determination, and he worked away on his petition as intelligently as the very "smart-est" man in Carley could have done.

By the end of the third day the Squire thought that all was done which was necessary, and he sent the budget off to Washington, with a few cautiously hopeful words to Solly, which made the poor fellow's heart beat almost to suffocation.

Every day now he felt the same courage and strength which had nerved him ever since he had read M'lancy's taunting letter. It seemed as though nothing could be too hard for him to undertake in order to get her back.

When the budget had started for Washington in the mail, Solly went up to see Mr. Murchison.

"You don't charge me much for that house of our'n, Mr. Murchison," he said, briskly, "but it leaks dreadful. I think it'll cost me 'most as much to fix it up decent as it would to build a new one, an' it wouldn't never be nothin' but an old one to the end of the chapter. Now there's that lot I cleared. You know you said I might have the wood from it if I'd get it away. I've been thinkin' that would be a good place for a house."

"Well, well," exclaimed Mr. Murchison, who was a good-hearted, well-to-do old farmer. He was so much surprised that he was hardly able to catch his breath at this announcement of Solly's temerity.

"O' course, I couldn't make such a grand one as Frank's," explained Solly, modestly; "but M'lancy an' me thought it would be nice to have a new house. I've got a few weeks now when I ain't drove, an' I might work on it, Alfid an' me."

"That would be very fine, Solly," said the old man, looking out inquiringly at Solly's excited, working face from under beetling gray eyebrows. "Very nice," he repeated; "but, like everything else, Solly, it costs money."

"How much would you charge me for the piece o' wood lot?" demanded Solly, with more manliness in his tone than Mr. Murchison had imagined that he possessed.

"Oh, I wouldn't be hard on you, Solly. I'm glad to see you're tryin' to do something for yourself. Well, call it twenty dollars, and you can pay me for it as you can work it."

"That's all I've got, sir," said Solly, but without any of his old hang-dog expression. "I ain't got no cash, but I can work it out. I'm obleeged to you, Mr. Murchison—very much obleeged."

"I'll have the deed made out right away," said the old man, half facetiously. His heart was touched by Solly's look and tone.

"I'm sure I'm obleeged to you!" cried Solly, with real enthusiasm.

"And you want to begin pretty soon?" inquired Mr. Murchison, waiving Solly's thanks, kindly.

"I'm goin' to begin to-morrer, Mr. Murchison," he answered, decidedly. "It's Saturday, an' Alfid can help me. You see"—coloring up a little, for Solly was as honest as the day—"you see, M'lancy she's off to Vermont visitin', an' I'd like to surprise her against she comes back."

"I'm older'n I was once, Solly," said Mr. Murchison, "but maybe I'll come round an' help you a little speck. Frank's house is all done but some of the inside work, an' I can come an' help you as well as not. I'd right down like to," he added, smothering Solly's delighted acknowledgments.

Solly went at once to the wood lot, which was about half way between his old home and the railroad station, and with a three-foot measure and a piece of string he staked out painfully the limits of the little cellar which he planned to dig. By the next night he and Mr. Murchison and Alfid had dug a trench all around the cellar, and a deep one through the middle.

"This woodland needs a sight o' dreenin'," Solly had said. "M'lancy ketches cold awful easy, an' I hain't goin' to have nothin' damp about our cellar, I can tell you."

On Monday—not to Mr. Murchison's surprise, for he had planned it, but very much to Solly's—six of the village men came around with their shovels, and asked Solly if he didn't want some help. By night the little cellar was dug, and a firm stone wall was built nearly around it.

"Mr. Reynolds is gettin' out a lot o' timber for me down at the mill," remarked Mr. Murchison to Solly, as he was turning homeward that night. "You might as well have it as anybody; I'll trust you, I guess. I've told him to fetch it around here to-morrow."

Solly looked at his friend, dumb with excess of feeling. "Now you're too good, Mr. Murchison, I swanny you be!" exclaimed Solly, with tears rising to his dull blue eyes.

Young Frank Murchison drew up beside his father and Solly just then. He was in a long wagon, in which he had been carrying supplies to his new house. He felt happy and generous, as a prospective bridegroom should.

"When you come to want your doors and sashes, let me know, Solly. I got out a good deal more of such stuff than I needed, and I'd be glad to let you have some of it for nothing."

The village storekeeper was sitting in Frank's wagon. "I've ordered a keg of nails for you, Solly," he said; "and I want to help you about door-handles and locks and hinges when you come to them. You've been a good customer of mine for nigh on to twenty years now, Solly, and you've always paid your bills. I'd like to chip in with the rest."

To say that Solly was overcome with these heaped-up benefits is a very mild way of putting the case. M'lancy was gone, but at this rate Solly felt that she would soon be back again.

When people came to think about it, everybody discovered that he liked Solly. As he had lived his honest, plodding life among them from day to day, no special occasion had arisen for displaying this liking; but now an occasion had arisen. Solly wanted a new house, and his neighbors were bent on helping him to get one.

Soon there was a "raisin'" in the wood lot. Early in the morning and late in the evening Solly was at work on the new house. He might not be able to "carpenter" as well as Mr. Reynolds, but he did his best in this emergency. The fever of his haste to "surprise M'lancy" infected everybody. There was rarely an hour in the day when some neighbor was not "chippin' in," as the Carley people expressed it, to help Solly.

Two weeks from the day when M'lancy had deserted her home, the roof—a good, tight one—was on a new house for her. In fact, the new clapboards were mostly on, and Solly, to use his own phrase, could "begin to see his way through," and his heart beat high with hope. As in the old Persian poem, the lover, with every stroke of the long work which he was fated to do, cried, "Alas,

Shireen!" so, with every nail that poor Solly had driven
in this tiny new mansion of his, he had cried, "It's for
M'lancy!"

"When the plasterin's on," he said to Alfid, "I'm
a-goin' to write her a letter, an' tell her to come home
an' see what we've been a-doin'. I mean to make her
feel some cur'osity, Alfid."

Nobody knew how Solly's brain reeled as he regarded
the progress which had been made upon his new house.
Every morning, as he hurried feverishly down to the
wood lot, he expected to find that there was nothing
there—that his house was but the baseless fabric of a
vision. But no, it stood there still, cheap and clumsy
to the eyes of an experienced architect, but palatial to
poor Solly's.

At the close of a certain day, the "plasterin'" being
nearly done, Solly and Alfid—whose school had been a
good deal neglected since the house came on, a boy being in great demand at the wood lot—were making their
weary way homeward, when Squire Mansfield drove up
behind them at a furious pace.

"Jump in, Solly; jump in, Alfid," he cried, joyously.
"I've got good news for you. It seems that your old
request for a pension had just come up on the calendar
when the new one was brought in. It wasn't likely the
old one would have amounted to much, but with the
new one on top of it, every respectable man in town
backing you up, as I might say, we've carried the day.
You've got your pension, and there's about a thousand
dollars back pay."

"What?" gasped Solly, climbing feebly into the carriage, and almost toppling over as he heard the squire's
words.

13

That gentleman repeated himself, in even more ex-plicit terms than before.

"I'm much obleeged to you, I'm sure, Square," Solly said at last. The gratitude which he had felt during the last few weeks, as he had never had occasion to use that commodity in bulk before, was almost killing him.

There was nothing in the house to eat when Solly and Alfid reached home but some crackers and cheese from the store, some vegetables, and some pork. Solly had ceased his day's work upon the house only twice since he had begun it, to earn money for the current expenses of Alfid and himself.

He did not want to get too deeply in debt. Now he wished he had laid in a greater stock of provisions, but he would do that before M'lancy came home. He ate some crackers and cheese, and then sat down to compose his letter, while Alfid puttered over the stove, getting himself up a more elaborate repast.

Solly's letter, the joint production of Alfid's and his own intellects, ran as follows:

"We wanter to see you awful bad. Alfid and me have missed you awful bad. It most seems as if you hadnt orter have gone so sudden"—this was the only word of reproach that patient Solly allowed himself. "We want you to hurry and come home, They's news for you. Youll be surprised, and Alfid and me think youll like it. I'm all stirred up. My head feels awful bad sometimes, I'm so stirred up. Hurry and come home to Alfid and me.   Your loving Solly."

It would be useless to try to picture M'lancy's coun-tenance as she spelled out her husband's letter. She was plunged into a condition bordering upon lunacy, her only clear convictions being that Solly really had news for her—agreeable news—and that she must start at once for home.

To this course "Cousin Em'ly and her folks" were amply resigned. M'lancy had never been a favorite among her relatives. She never received special invitations to pay them visits, and Cousin Em'ly had been pondering for days upon some means of getting rid of her obnoxious guest, whose visit seemed destined to last all winter. She hailed with alacrity the present crisis therefore, and all her resources were brought into play to get M'lancy to the railroad station in time to take the very next train for home. Late in the afternoon of the second day after Solly had sent his letter, she alighted at the station in Carley.

There had been nobody on the train whom she knew, or else she would have inquired concerning the welfare of her family, and thus perhaps have received some hint of that "news" of which Solly had spoken.

The station agent nodded pleasantly to her as she lumbered down from the cars with her satchel. She did not know him very well, and a sudden feeling of shame came over her as she realized that everybody might know by this time how she had run away from home. She thought she would not say a word to him, but he did not wait for her to ask him any questions. Just as she was hurrying past him he sang out, good-humoredly:

"Hullo, M'lancy! You and Solly have come to your luck at last, hain't you?"

"Come to their luck at last"? What did he mean?

It was a wonder that M'lancy did not stop then and there, and demand a full explanation of his words from him. But something kept her silent.

"Yes," she said, coloring up, and with a nervous little laugh—"yes, we have."

She stumbled along the road as fast as she could, past the few houses near the station, then into the woods which intervened before the next little group of dwellings.

Suddenly she came upon the cleared space in Mr. Murchison's wood lot. There had been nothing upon it when M'lancy had left Carley little more than three weeks ago, but now a little house stood there nearly completed. Men were bustling in and out of the doors. There was a sound of pounding and scraping from within it. Things were not usually managed with such rapidity as this in Carley. What did it mean? M'lancy dropped her satchel, and gazed upon the phenomenon open-mouthed. Suddenly Alfid appeared at the door.

"Oh, ma!—oh, ma!" he cried, joyously. He started to come to her. Then he turned back toward the house. "I wanter tell pa you've come!" he shouted.

M'lancy picked up her satchel again, and trudged toward the unfinished door. Solly was shuffling along to meet her, his hat upon the back of his head, his whole plain face glorified with his delight. He extended his arms toward her, when suddenly he seemed to trip upon a pile of rubbish which stood between them, and fell heavily forward at her feet. She waited a moment, with a broad smile upon her face, but he did not rise. Then she saw that a stream of blood was flowing from his mouth.

Screaming for help, she sat down upon the heap of shavings and broken scantling over which he had fallen, and took his head in her lap. As he did so, the loving touch for which his soul had longed seemed to revive him, and he opened his eyes feebly.

"I ain't pieced none sence you went away, M'lancy," he whispered. "You needn't be afraid, I ain't goin' to never do it no more."

"Oh, you may, Solly!" sobbed M'lancy, her hatefulness banished by the sight of the pale face in her lap, and possibly somewhat mitigated also by the spectacle of this mysterious new house. "You may piece bedquilts all day, if yer wanter, Solly."

But poor Solly never spoke again.

M'lancy tried to think that it was the fall which had killed him—that he had stumbled in full possession of his faculties; but the doctor said:

"No; it was a case of apoplexy. He fell because everything turned black before his eyes, and his strength departed."

Yes, it had been too much for poor Solly, this "stirrin' round to try to be smarter, and to "git M'lancy back."

Tid's Wife.

WHEN "Tid" came into the Tom Lake Range, he had but one acquaintance in the settlement there. This was a man whose name was really Peter Brown, but from "Pete" his habits of universal curiosity had gradually changed it to "Peek"—and as "Peek" Brown he is forever distinguished in the annals of the place. "Peek" had known "Tid" over on the Wisconsin side, where his steady attention to business, lack of "luck," and uncommunicativeness had made him a marked and mysterious character.

"What's his name, anyhow, Peek?" asked Handy Graham, one of the old settlers.

"How should I know?" demanded Peek impatiently. "He ain't the sort o' chap to tell his affairs to everybody. They did say over thar—mind ye, 'twas only 'say'— that his last name was 'Slocum;' but the 'Tid' part, by ——, that's too deep for me!"

"Likely it's short fer Timothy," suggested Handy, speculatively.

"'Timothy!'" Mr. Brown gazed at his companion as though he suspected his sanity. "Short fer that's 'Tim.' Didn't ye know that?"

Peek's manner was overbearing, and Handy did not attempt to push his case, or to advance a further theory which had its origin in a certain sarcastic streak in his nature, and which derived Tid from "tidbit," Tid being almost a giant in stature. And thus it happened that Tid came to be unquestioningly accepted throughout the

Tid's Wife.

Tom Lake settlement as "Tid," and nothing else, until a certain day, when the "Slocum" postulate received absolute confirmation.

That day was one of great excitement on the Tom Lake Range. In order to understand this excitement in all its bearings, we must premise that among the hundred and fifty-odd denizens of the little mushroom village there were but half-a-dozen women. One of these was the wife of "Old Bill," the veteran of the place. She was old and infirm, and seldom seen beyond her cabin door. Another was a staid and respectable matron, the mother of a row of sturdy urchins, and the wife of Jack Peabody, known as "Copper-bottom Jack," who had amassed a moderate fortune by mining and speculating, and talked of "retiring" before long. The other four women resided at "Gulick's"—a long, low shanty of the general character of a hotel, and with a barroom attachment, which, in point of earnings, quite eclipsed all the rest. Mrs. Gulick was a weak but well-meaning woman, while of Bridget and Jane, the kitchen girls, and of "Lize," the tawdry barmaid, perhaps the less said the better.

As the winter and spring wore away, Tid was observed to be fixing up his already comfortable "shanty" a good deal, and then he disappeared for a full month. May was well along, and the straits were open, when he reappeared, riding in on the Houghton stage straight from Detroit, via the "Soo," in company with a woman—a young woman—a pretty woman—whom he introduced to the stage-driver and the one or two passengers whom he knew as "My wife, Mis' Slocum."

Now, Tid, though possessed of sterling and acknowledged virtues, had not had generally accredited to him the power of captivating the female sex. "Lize" and "Jane" had unmercifully made fun of him, and it was commonly supposed that he cared as little about women as the representatives of the softer sex at Tom Lake cared about him. Consequently, as the stage conveyed Tid and his bride to their humble home, the "residents" to a man surveyed the sight with open-mouthed wonder.

"Darned ef he hain't took us in like thunder!" said Peek Brown, who had suspected nothing, and owned up to the oversight like a man.

"She looks like consid'able of a gal." This was Gulick's opinion, and fell with weight.

"What you good-lookin' fellers doin'," said Handy Graham, poking Dan Morey, the handsomest man in the place, facetiously in the ribs, "lettin' a chap like Tid get ahead of ye like this?"

The idea of Tid's coming out in advance of Dan in such a contest was indeed absurd, and made the good-natured miners laugh. Enormously tall, large and ill-built, with a gait like an elephant's, a hanging head, a shock of tawny hair and whisker, dull blue eyes, and a mouth always full of tobacco juice—there was certainly nothing attractive about Tid; while Dan, tall, straight, with curling hair and beard, and a bearing like a king's —Dan Morey, though not implicitly to be trusted, was certainly the sort of man in his appearance of whom women are traditionally fond.

"I see her," said Dan, sententiously, "and, by ——! she is harnsum."

In reality, Mrs. Tid Slocum was simply a good-looking, healthy and well-built young woman of twenty-five or thereabout; but to the rough men of the place, who had nothing at hand to compare with her but the senile wife

of "Old Bill," the faded and flavorless charms of Mrs.
Peabody and Mrs. Gulick, and the slatternly pertness of
the "girls" at Gulick's, she seemed a species of angel, as,
in her dark print gown, with a collar—a veritable, shining, white linen collar—her hair neatly brushed and
wound about her head, and a mien that commanded respect, she took up her daily life among the disorderly inhabitants of her husband's adopted home. Numerous
theories were hazarded as to the mystery of her accept-
ance of Tid, but no satisfactory conclusion was ever
reached, and, like the agitation in regard to her husband's
name, this also subsided, and the fact was gradually accepted as stubborn but irrefragable.

Mrs. Jack Peabody, except for now and then "running
in" to see "Old Bill's" wife, did not consider it expedient
for her to recognize socially the other women of the settlement. After weighing the matter for a fortnight, however, and having watched Mrs. Slocum approvingly in
her daily peregrinations between the grocery and her
home, she mentally decided the important question,
"Ought we to visit her?" in the affirmative. Accordingly,
the very next day, arrayed in a well-preserved black
alpaca dress, and after a period of trying indecision between a faded straw bonnet, elegant a decade before, and
a marvellous new slatted sun-bonnet of her own manu-
facture and of recent date, she donned the latter article
and made a state call upon Mrs. Slocum.

While there—— But Mrs. Peabody's own graphic de-
scription, given later to her faithful spouse, covers the
ground much better than any other could possibly do.
"I set down," said Mrs. Peabody, "an' I sez"—Mrs. Peabody had been born in the State of Maine, and East and
West battled for the victory among her idioms—"I sez,

sez I, 'You come quite unexpected like,' sez I, 'but,' sez I, 'I'm sure we're glad ter see yer,' sez I. 'Thar ain't much time fer sercierty ter Tom Lake,' sez I. 'No,' sez me, an' she talked along a spell, quiet an' purty enough, when, aller a suddent, I heerd a voice say, kinder gentle in' pleasant-like—couldn't ermagine whoser 'twas— Lucy, say, whar be yer?' 'n' she jumps up, 'n' sez she, quite perlite, 'Erxcuse me, my husband's a-callin' me,' in'—do yer believe it?—that was Tid a-callin', soft 'n' sweet—ye'd never 'a s'posed in yer life 't he could 'a made sech a little noise ef he'd 'a tried. Wal, thar's a keyhole in the door, 'n' I jumped up 'n' jest kinder happened ter git in the line o' that yer keyhole—w'at yer laffin' at?—'n' that Tid he kissed her, 'n' I see him kinder smooth her hair-back—from her face, 'n' he kinder whispered to her what'd she been a-doin', 'n' who was in thar, 'n' she said, 'A-visitin' with Mis' Jack Peabody'—'n' all these goin's on, his kissin' her, 'n' all—that great, humbly thing—she acshally 'peared ter like it! 'N' ef he don't jest worship her, I ain't no prophet."

Mrs. Peabody's notion of the functions of a prophet was somewhat vague, but she evidently understood a good deal ￼of human nature. Her narrative had been heard and repeated by everybody in the place before a week passed away, and Tid suddenly found himself treated with unwonted consideration. The man who could caress a young woman like Mrs. Tid Slocum, and have her " 'pear ter like it," was unmistakably no common character, and his claims were respected the more deeply because he made no pretensions on account of his superiority. There was the same swing to his awkward gait, the same impassive look in his dull eye, the same strict attention to business. Only now—impressive change!—the men recognized self-control in what before had been a supposed lack of controllable material.

A month after Mrs. Tid Slocum had taken up her abode at the Lake, a troupe of strolling players came along and gave an entertainment at Gulick's dancing-hall, where once or twice a year a grand ball mingled the society from half-a-dozen neighboring settlements with that of the Lake. To this entertainment the populati of the place turned out en masse, and it so chance.! (though there was really no chance about it) that the seat next to Mrs. Tid Slocum was picked out and persistently occupied, even when the rest went out to refresh themselves during the entr'actes, by Mr. Daniel Morey—not the ordinary, rough, good-looking miner of every day, but a positive dandy, arrayed in a sleek black coat and a starched white shirt front, in which glittered a remarkable diamond pin. His ambrosial locks were tossed with fascinating grace from off his forehead, and his moustache seemed to have acquired a new distinction. Mr. Daniel Morey in the long-unaccustomed costume and manners of older civilizations yet carried both so well that even the jeers of his companions were not unmixed with admiration, and could not discompose him. Whenever Mrs. Slocum turned in his direction that evening, she encountered a pair of melting masculine eyes fixed full upon her, and, though she rather shrank away toward Tid and maintained outward calm, yet the admiration of so distinguished an individual could hardly have been lost upon her.

The weeks wore away, and it began to be whispered about among the miners that Dan Morey was getting to be a frequent visitor at Tid Slocum's cabin; but Tid preserved the same imperturbable demeanor toward the

Adonis of the place as toward everybody else. It was rumored by some imaginative person that his heart was breaking. But even this blood-curdling suggestion failed to throw any light upon the situation. Mrs. Jack Peabody, however, who was propriety itself, resolved upon breaking the social bond with which by her visit, and, indeed, by a subsequent one also, she had united herself to the fair new-comer, and she consequently visited her no more. So that Mrs. Tid Slocum, except for the unremitting faithfulness and devotion of her husband and occasional observed and more presumed calls from Dan Morey, must have led a rather lonely life. But she was not one of the kind to be pitied. She carried her head high, worked briskly all day—no such housekeeper and seamstress had ever been seen at the Lake—and appeared not to observe even the disapproving defection of Mrs. Jack Peabody.

Six months after the bright spring day when big, lumbering Tid Slocum had astounded his neighbors by bringing his bride among them, Dan Morey was missing from his place beside the genial fire at Gulick's, and "Old Bill," with whom he messed, could give no account of him. Tid Slocum went regularly to work every day, but shortly after Dan Morey was missed, some one remarked that Mrs. Tid Slocum "had been keepin' mighty quiet lately."

The temptation to investigate the mystery was too much for Peek Brown, who, as soon as Tid started for work the next morning, stole up to the back-side of his little shanty and made as thorough an examination as was compatible with a tightly-locked door and uncommunicative shutters. Tid had, evidently not without a pur- pose, left behind him a slow fire, for the chimney gave off a gentle smoke all the morning. Peek determined to go quite around the house, even at the risk of being seen, for it stood upon a knoll and close against the hillside. Tid had put solid wooden shutters on every window of his stout little cabin, but they were open in front, and neat white curtains, hung shortly after Mrs. Tid's arrival, were adroitly looped inside, so as to suggest some occupancy of the place. Everything was in profound quiet. The woman might be ill, but, ill or well, Peek was morally certain that she was not there.

That night Tid went into Gulick's, still and unapproachable as usual, and ordered a stiff glass of rum-and-water. While it was preparing, Peek stepped up and remarked drily, "Wife ain't sick, is she? Lef' town?" There was quite a crowd present, and the answer to Peek's question was awaited with breathless interest.

Tid took up his glass of rum-and-water and drained it at a draught, his face meanwhile growing whiter and whiter. Then he turned toward Peek, who instinctively began to shrink away from him. His dull eyes emitted a single sulphurous flash. Then he gathered up his brawny fist like lightning, and planted a tremendous blow in the middle of his interrogator's face. "Darn yer picter!" he shouted, in a voice so hoarse and unnatural that none of the men would ever have recognized it; "ef ye speak of her, 'n' mostly ef ye speak ag'in her, I'll kill ye!" Then he turned sharply, and walked off to his lonely cabin. The blow that he had dealt to Peek was attended with permanent and disfiguring results, and Tid Slocum's request was ever after respected, at least in his presence. But his wife had undoubtedly deserted him.

A year and a half passed away, and as spring opened —the second spring after Tid's marriage—the brisk

sounds of reviving labor echoed through the Tom Lake
settlement. A newly-opened iron mine of untold rich-
ness had been located on the range, and owners of land in
the vicinity had sold it at a handsome advance. "Old
Bill" had died, and Jack Peabody had "sold out" and returned to his native place in New England to begin life
again with a hundred thousand dollars in his pocket.
With these vicissitudes, and with the influx of new-
comers, there had been considerable change in the little
settlement; but still Tid Slocum, who had been more
prosperous perhaps than any of his old mates, grim and
silent as ever, lived alone in his trim little cabin. His
"luck" in worldly affairs had evidently "turned," and,
isolated and friendless though he was, he had yet sufficient
cause to congratulate himself.

One night, the chill in the evening air having driven
Gulick's guests inside, they were listening to the exciting revelations of one of their comrades who had been
down in Chicago for the winter. The narrator was de-
tailing consequentially some triflng personal adventure,
when he suddenly broke off short, looked around cautiously, and exclaimed:

"But, Lord, boys! I hain't told ye the biggest news of
all! I seen Tid's wife!" Amazed ejaculations broke from
one and another, and the little circle gathered closer.
"Yes," continued the man, in the same circumspect manner, "I seen her, 'n' she seen me, 'n' she pulled her veil
over her face, and herried along. By George, but she
looked 's ef she was poor!" The excited interest of his
hearers led the narrator into a little display of human
nature, and he began to dwell with unnecessary minute-
ness upon the details of his story. "She had a bundle in
her hands, like sewin'-work, er suthin er other, 'n' I fol-

lered her, ter a number"—and the speaker took out a
notebook, and pronounced the number loudly by way of
corroborating his story—" 'n' then, bein' kinder thirsty,
I stepped inter a saloon close by, 'n' a kinder good-lookin' feller he cum in, 'n' we struck up quite an acquaintance; 'n', bein' flush, I sez, sez I, 'I hope ye'll jine me?'
'O' course,' he sez; 'don't care 'f I do.' "

"Wal—Tid's wife?" interrupted an auditor impatiently.

"Good Lord!" snapped the taleteller, crossly, "who's
a-tellin' this story, anyhow? Ef I ain't——"

"Go on! go on!" cried the crowd, and Handy Graham
took hold of the interrupter's shoulders with an emphatic
shake and a "You shut up!" which quite restored the
equilibrium of the injured hero.

"After we'd treated back and forth a few times,' I sez,
sez I, p'intin' to the house I seen Tid's wife go in, 'Know
'em?' 'Yes,' sez he. 'How 'bout that woman 't jest
went in?' sez I. 'I've seen her often,' sez he; 'a sewin'-
woman 't sews fer 'em—they're dress-makers,' sez he.
'I noticed her,' sez he, 'bein' uncommon good-lookin'
'n' sorter sad-like. Know her?' 'Wal,' sez I, 'middlin'.
Run away from her husband up in the mines with another
man. Hain't never seen no man round with her, have
ye?' sez I. 'No,' sez he, 'he must 'a left her—fer I see her
often, bein' here frequent, 'n' I hain't seen no man near
her this winter: he must 'a left her.' 'He was jest that
kind,' sez I: 'I'll bet my pile he has gone and left her.' "

At that moment a muffled sound came from the doorway, and Tid Slocum, with the same white face and flashing eyes that some of the crowd remembered to have
seen once before, entered and walked up to the bar. Peek
Brown, who had been among the most absorbed of the
spell-bound audience of a moment before, shrank to half

his usual size, and hid behind his companions; but he need not have been frightened, for Tid simply ordered a dram, which was served quietly to him by the brazen Lize, and then walked stumblingly away. The next day there was silence and gloom in Tid's little cabin, and his face did not appear at Gulick's. In fact, Tid had "vamosed," and the inhabitants of Tom Lake village never saw him there again.

Ten years later, Jack Peabody and his wife, whose well-earned wealth had been doubled and trebled by fortunate investments, visited the opera in grand style in one of our great Eastern cities. The music was fine, and Mr. Peabody and his wife, who had not misused their recent opportunities for "culchah," were listening attentively and with an acute admiration, when suddenly a couple in an opposite box attracted Mr. Peabody's observant eye. He raised his glass and called his wife's attention to the objects of his gaze, whereupon a prolonged scrutiny and discussion followed.

They saw a gaunt, enormous man, with dull blue eyes, and a mass of tawny hair, which had evidently been the despair of some unhappy barber. He was attired in a rich but ill-worn suit of broadcloth, and by his side was a woman, whose well-featured face, expensive dress, and flashing jewels made her harmonize well with her sumptuous surroundings. She looked with a calm interest upon the scenes which were being depicted before her, but the man's rapt gaze never wandered from her face, and to the bewildered pair who were surveying him he was a mute but eloquent statue of love, adoration, forgiveness.

"Yes," whispered Mr. Peabody to his wife, after a protracted and earnest canvass of the question, "it's them— by George, it's them!"

"*Ye Christmas Witch.*"

A TRUE NEW ENGLAND STORY OF THE LAST CENTURY.

"I TELL 'ee 'at she do dawnce aroun' it!"

Old Laban Trewis opened wide his solemnly blinking eyes as he said this. His audience, the men and boys gathered around the fire at the store of Mr. Mellen, one of the chief citizens of Fenmarsh Village, looked awe-stricken. Mr. Mellen himself, with the air of one who had not suspected anything so bad as this, ejaculated, "You don't mean to say so!"

"Aw, she do!" pursued old Laban, who, in spite of many years' residence in the new world, still retained his strong north-of-England vernacular. "She do thot! An' they say she do burn candles to the front of an image-like when she do say her prayers. Aw, she do be a Papist, sure!"

The old man leaned back, proud of the attention which had been yielded him, and convinced that his case was proven.

"I seen the bush-like, out in a big box, settin' to the right o' the door-stone all summer," drawled Lysander Mingins, a young farmer from the Height-O'-Land part of the town. The road by which he usually entered the village ran past the small house, just on the outskirts of it, in which all these strange events had taken place. "I seen it," he went on, "but I didn't know nothin' about its bein' a holly-bush."

14 209

"You was too young when you come over," said Mr. Mellen, the storekeeper. "You'd a' known a holly-bush if you'd a' lived long enough in Old England."

"Wal, she do dawnce aroun' that holly-bush," chirruped old Laban Trewis, again. "Fairweather folks can tell 'ee of queer doin's enough over to their side 'e river. It's bad luck for Fenmarsh they ever coom here."

"I should think they'd find out when they'd been struck with lightning a few more times, and when they'd lost a few more sheep and cattle by the foot-rot,—I should think they'd find out 'twa'n't no use goin' contrary to the Almighty," said Mr. Mellen, solemnly. "An' wa'n't the son's wife ravin' crazy before she come down sick on her bed? That was before they left Fairweather, wa'n't it?"

The door opened, and a stately figure entered. There was a sort of a straightening up, and a putting on of dignity among the gossiping group. It was Parson Bement who was coming in—grave, reverend, stern. As he closed the door behind him, he took off his heavy woolen cap and shook the snow from it. His high, narrow forehead, his small, cold, deep-set eyes, his close-shaven, firm-set jaws showed him to be a typical Puritan. Parson Bement exacted his rights of everyone, and he meant to do justice to all; but he felt that Papists, and other sects who did not interpret the Bible as he himself did, were sinners against high Heaven, and that they should be treated accordingly. If Parson Bement had lived in another land and in another age, he might have been that merciless Abbot, to whom the fearless Constance de Beverley aided even by St. Hilda's gentle Abbess, and the "haughty" but relenting Prioress of Tynemouth, appealed in vain.

The parson saluted them all with serious politeness, and made purchase at the counter of a pound of good tobacco.

"And what is the news to-night, good Master Mellen?" he asked, as his package was handed to him.

"They was jest sayin' as how the Mistress Maitland have lost the only good cow she have left, sir."

The parson raised his eyes to the ceiling, and shook his head. The eight or ten men and boys sitting on the boxes and benches around the fire, eyed him narrowly.

"And the son—is he no better, Master Mellen?"

"Worse, sir. He walks out, and can shovel the paths, I see, but he do cough dreadful."

There was a suggestion in the storekeeper's tone that it was to be expected that young Maitland's cough should be worse, and that, perhaps, it was just and right that it should be.

"I fear," said Parson Bement, in slow and measured accents, "that the young man will follow his poor wife ere many days. It may be that this severe climate does not agree with them."

A grim smile played over the parson's hard face. The men laughed a little. Old Laban Trewis seized this opportunity for repeating what he felt to be the most impressive and sensational fact which had yet been elicited concerning the Maitlands.

"I tell 'ee, Parson Bement," he hurried to say, "I tell 'ee, she be not a right-minded woman! She do have a holly-bush in a box in her kitchen, an' it do have red berries on it. I warrant she will pick 'em and hang 'em about her house for 'e Christmas time them Papists set such store by—an' as I was coomin' by her house to-night, I seen her, big 'n proud as she be—I seen her, sir—I seen her a-dawncin' aroun' her holly-bush. I seen her mysel' through the kitchen-pane."

The parson's features betrayed the keenest interest, but he merely shook his head.

"They hain't been to meetin', hev' they, sence they come to town?" asked the Height-O'-Land farmer.

"They have not entered the house of prayer, to my knowledge," said the minister, oracularly, "during the two years since they came to Fenmarsh. My friend and co-laborer, Dr. Dummer, the pastor of the Fairweather church, said that all their losses and afflictions while in his parish did not seem to soften their hearts. If they prayed at all, it was by forms and in their own apartments. They never worshipped with God's people. I could not refuse to bury their dead for them, but I know that they had read their Church of England service over her body, very likely with the burning of candles and other Papist mummery, before I came to pray. I fear all is not well with them."

The parson drew his face down, but his air expressed, after all, a certain sacred sense of triumph that a deserved fate was overtaking miscreants.

"They're awful poor—I know that," piped up a boy's voice. It was that of Levi Fuller, the son of the town constable, whose house lay near the small cottage of the Maitlands. There was a strain of indignant pity in the shrill half-protest. "They've mostly lived on the milk of the cow," he went on, "an' now they hain't got nothin'."

A little qualm passed over the face of the pastor. Then it resumed its usual expression of inscrutable calm.

"They that live against the Lord, from His wrath may they not hope to be delivered!" he ejaculated, fervently.

"Mother sent 'em over a hunk o' dried beef this mornin'," proceeded the boy, as though driven by some fateful force to tell the secrets of his family. There was a certain defiance in his tone, too, as though one should say, "If there is any heart in you, you, too, will pity these unfortunate people."

"If old Lady Maitland is what some thinks," said Lysander Mingins, significantly, "an' this dancin' an' the rest looks mighty like it, them that helps her had better take care. I believe."—his voice grew thick and low— "I believe the's a curse on 'em."

Old Laban Trewis leaned forward and struck the floor with his heavy cane.

"Did they keep a Thanksgivin'?" he thundered. "Naw —they never even coom to the house o' Gawd! But what is it they'll keep so solemn 'n so gay, too? I tell 'ee it's the Christmas time coomin' nex' week now! I tell 'ee, they'll both on 'em dawnce aroun' the holly-bush then! An' when I fust coom to this country, 'n lived down Salem way, there was death 'n blight there among them that had dawncin' roun' holly-bushes and Christmas-keepin',—an' they wa'n't no mincin' names then, I tell 'ee—they was called by their right names then—they was called Witches!"

The old man sank back into his seat, almost exhausted by his long and fiery speech. There was a rapid mingling of talk as he concluded, during which he seized a chance to order a glass of rum-and-water. In the midst of the hubbub the door opened again, and there entered a slender and singularly handsome young man. His face, in spite of its high-bred beauty, was very sallow, and the expression of his sunken eyes and the sharpness of his long, straight nose made him as one on whom the seal of death is set. He coughed as he came in—a cough which made

even the hardest of the group about the fire to shudder.
On his head was a worn but still elegant cap of fur. His
cloak, though old and shabby, was of the richest materials,
and on its broad collar was embroidered a coat of arms.
His bearing, though that of a man whom illness has en-
feebled, was still proud and noble.

He bought a few cheap groceries, taking the packages
from the tradesman's hands as a duke might receive a
gift from his dependents. The parson deliberately turned
his back upon the youth. The sudden cessation of the
excited talk as he came in must have been noticed by
him, but his marble face expressed nothing beyond a
half-defined contempt.

As he closed the door behind him and went out into
the snowy night, the Fuller boy followed him. The storekeeper quietly slipped out upon the big stone step of his
store to see what should be done. He saw the Fuller
boy take the sick man's parcels and offer him the strong,
if clumsy, support of his young arm, which was not re-
jected. The Fuller boy had a mother, who, while trying
hard to follow the severe theology of the day, still allowed her somewhat strong mind, and her kind and
gentle heart to dwell chiefly upon the precepts of the
merciful Jesus. In the first place, she did not believe
half the stories which were afloat about the Maitlands.
In the second place, even if these stories were all true,
there was no excuse, she declared, for treating the unfortunate family inhumanly. That the Maitlands were
proud and scornful, was true. They had been treated
in a way to make them so, reasoned Mrs. Fuller. But,
if they were poor, misguided "Papists," why not try to
win them over to the true faith by kindness and love? For
her own part, Mrs. Fuller—and she was not the only one

—loved to go by the little wooden house in which the Maitlands lived, and see through the window the white-haired, beautiful-faced old woman, as she sat sewing; or hear her, as she played upon her spinet—the only one in town. Everybody loved to watch her, too, as she tended her flower garden. Nobody had such flowers as she.

The men in the store, who separated to go to their various homes shortly after young Maitland left, commiserated the Fuller boy, and expressed fears—when they saw Parson Bement's shocked look, as the storekeeper related what the boy had done—that a new subject was making ready to serve the Prince of Darkness. But the boy did not know this, and as his mother told him—in few words and without emotion, as was the way with New England mothers—that he had done right—this, with the warm thanks of the sick man, when he had parted from his young benefactor, made Levi Fuller quite easy in his mind.

The heavy snows began to melt. One of those delightful, sunny seasons which the stern New England winters sometimes grant about Christmas time, came over Fenmarsh. Young Maitland seemed to revive somewhat under the gracious influences of the kindly sun. One morning, warmly wrapped, he sat out on the porch of their little cottage, while "Lady Maitland," as his mother was generally called throughout the village, brought forth her boxes of chrysanthemums and set them in the sun beside him. There were five of the plants, large, strong, and covered with nodding blossoms. Nobody else in Fenmarsh had anything like them. The women there envied "Lady Maitland" far more than her air of distinction and the experiences of splendor which it was rumored that she had had—her wonderful success with plants. What would they not give for such "artemishys" as those!

The old lady, high-headed, perfectly erect, stern-faced, but regally handsome, went on with her work as she talked with her son.

"I was hoping," he said, "to go down to the graveyard once more before the winter fairly closed in, and put a bunch of flowers on Edith's grave."

Her face grew pale, and she fetched out another box of tossing, beautiful flowers before she dared to speak.

"You must not think of it, Gerald," she said, calmly. "In the spring you will be stronger. Our fortunes must look up by that time. We shall hear from Elizabeth, and she or some of our friends must come to us. We can manage in some way to get through the winter—but you must keep quiet and warm. I am afraid it overtaxed you, going out the other night."

"Not in the least," he hastened to say. "If you think I am so far gone that my mother must go without her morning cup of tea because I cannot face the night air——"

"It is no disgrace, Gerald," she hastened to cry, with a note of exquisite pain in her voice. "Think what you have been through—the little one's death in Fairweather —then Edith's slow decline—our losses of property—the burning of our buildings—oh, you would be more than human if you could endure it without breaking down. You know you have always been delicate."

"But you—you have endured it." He looked at her with fond pride. They were all in all to each other.

She buried her face in a mass of yellow bloom, to hide a tear which would trickle down her cheek. "He does not know how my brain has reeled!" she murmured.

"Oh, yes!" she said brightly, turning her face from him, and leaving the tear to shine like a drop of dew upon the golden blossom, "I feel as strong and fresh as ever. I have always been so strong, you know, dear!"

Two little children, muffled in stout, home-spun woolen, had come along the street, and now they were leaning against the gate and looking covetously at Lady Maitland's wonderful chrysanthemums. She always regarded the village people with unconcealed scorn.

"What do you want, little girls?" she called out now. Her tone was very cross.

The children dropped a courtesy in careful unison.

"Please, forsooth, a flower, mum, for Vashti and me."

Lady Maitland broke off the spray of yellow chrysanthemums on which the tear was still glittering, shook it, and gave it to the child. To little "Vashti," she gave a red one.

The children took them with eyes glowing, and sniffed in their spicy odors. The old woman's set face softened. It was a mitigation of their vulgarity that these children should so love flowers.

"You poor little things! how you do enjoy them!" she said, kindly.

This encouraged them. Little Vashti came nearer.

"Please, forsooth," she said, trembling, "can—can— Lois and I—have you got a holly-bush?"

"Indeed I have," replied Lady Maitland; "and it is all covered with beautiful red berries."

"He said so!" cried the child, clapping her hands and then putting on a frightened look, as she saw that she had almost broken her cherished spray of flowers by so doing; "Uncle Laban Trewis said you had. Where is it?"

She began to push, child-like, past the stately figure,

little Lois following hard after her, but the strong arm of the mistress barred the way.

"What rude little girls!" she exclaimed, with a look which made the innocent little things shrink back aghast. "You should never enter a house without an invitation. Did you never hear of such a rule as that?"

Little Vashti began to cry.

"I want to see the red berries," she sobbed.

"Oh, let them see it, mother," interposed the young man, wearily. "It's little enough we have to please anybody."

"Well, come, then," she said, impatiently. She led the way in. "Here it is.'"

There, in the full glory of a south window, stood the famous holly-bush, as tall as little Vashti's head, and looking brave enough, with its spreading, prickly leaves and shining berries.

"Oh-h-h!" sighed the little ones, gazing with eyes like stars upon the brilliant spectacle.

"I will cut a spray for each of you," said Lady Maitland, graciously. This done, they did not forget to thank her, but even after they had done this, they still stood gazing at her. ·

"Well," said the old lady, whose opinion of the manners of the neighborhood was confirmed by the conduct of these heedless little ones, "What now?"

They were very small—probably not more than seven years old, and their solemn aspect, as they looked from the holly-bush to her, and from her to the holly-bush. seemed unutterably ridiculous to her. She began to laugh nervously.

"What now?" she repeated.

"Please, forsooth," began little Lois, timidly, and with

the awe-struck look in her big eyes growing deeper. "Please, forsooth, would you dawnce around the holly-bush for us?"

The usual pronunciation of the word "dance" was short and flat to a degree in Fenmarsh, but the child had heard Uncle Laban Trewis use the word in this connection, and she copied his manner.

Lady Maitland looked at her for a moment in indignant bewilderment. Then a partial vision of the situation came over her, and she burst into a harsh, wild laugh. Any one hearing it would surely have thought it the laugh of a crazy woman. Her son came hurrying in from the porch.

"Fancy, Gerald!" she cried, amid hysterical sobs, which were half of sardonic laughter, "these impertinent little things! What can they mean!"

She sat down in one of the stiff, high-backed chairs against the wall, and fell to laughing again that dreadful laugh.

"What is it?" exclaimed the young man, pulling little Lois toward him. "What did you say to her? Tell me quick."

The child choked up and began to cry bitterly, hiding her face behind her flowers. Little Vashti came to her assistance.

"She said," she began tremblingly. "She said, 'Won't you dawnce around the holly-bush for us?'"

The young man looked puzzled and distressed. "Go now," he said.

The little things, both of them sobbing by this time, went slowly down the path to the road. As the young man gazed after them, his face darkened. He and his mother were, then, objects of suspicion as well as of dislike. He had not cared for the dislike of the people—a Maitland could only disdain these lowly folk and all their ways, but could it be that they thought his mother a— witch?

A cold sweat gathered on him as he recalled the Salem murders, and the other outrages on helpless and inno- cent unfortunates which had occurred nearer Fenmarsh. The excitement over witches had died away, he thought. Could it be that it was to start up again now, and that the lightning strokes which had twice burned their build- ings—the death which had carried off his child and then his young wife—the plagues which had destroyed their cattle—that these were going to be laid to a curse from the Almighty? "Ah," his soul cried in its anguish, "if there be any foundation for the belief that misfortunes follow those who are hated of God, then are we, indeed, the objects of His sore displeasure!"

As the children departed, his mother had thrown her head upon her arms, and, leaning on the plain kitchen table, was weeping violently. As he thought, he stroked her gray hair and tried to soothe her.

"Forget it, mother," he pleaded, "think of what the future holds for us. It cannot hold anything worse than we have suffered. I believe it will be like the beautiful old times. Think of them."

"I can see it all now," she said, brokenly. "I did not understand it before. I know now why the children look so at me when I pass along the street; why people cross over; and why the horses are whipped up when they go by the house. They think I am a witch, and that I hold or- gies, like the witches in 'Macbeth!' Oh, Gerald! isn't it absurd!" she laughed wildly, "and yet isn't it awful!" Now she began to weep.

"Don't, mother," he begged, "just think how it is almost Christmas-time, and remember what beautiful times we used to have at the Hall—how Elizabeth and I used to trim the mantels, and how Edith would come over so early and sing carols with us, and what lovely gifts we used to have."

"Yes," said his mother, bitterly, calmed by his gentleness. "But what do these recollections bring to me? Memory seems no friend—only a lash to sting me. Edith and her beautiful babe are dead. Elizabeth—where is she? When we heard last from her—and, just think, Gerald, that was three years ago—she was very ill at your Uncle William's, and she, too, may be dead, for all we know. Maitland Hall is wrested from us by a false claim. I know your father never owed your Uncle Richard any such sum as he claimed. I know he had no right to take our home from us—though he did produce those dreadful papers in court to prove it. Then our money is nearly gone. It is only by the closest management that we can get through the long, hard winter which is just beginning. You are ill, and need delicacies which we cannot buy. Why, Gerald, my brain whirls so, when I think of it sometimes, that I can readily believe of myself that I am as crazy as these low village people think."

"Poor mother! Poor mother!" he said, with streaming eyes.

"Oh, my brave, beautiful boy! Forgive me!" she cried, as she saw the look which crept over his stern, sunken face. "Let us forget it all! We shall hear from Elizabeth. She is well and strong. She and Uncle William have succeeded in getting back our home. They will come to us with plenty of money, or else they will call us back to England. We cannot make the dead to live, but there will be much comfort and happiness for us yet."

"How could I excite him so!" she murmured, as she turned away from him. In her heart she felt that she was but hastening the end.

"Bring in your chair, Gerald," she continued, brightly, "I will cook the potatoes and cut the loaf."

With an air as though she were serving for her pleasure the sovereign of her country, the stately woman moved about the little room, performing the menial duties which seemed so ill-suited to her; and thus the day passed on. At nightfall, she saw that her son had visibly failed. The exciting events of the day—the startling glimpse into the true feeling of the people around them, which had been afforded by the little girl's absurd question about the holly-bush, had unnerved and exhausted him. But before they went to bed, the old woman sat down at her spinet, and sang a tender Christmas song.

"Forget everything that is sad, Gerald," she said, cheerily, as she kissed him good-night; "we will have a happy Christmas to-morrow, in spite of everything. We still have each other. Those who have passed away are happy in a better world. We shall join them some time, and how beautiful that will be! There is nothing sad, any way you look at it. It is all bright, and by another Christmas things may be so different with us!" She laughed a laugh that had tears in it, but it was not grating and strange, like her laugh in the morning. He kissed her.

"Good-night, mother," he said, "the brave mother who will not be cast down."

The lights were put out, the little home was still, but angels entered that night through the closed doors. The messenger came, and, as ever, he found no resistance, for who can resist the Angel of Death?

The Christmas morning broke clear and quiet. "Lady Maitland" had fashioned, out of materials saved from the wreck of their fortunes, a rich, embroidered garment for her son, and, with her hands piled full of gay chrysanthemums, she went into his room to take to him her Christmas token.

"Good morning, Gerald!" she exclaimed, as she entered his chamber. "Let me throw open the shutter. See how the sunlight streams in. Is it not wonderful?"

There was a strange stillness. The smile with which she had wreathed her face faded. With a cry of utter despair she threw herself across his silent body, scattering the flowers over the coarse white counterpane. The warm, embroidered dressing-gown, over which she had toiled so hard in secret, weaving in her desperate love with every pictured blossom, fell to the floor.

It was thus they found her, hours afterward.

"They ain't been no smoke outer Lady Maitland's chimbly this mornin'," said Mrs. Fuller to her husband, the constable. It was ten o'clock, and he had just come in from the barn. The soft weather had gone by. It was blowing up cold from the north—a bitter Christmas day. It had not occurred to the Fullers that it was Christmas day at all.

The stiff-legged, clumsy farmer walked to the last window, which overlooked the modest home of the Maitlands. The plain curtains had not been raised. Everything looked still and deserted.

"I guess I'll go over," persisted Mrs. Fuller.

"I wish you'd let them pesky folks alone," snapped her husband. "Fairweather folks is glad enough to get

shet on 'em. Over there they call 'em Papists out'n out.
I seen John Gerrish yisterd'y. He says Parson Dummer's right outspoken about 'em, same as Parson Bement is here. Parson Dummer, he hain't so hard on
nobody as Parson Bement is, but Gerrish says even he
says the Maitlands ain't what they orter be!"

"I'm reely worried, Tobias," went on Mrs. Fuller, as
though she had not heard a word her husband was saying,
"about Lady Maitland. I don't mind her airs. She
never puts on none on 'em along o' me. She's good to
her friends, same as the rest on us be. When folks treat
her mean, she pays 'em back, o' course." As she spoke
she was winding a woolen comforter around her neck,
and donning her "camlet" cloak and hood. "I'm goin'
over," she said, shortly. "Levi saw Mr. Gerald out in
the storm the other night, gittin' groceries to the store.
He hain't been out much sense. I'm afeared they're both
on 'em down."

Mrs. Fuller did not mention to her husband that she
proposed to take with her a pail of milk and a package
of doughnuts, but she took them, just the same.

Repeated knocks at the Maitlands' doors produced no
effect. Mrs. Fuller came back for her husband, and, after
some reasoning, induced him to return with her and force
an entrance. Then the sad truth was known. Young
Gerald Maitland was dead. His proud mother, whose
brain, in the opinion of most of the village people, had
always been more or less cracked, was now undoubtedly
demented.

Mrs. Fuller would not call in any neighbors, till she
had first made a thorough investigation of the case and
of the house, herself. They had raised up the poor, fainting mother, and had laid her upon a chintz-covered couch

in the little sitting-room, but she was in such a fever and seemed so weak and helpless that it was plain she must be undressed and put to bed. Mrs. Fuller hurried upstairs to see that a room should be made ready for her. The good woman's heart beat as she ascended the stairs. Should she find in that secluded apartment any of the strange charms and cabalistic manuscripts which were rumored to belong to poor Lady Maitland? She opened the door carefully. The light of noon poured in upon the plain furnishings of the room, which were not unlike those of Mrs. Fuller's own, excepting that, between the windows, hung a crucifix, and in sockets placed on either side of it in the wall were unlighted candles. A cushion was beneath it in which there was a fresh impression.

"She's said her prayers there this blessed morning!" sighed Mrs. Fuller. "I should think she'd a' found out before this that prayin' in that way wouldn't avail." But, still, in Mrs. Fuller's secret soul arose the unbidden question, why, if the heart were sincere, prayer offered before a crucifix should be not as acceptable as the same prayer offered somewhere else? There was something of the nineteenth century, as well as of the eighteenth, in good Mrs. Fuller's make-up.

"Any way," soliloquized the good woman, hurriedly, for she heard a voice below which she recognized as that of Mrs. Mingins, little Lois's mother, "I'll hide everything, so that nobody else shall see it." So crucifix, cushion, candles and all were hastily thrust between the feather mattresses. The candlesticks alone remained to tell the story, and they were not necessarily incendiary. Mrs. Fuller was none too soon. She had scarcely time to open an oaken chest near her, and pretend to be ex-

15

amining its contents, when Mrs. Mingins' face appeared at the door.

"Here's a clean nightgown for her," said Mrs. Fuller, stopping for no conventionalities. "I'm so glad you've come, Miss Mingins. Tell 'em to fetch her up, if they can. I can manage her, if they'll get her up here."

"Who's goin' to take care on her?" said Mrs. Mingins, doubtfully. "I'll tell ye frankly, Mis Fuller, I wouldn't stay here for no money."

"I'll stay," said Mrs. Fuller, promptly. "I'll stay till to-morrow, sure. Sarah Jane an' Levi can do the work up to my house. Tell 'em to hurry up."

An hour later, thanks to Mrs. Fuller's judicious nursing, the poor, lonely mother lay in a gentle sleep.

Downstairs there was a great consultation; Parson Bement, Doctor Dow, Tobias Fuller, Mr. Mellen and several others from among the leading men in the village were talking about the Maitlands. Nobody wanted to watch overnight with the dead man. Nobody was clear what sort of a funeral should be given him; but after discussing the subject for a half-hour, Uncle Laban Trewis, who had dug the graves in the village churchyard for twenty years, was set to work digging a grave, a plain coffin was procured, young Gerald Maitland was placed in it, a prayer was said over him, and before the darkness fell that night, his body lay at rest beside that of his young wife. Mrs. Fuller had not been able to join much in the discussion, but she was indignant when she found how summarily matters had been settled.

"What if she comes to in the night?" she asked, warmly. "What should I say to her? It's a shame to bury him so quick! You hadn't orter a' consented to it, Tobias! Wal, the least you can do is to lay the flowers that was scattered on the coverlid, on his grave. Freeze? What if they do freeze? It's a little mite o' mercy, any-how."

Parson Bement thought this outburst anything but truly pious, but Mrs. Fuller was not very amenable to his counsels, and broke away from him as soon as she could, on the pretext that the poor woman upstairs was in need of her.

The nailing of the coffin had disturbed the sleeper. When Mrs. Fuller came upstairs she found Lady Mait-land sitting up in the bed, and gazing about her in be-wilderment.

"What was that noise?" she said, faintly. "I thought the Christmas greens had been put up long ago. I did not order any decorations upstairs."

"No, no!" said Mrs. Fuller, soothingly. "That's all right. You lie down."

"No," said the sick woman. "It is time for me to get up. Did you hear the children sing this morning? I must have slept through it myself—but I know it was lovely. What a charming voice Edith has! And Eliza-beth's is almost as sweet."

"Yes, yes," said Mrs. Fuller, "but don't talk now. It is growing dark, and it's cold. You'll ketch cold if you set up so. Do lie down. You can't get up 'n dress now. 'Tain't time."

"Why, Susan, is that you?" said the wandering woman, cheerfully. "I thought it was—who did I think it was? I feel confused, some way. But I'll do as you say, Susan."

She lay down quietly enough. After this Mrs. Fuller was constantly "Susan" to her. She went on with her prattle.

"Are the children's gifts all ready?" she asked, peremptorily. "I told you to set them in order in the great hall. There was an embroidered gown for Gerald—but for Edith—did I get anything for Edith? What was it?"

Her tone grew helpless and inquiring. There was something very touching to Mrs. Fuller, who had never seen Lady Maitland except in the proud, unbending character which she had chosen to assume always before the village people, in the sweet, appealing looks she gave her now, as a certain evidently much-trusted "Susan."

"Oh—yes—that's all right," she answered, half sobbingly. "There's something for everybody, I guess."

"And did you ever see anything so pretty?" pursued the distracted invalid. "Elizabeth made the holly wreaths, and wound in the mistletoe. I never saw anything so pretty. Oh, it will be the best Christmas that the children ever had. I am so glad!"

"You must not talk so much," said Mrs. Fuller, gently, "Your fever is coming on again. Now try to keep still."

"You see," went on the sick woman, paying not the slightest heed to her nurse's words, "You see, Edith and Gerald are very fond of each other. She is a sweet girl, and they have always loved each other. If they should marry, it would be well enough. Edith is not rich, but Gerald will have the Hall, and there is an abundance—an abundance."

She repeated the words emphatically, as though to dare Mrs. Fuller to deny them.

"Poor thing!" cried Mrs. Fuller, "I wonder if she will understand to-morrow."

For she knew already, from what she had been able to see in the short time she had been in charge of the house. that there was little enough to pay for the keeping of even this one poor creature in it. There were vegetables and apples in the cellar, a few supplies in the pantry, a little money, but beyond something which, it had been learned, was yet to be paid upon a mortgage which had just been put upon the place, there was barely enough of the whole Maitland estate to cover the young man's funeral expenses, and to provide for the mother's wants during the winter.

"She will have to go to the poorhouse," murmured Mrs. Fuller, turning white about the lips herself at the thought. The fall of pride involved seemed to extend somehow to her, too—at least, so that she could feel something of the twinge which the proud woman on the pillow would feel if she knew.

Levi slept that night on the couch in the little Maitland sitting room, while his mother watched upstairs with the sick woman. They both slept late the next morning. It was nearly eight when Mrs. Fuller was awakened by a violent shaking. Lady Maitland stood above her, with an impatient expression on her face. She was quite dressed, and with neatness.

"Susan!" she said, sharply; "why do you not wake up? I have dressed entirely by myself. The children ——" she looked around vaguely, "the children must be out singing carols. It seems very lonely."

"Don't talk about 'carols' to-day," said Mrs. Fuller, springing up and beginning to make her toilet. "Christmas is over. Folks around here don't think much of Christmas any way. I wouldn't say much about it if I was you."

"Not Christmas to-day!" exclaimed the old woman, severely. "Susan, you are insane! It is Christmas to-day—it is Christmas always. What are you thinking about?"

To this, the poor, weak mind was henceforth consistent. With her it was indeed, "Christmas always" and, alas! —she could not know enough to heed kind Mrs. Fuller's well-meant suggestion as to reticence, but babbled continually of Christmas and Christmas scenes—but always in the past.

In the town records of Fenmarsh for the year 1788, appears the following:

"On ye 25 of Dec. 1788, died: Gerald Maitland, aged about 27. Ye mother of ye young man, who is strange to ye most of ye townsfolk, is much distraught by his death. She was taken on ye 29 to ye town farm, where she could be cared for. Some say she do hold a pasture lot in ye town of Fairweather. If it can be done, ye charge for her keepe will be put on ye towne of Fairweather. Ye Doctor Dow pronounces her very crazy. Her friends be not known, but ye Mistress Tobias Fuller have writ a letter to one Elizabeth Maitland in England, according to a letter found in an oaken, silver-banded chest which was in ye house. If she heare not from said Elizabeth Maitland, ye woman will come for a charge on ye town of Fenmarsh, unless ye town of Fairweather will take her up. Ye property of ye woman Margaret Maitland is but ye oaken chest aforementioned, some good old clothing, a spinet and some other good furniture, some foolish flowering plants, and ye pasture lot in Fairweather, which some say be mortgaged for all it be worth. Ye house and place here be mortgaged, also. It is feared ye woman, who be not more than sixty years of age, and strong and well, but for ye sickness of her mind, will come to be a pauper for ye rest of her life, and a charge on ye towne of Fenmarsh."

In the records of the town of Fairweather, which were

kept evidently by a much less scholarly person than those of Fenmarsh, appears the following entry at about the same time:

"Ye crazy woman, Margaret Maitland, be on ye town of Fenmarsh. Said woman did lose her mind on acct. of loosing her son on ye 25 of December. This being ye Christmas Day, she do gabble of ye Christmas all ye time. Said Margaret Maitland be a Papist and a witch. Said woman have always had bad luck upon her. Ye towne of Fairweather have no righte to take her from ye towne of Fenmarsh. Her pasture lot be only 1,000 feet square out of Square Ewing's large pasture lot. Square Ewing held a mortgage on it, which be now foreclosed. So it do be plain to ye lawyers of Fairweather yt ye witch belong not to this towne, but to ye towne of Fenmarsh."

Each town employed lawyers in its behalf, and all through the winter raged a violent fight between them regarding the keeping of poor Lady Maitland, whose fallen estate began to be denoted by making her title "Mother." She was usually quiet and docile. The poormaster could not complain that she made any trouble. Through the intercession of Mrs. Fuller, who had been faithful to the Maitlands' interests through everything, the old woman's spinet had been carried to the town-farm with her, and she amused herself a great deal with playing upon it. Nobody had wanted to buy the instrument, so it was not strange that the privilege had been permitted. She had her flowers, too, and seemed to tend them as skilfully as ever. Common work, however, she would not do, and her tone and manner toward those around her were always superior and condescending. She seemed perfectly well, and offered no violence to anybody. There was money enough realized from the sale of her effects to pay her board for a few weeks, for everything that could be had been turned into money, excepting the spinet and the oaken chest. Consequently, for the first two months the controversy between the towns was not so very violent. As the spring came on, and the money began to give out, however, Fenmarsh redoubled its efforts to get rid of its unwelcome burden. There had been much illness among the paupers in Fenmarsh. This was attributed by "Dick" White, the poormaster, to the presence of poor Mother Maitland. Early in March, Polly Staunton, one of the oldest paupers, died with consumption. This might have been regarded by Fenmarsh, under some circumstances, as an event not to be especially mourned, but, as things stood, they declared it to be largely the work of the evil spirits under the direction of Mother Maitland.

"So she's dead!" said Mrs. Fuller, who, not having seen Mother Maitland for some weeks, was paying her a short call. "It's rather of a mercy—poor soul! I've known Polly Staunton this forty year, and she's always been a poor, ailin' critter. She's at rest, thank the Lord!"

"Dick" White looked at Mrs. Fuller mysteriously, and pulled her to one side.

"I ain't never had sech luck with sickness sense I took the farm," he said, complainingly. "They ain't no chance o' sendin' Mother Maitland off to Fairweather, I'm afeard, and the Lord only knows what'll happen to us. What do you think, Mrs. Fuller? Is she a witch, 'r ain't she? I'd like to know your opinion."

"Witch!" cried good Mrs. Fuller, impatiently. "She ain't no more a witch, Dick White, than you or I be— not a mite. She's a poor, crazy woman—that's all. Dr. Dow says she won't never git right again, but Dr. Dow don't know everything, no more'n anybody else. For all you or I know, she may wake up some mornin' as bright as ever. She's had trouble; but this witch talk! It puts me out o' mind with the whole o' ye. I s'posed witches had gone out er fashion. I hain't heered nothin' on 'em sense the war. They ain't no use trumpin' 'em up again, to my notion. I don't believe they ever was witches, any way. I aint no believer in ghosts, nor witches, nuther. Don't you be scart by all this talk, Dick White. Mis White's good to Mother Maitland, 'n I'm glad on it. 'Tain't clear whether it's Fairweather or Fenmarsh had orter keep her, but as long as she stays with us, you be as good to her as you hev been, 'n there won't no harm come to ye. Now, you mark my words. I can't help a-hopin'," she continued in a low voice, "that a letter or somethin'll come from her folks in England. I believe they'll pay suthin' sometime. Her money's pretty much gone, I know, but I wouldn't wonder if the pay came from somewheres or other."

The strong convictions of Mrs. Fuller had for a while their effect upon Dick White. Then a sudden succession of calamities fell upon the town-farm. The White's eldest boy, a lad of fourteen or fifteen, fell from a beam and broke his arm; one of the cows cast her calf; and a child carelessly took a burning brand into the barn and it was destroyed by fire.

Now Fenmarsh was all awake. The witch belonged to Fairweather, and to Fairweather she must go. Accordingly, one sunny May morning, poor Mother Maitland, with her spinet, her oaken chest and her boxes of plants, was unceremoniously bundled into Dick White's long wagon and carted across the Connecticut River to the town-farm of Fairweather.

She was cheerful and composed over the move, and chatted incessantly as she passed along. She always called Dick White, "Richard," and as he was never harsh with her, she treated him with benignant condescension.

"It is a pleasant day for Christmas," she said, dreamily, "but I don't like to have it quite so warm at this season."

"A little while ago you was findin' it too cold for Christmas," said Dick White, good-humoredly; "you're kinder hard to suit."

"The weather is too warm for Christmas Day," repeated Mother Maitland, with emphasis. "I fear the church will be uncomfortably warm. The children have been busy trimming it all the morning. I hope the exertion has not been too much for them."

"I guess not," interposed Dick White drily.

"If it is too warm when we get there, Richard, I wish you personally to see to having the windows opened. My head will ache if the air is too close. You will please attend to it, Richard."

"Wal, I ain't a-runnin' this here 'church' that we're goin' to," said Dick White. "It's John Gerrish that runs this concern, 'n I don't know how he'll feel about givin' you plenty of air, I'm sure. I'm afeard he won't step around so lively as to please ye as Laury 'n I hev."

She paid little heed to his warnings, but kept on prattling of Christmas trimmings and the Christmas service, until the good man was almost wild.

"Now, see here," he said kindly, "John Gerrish 'n his wife won't put up with so much of this Christmas nonsense as I do. You want to keep kinder quiet over here. Fairweather folks don't like ye none too well. You was kinder airy when ye used to live over here 'n they don't forgit it. Now, Mother Maitland," he went on impressively, "you're sensible enough about your plants 'n takin' keer o' yerself—why can't ye understand me? You want to quit this Christmas talk, now you're going to Fairweather."

She looked at him with vacant, unheeding blandness.

"I think if we pass a shop," she said, "I will stop and buy a few more Christmas gifts for the tenants. I'm sure I haven't enough."

"No; I guess ye haint!" ejaculated Dick White. " 'N ye haint got no money to buy none with neither. Lord!" he continued, under his breath, "crazy folks is funny! I can't get an idea into her noddle to save me."

They rode on. John Gerrish met them as they drove up to the door. He had no mind to receive this gracious, queenly-looking woman, with her wandering far-away eyes, and her tone of lofty condescension—but the judge had decided that Fairweather must take her; so that nothing more was to be said.

"We're goin' to have another trial, mind ye, Dick White," he said, crossly. "They all say they wa'n't fair-play this time. She'll go kitin' back to Fenmarsh before many weeks. Now, you mark me!"

"Be careful how you move the chest, Richard," said Mother Maitland imperiously. "The Christmas gifts are in it, and some of them are frail. Christmas Day will be entirely spoiled if the gifts are injured."

"All right," said Dick White, pleasantly.

"Lord! does she go on like that?" asked John Gerrish. "How did she get so much Christmas in her head?'"

"You know her son died on Christmas Day—and it was Christmas Day that she went crazy," said Dick White soberly. "You wanter kinder humor her like— 'n she won't make ye no trouble."

"No broken arms, no cast calves, nor burnt barns, I s'pose.". John Gerrish spoke very sarcastically.

"She didn't break no arms, nor cast no calves, nor burn no barns, as I know on," said Dick White doggedly.

"Ye know she did," said John Gerrish under his breath and through shut teeth, as he thrust his face close against Dick White's. "Ye know she did: 'n I'd a sight rather see the old black man himself comin' in at my door, than yonder crazy woman—'n nobody knows why better than you do, Dick White, you know it!"

"Don't be a fool!"

Dick White turned a little pale as he heard these fearful words, and with just this brief exclamation, he gathered up his reins and hurried off.

In the meantime, down the village street of Fenmarsh paraded a procession of men and boys ringing bells, beating tin pans and shouting till they were hoarse.

"Good riddance to the Christmas witch!" they cried. "Down with the Papists! Over the hills and far away goes Mother Maitland!"

The church-bell was rung. The town had the aspect of a holiday.

In the middle of June the case was tried again, and this time it went against Fenmarsh, as John Gerrish had predicted. No calamity had occurred in the poor-house at Fairweather, except the breaking down of a pantry-shelf loaded with dishes. The shelf was old and weak, but no matter. Mother Maitland was at the bottom of it, in spite of the fact that she was picking strawberries for a barmecide Christmas feast, at the very moment when the helf gave way.

Then John Gerrish with a great ado carted back the

poor little woman, with the spinet, the chest and the plants, to Dick White.

"You'll have to keep her now," he said triumphantly, "till after the first of January, sure, for the case can't be tried again till then, if it ever is."

So, unwillingly enough, Fenmarsh accepted the charge again, and the Summer passed on without further incident.

It was three o'clock of a pleasant afternoon early in September that the dwellers on Height-O'-Land saw a cloud of dust rising on the Boston turnpike leading into Fenmarsh. Out of the cloud of dust glimmered a sheen of gold lace, cockades, and red uniforms.

On came the cavalcade, attracting immediate and universal attention as it swept along through the village street. Small boys gathered as if by a miracle, or as if a new Roderick Dhu had taught them to arise, as it were, out of the ground. Heads appeared at windows. All Fenmarsh was agape.

First came two outriders in red uniforms and gilt trappings. Their horses were fine and fresh. Then came a coach which was the grandest ever yet seen, at that time, in Fenmarsh, though it would look clumsy and lumbering enough to modern eyes. On the box was mounted a liveried coachman with powdered wig, while a gorgeous footman rode at the back of the vehicle. Two outriders followed at a little remove behind the coach.

They paused in the village street but once, and that was in front of Mr. Mellen's store, to ask if it were known to him where dwelt a certain Mr. Tobias Fuller.

It was the footman who sought this information, and when it was given, he sprang back to his place, and on went the procession till it turned the curve leading to the Height-O'-Land road, passed the small white cottage once occupied by the Maitlands, and paused at last before the low, comfortable farm-house of Constable Tobias Fuller. At a discreet remove lingered the motley crowd of curious villagers. Who, in the name of the Continental Congress, were these lordly people, and what could they possibly want with Tobias Fuller?

The footman opened the carriage-door and a gentleman, elegantly but plainly clad, sprang to the ground. He, in his turn, assisted a lady to alight. Her fair young face and stately bearing impressed at once the curious lookers-on.

"You are Mistress Tobias Fuller," said this beautiful creature graciously, "I am Elizabeth Maitland, of Maitland Hall, Warwickshire, now the Countess of Ellerslie. Your letter to me was long delayed by falling into the hands of a wicked man, who had doubtless received and destroyed many others. At last it reached me, however, and I hastened, as soon as illness would permit, to come to America. Where is my mother?"

Her tone was piteous. She evidently feared the worst. Could Mrs. Fuller tell her that her mother was a mindless pauper at the Fenmarsh town-farm upon the hill?

That excellent woman, who had been thrown into a condition approaching panic by the sudden appearance of so much scarlet and gold, was now thoroughly off her balance. Her honest face grew red and white by turns, while she dropped bewildered curtsies from time to time. A countess, too! Merciful heavens! Poor Mrs. Fuller felt that her cup was full!

"Do you not know where she is?" began the Countess of Ellerslie again in a tone of the keenest distress. This lent Mrs. Fuller a tongue.

"I do indeed, your honor—forsooth," she commenced in painful embarrassment. "Your mother is alive, and she is livin' with Mr. Dick White, in the low red house, with six maple trees before it, as you go along the first road from here that turns to your right."

Her manner suggested something more than the embarrassment which might naturally be expected in an humble village matron encountering a great personage.

"Is—is—she ill?" stammered the lady anxiously.

She—that is—she is not quite well, mum—you will see," was all that good Mrs. Fuller could say, and the lady, handing over the directions with great plainness to the coachman, was shut into the carriage again, and the superb cortège swept onward up the hill.

At the poor-house reigned the traditional calm which is said to precede the tempest. Two of the older pauper women, gaunt, hollow-eyed, unsightly, sat on a bench beneath the maple trees. The only old man among them was raking up a little pile of rowan in the field near by. A half-witted young woman, whose dull-faced, fatherless child stood staring, thumb in mouth, at the robins in the trees overhead, was helping to tidy the kitchen. Her name was Letitia, commonly abbreviated to Tishy.

All of these were struck by a sort of an electric paralysis, as the magnificent escort of the Countess of Ellerslie hove in sight, climbing wearily, but with a certain eagerness, the long, hard hill. The noise brought Mother Maitland to the front door. She had been in a garden-plot behind the house, attending to her plants. As they drew up, she stood there in placid dignity, her lips moving as they always did, and her whole air, as usual, as of one in a dream.

Elizabeth Maitland could not wait for the door to be opened for her.

"Mother!" she screamed, "Oh, mother! I have found you at last. Don't you know me? What is it? What makes you look so? Oh, Arthur, Arthur, make haste— she is fainting——!"

The Earl of Ellerslie was none too soon. As he rushed to aid his wife, the old woman, white as the soft summer clouds floating in the calm September sky above her, fell, like one dead, into his arms. "Tishy" brought water. She was quite collected, but if she had known that she was waiting upon a live earl, she would have fainted away more completely than had Mother Maitland. The maid of the Countess ran hither and thither, wringing her hands. She was far less useful than "Tishy."

It was a long time before the poor mother came to herself. The scarlet-coated outriders dismounted, and lay down under the trees. The grand coach was drawn up beside the grassy road, and the horses were tethered to a stout sapling. Yet, still on the plain couch in the rag-carpeted sitting room of the poor-house, large and small bustled about, endeavoring to restore the poor demented creature, whom, but a few moments before, they had considered as hardly worth lifting a finger for. Dick White, himself, had gone for Doctor Dow, and before he could return with that functionary, who was, it is needless to say, in a white heat of excitement, a goodly portion of the population of Fenmarsh, and even of the adjoining towns, were gathered in the vicinity of the house, awaiting developments.

At last, when they were beginning to despair of ever rousing her again, the eyes of Mother Maitland opened wide, and rested upon the beautiful face of her long-lost daughter. Then there came a strange look in them. The terrible blow which had been given to the tilted brain had restored its balance. The look was not the wild, far-away, dreamy look of the last few months—it was the old, sane expression of the years gone by. Mother Maitland was herself again.

"I have been in a dream, Elizabeth," she said, looking about her with dilated eyes. "I thought, dear, that it was the Christmas morning, and I heard you and Edith and Gerald singing carols under my window, and it woke me up."

Thus the long dream of Christmas was ended, and the kind, kind saint, who watches over the Christmas-keeping, had restored this poor deluded one to her own.

"Poor mother!" sobbed Elizabeth Maitland—but how poor she did not know until the next day, when she extracted the full history of the trials of her family from the reluctant lips of the worthy Mrs. Fuller.

The blunt, curt annals of the town furnish the sequel of the story:

"Ye most strange happening of ye yeare 1789 hathe beene ye law-suits over ye keepe of ye Christmas witch, so-called, ye Mistress Margaret Maitland."

Then, after describing at length the law-suits between Fairweather and Fenmarsh, the chronicler continues:

"Ye suit would have been opened again in ye winter courte, but yt on ye 3 day of September, ye daughter of ye Mistress Maitland did come, with many servants and a great noise of horses and carriages, and take away ye Mistress Maitland to England. Ye daughter, yt was hight ye Countess of Ellerslie, is of great wealth and power. Ye letters from her to her mother were stole by

ye wicked uncle of ye Countess" (the word Countess
appears to have filled the soul of the town clerk of Fenmarsh with the keenest delight, as he lugs it in wherever
he can). "Ye Countess hathe paid everybody in hard
gold for ye care of her mother. Ye Mistress Fuller she
hath give two flowered gowns and a great amber comb
and some spoones of solid silver. Ye young son of ye
Mistress Fuller, ye Countess will send to ye college at
Hanover, yt he may have good learning. Ye Countess
hath begged ye Mistress Fuller yt she would go to keep
Christmas at ye great house of ye Countess in England.
Ye minde of ye Mistress Maitland hath beene clear and
bright since ye Countess hathe come. Ye Parson Bement and other Godly men held a sitting to find out for
themselves what proofs were offered yt ye Mistress was
a witch. It is now thought yt she was no witch. Ye
Countess hath ordered yt ye bodies of her brother and
his wife and child be dug up and carried to Boston, to be
put on ship for England. Ye Countess hath got back
ye inheritance ye wicked uncle would have got from her
family, so ye Mistress Maitland is rich again. A great
crowd came together to see her start away for England
in ye carriage with ye Countess on ye 6 day of September. Ye Countess threw out handfuls of silver money
as they passed away out of the village. Such grand
doings were never seen in ye town of Fenmarsh. Ye
Grandsir Laban Trewis, yt was sure he saw ye Mistress
Maitland dance around a holly-bush in ye kitchen of her
house, when ye Godly men asked him sharp about it, did
saye yt it might be the light of ye fire upon her, while
she did walk about, so it is thought yt she be no witch."

Which is no more of a "flattening-out" than befalls
many another sensational story of to-day or yesterday—

but Uncle Laban Trewis felt it keenly, and never again occupied so important a position in Fenmarsh, as on that eventful night in the village store when he made the blood curdle in every heart by telling of poor proud Lady Maitland's holly-bush, and how she did "dawnce aroun' it."

And to this day the old people of Fairweather will tell you how the tradition has come down to them, of the grief which was felt by the whole town, that the Countess of Ellerslie should not have had to drive with her out-riders to Fairweather, instead of to Fenmarsh, to find her mother. Thus signally do poor, fallible mortals often fail to recognize in time the quality of Fate!

Direxia.

IT was a great change for Eliezer Denham and his wife Eunice to go from Maine to Arkansas to live; but a distant cousin, who had enticed them thither early in the fifties, helped them through their "chills," and put in their first "craps" for them. It took them a long time to become acclimated, and two of their four children died in the process. It seemed for a while as though Direxia and Cyrus, the remaining two, must succumb also, but they were evidently made of sterner stuff than the others, for they came out strong and healthy in the end—as health went on the Allowee River.

It was a little black, unhealthy-looking river, very different from the sparkling, rapid New England streams to which the Denhams were accustomed; but they gradually became used to it, and, in a way, proud of it, for they soon learned that it was the centre of everything in their new home. The cluster of houses, a mile or more away from Eliezer's modest, not to say shackly, farmhouse, was known as Allowee Fo' Corners. The rolling elevations in the distance were the Allowee Hills, the county was Allowee County, and the people were "Allowee Folks." By the time that Eliezer and his wife had lived among the Allowee Folks for ten years, they were as much a part of them as though they had been born there. Eunice "dipped" with zest, and Eliezer, who had been guiltless of tobacco in their Maine home, went about now with his mouth full, and with the regulation Allowee rivulets of tawny juice oozing from each end of that irregular orifice. They were naturalized now without a doubt, though they still retained the industrious and orderly habits of their old home.

It was amusing to hear the Yankee and the Arkansas idioms struggling for the mastery in the speech of Eliezer and Eunice during these ten years. They had been plain, poor farmer-folk up in Maine, and their talk had been the essence of New England dialect, uncorrupted by the learning of the schools, of which neither of them had had more than a weather-beaten red school-house, dating back to Revolutionary times, had given them. Direxia and the baby Cyrus grew up with a pretty straight Allo-wee vernacular.

Direxia, at fifteen, was long, lank, hollow-cheeked and hollow-chested—a typical Arkansas girl. She had ceased to attend school at the log school-house, and was engaged to "stan' up" in a few weeks with Derry Driggs, the twenty-year-old son of a neighboring planter, of about the same status as Eliezer Denham. She was of the sort that matures early in body, but late in mind. Outside, though it was different inside, she had taken on the semblance of the girls about her. Her dark hair was drawn back tightly from her face, and done into a "waterfall" at the back, which was in its turn covered with a "net." Thus there was, as Mr. Howells says, ample scope afforded for the expression of character. And Direxia had character. Her full, rather bulging forehead, long, curving nose, and square chin showed this. But chiefly her eyes, gray, deep-set, and glowing, revealed, even in the undeveloped state in which she re-mained when she married Derry Driggs, that there was a gleam of fire in her, inherited from some New England ancestor. She was true to the core to the State of her adoption, and would not have admitted the New England strain; but it was there, and in due course of time it came out.

One evening in early October, Direxia and her husband, who was universally known along the Allowee as "Dank" Driggs, were sitting in front of a bright pine-knot blaze. A chilliness had come on since the sun went down, and Dank had graciously seconded Direxia's suggestion that they should have a fire, since she evidently proposed to make it herself. They had been married five years now, and there were two children, who were properly sleeping at this moment in their trundle-bed.

As Direxia went out to gather a fresh apronful from the pile of loose "wood-trash" which lay beside the door outside, a carriage rolled by. It contained a lady, a fine-looking, elderly gentleman, and two or three young people. Direxia knew that they were Judge Burnley and his family, and that they were from the county town of Thrall ("T'rall"), ten miles away.

She came in, threw the contents of her apron upon the little fire which she had started, and then sat down reflectively in its light. Dank was smoking stupidly.

"Yer a ornary houn', Dank," began Direxia at last, with perfect good-nature.

Dank dropped his smoking and looked at her out of his wide, gentle eyes, which sat in his hairy face like twin lakes in a region of unrestrained brushwood.

"I don' come at what you-uns er aimin' after," he admitted, frankly.

"Yer promised me ye'd nail that clapboard, that's been hangin' off this six months, and tinker that front door so't I could shet it. An' hyar comes along the

quality from T'rall, ridin' in their carriages, an' seein'
it all, same's we-uns was ornary niggers. Pap don'
hev no sech goin's on—not if mammy's roun', he don'."

"I ben so durn druv, Rexy," pleaded her husband,
tacitly admitting the justice of her rebuke.

Direxia sighed.

" 'Tain't that," she said, shaking her head as though
the problem **were one** which she had long wrestled with,
and had found difficult. " 'Tain't that. It's long o' yer
bein' Allowee folks. Lord knows they-uns all got thayer
clapboards hangin', an' thayer doors out o' jint. I 'lowed,
when I was little, that everybody was thataway. Pappy
was a heap more keerful'n the rest—but he war'n't so
durn keerful nayther. An' when I come to go to T'rall
—when I got big enough so's I war'n't skeert to death,
an' could notice how they-uns had things—then I see't
wa'n't any need o' this yer lettin' things go so—no more'n
o' lettin' things go in the house yer. They's plenty as
says 'tain't no use tryin' to keep a kitchen up right along
—but you-uns know, Dank, I kin do it. It's shif'less-
ness, when women folks can't. I heer'n my mammy tell
how up to Maine, whar she was raised, they have things
slick right along. Lord knows, Dank, I hate the Yan-
kees bad as you-uns do. My Uncle Gid up thar, he wrote
my pap the meanest kyind of a letter. He called him a
'clay-eater,' an' Lord knows what, long o' his writin' up
thar that they-uns better not be helpin' our niggers to git
to Canady. Oh, he run on jest turrible. We-uns don'
kyar for Maine—but min' you, Dank, they-uns has things
slick up thar, mammy says."

Dank gave a sleepy, indifferent grunt. Direxia bestowed a reproachful look on his hairy face in the flick-
ering light

"You-uns was a turrible smart scholar, down to the old school-house, when I fust knowed ye, Dank. she began again, reflectively.

Dank grinned.

"So I heern ye say, Rexy," he acknowledged, with shame-faced delight.

"Yes," went on Direxia, still musingly, "I 'lowed ye was goin' to turn out a powerful smart man, somehow. I do' know what I thought ye was goin' fer to do, but I reckoned ye was goin' fer to do somethin' o' yuther."

Dank was not so happy now, but he still gazed at his wife kindly enough from under his shock of black hair.

"Lawyers seems to be powerful likely sort o' fellers," she pursued, tentatively. "I 'low ye never let on, Dank, how as ever ye could be a lawyer now?"

There was a pathetic look on Direxia's colorless face, which gave her large features a certain softness. It seemed to touch her impassive husband as he watched her curiously in the light of the fire.

"Sho, now, Rexy!" he began, deprecatingly, "who'd ever 'a 'lowed ye was thinkin' thataway!"

"I heern Jedge Burnley down to T'rall, you know, talkin' how, if the Yanks don' quit foolin' with we-uns' niggers, we-uns was goin' fer to give hit ter 'em—an' them other fellers talked too, an' they said they was mostly lawyers. Ever since then I've thought a heap about they-uns. They had on good clo'es, Dank, and they talked so sort o' perlite like—it was nice. I remembered how you-uns used to speak pieces down to the school-house, an' I' lowed ye could have made a likely speech same as they-uns, if you was only a lawyer long o' them. What do they have to do, Dank, to be a lawyer? Couldn't you be a lawyer?"

"Oh, gawnamighty, Rexy!" cried her husband, appalled by the height of her ambitions, "you-uns are crazy—fer a fac', I 'low ye be! Why, gal, lawyers has to shave ev'ry durn day o' their lives, an' ye said yesself they had to wear good clo'es. An' they have to read stiddy, I reckon, in them great leather-covered books on a shelf in the court-house. I 'low it takes 'em nigh onto a lifetime to git to be a reg'lar lawyer—an' most on 'em has to go to college, an' Lord knows what all. Then they've got to be 'admitted to the bar'—I don't rightly yunderstan' it, Rexy, but thar's a heap o' trash like that yer. Why, thar wan't never none o' my folks lawyers. I couldn't be a lawyer, no more'n I could be a—a—dawg, Rexy. Who'd take keer o' you-uns, an' the young uns in thar, ef I was to go off tryin' to be a lawyer! I reckon all the folks on the Allowee would think I'd gone plumb crazy!" Dank gave a great guffaw, and relapsed into the depths of his whiskers again, whence clouds of smoke soon began to reissue, indicating that he was regaining his composure after the excitement to which his wife's insane fancies had subjected him.

Direxia sighed a long, quivering sigh. Nobody would know how she had tried, since she had married, and had begun to think, as she had never done in her slow, unripe girlhood, to work out a grand destiny for her yielding, good-natured husband—in her mind. He had been a good scholar for Allowee folks, as she had said, and as she had grown older, and had begun to dimly comprehend the little world in which she lived, on which a new light had been thrown by her motherhood, she longed for a glimpse into the enchanted region in which it seemed to her that these people from

T'rall must live. If her little "Voylet," and the baby Earl could go with such people, could ride in such carriages—why, life would be a different thing to them from what it was to her, and to the dull and earthy folk along the river valley. Thus dimly she had groped through mazes of reasoning, until she had come to the conclusion that, if Dank could occupy a different station in life, her children's future would be assured.

Her husband marked the frown of reflection which still lingered upon her brow.

"Yer pappy'd laugh, I reckon, Rexy, if I should tell him what you-uns been sayin' to me," he began at length, hoping good-humoredly to dissipate the shadows which hung about her.

"Don't ye tell him," she exclaimed, earnestly. "Now, don't ye go fur to be that mean!"

He promised her, chuckling over the idea of her pappy's dismay, if his daughter's wild project should ever reach his ears—but she paid no heed to his mirth. She was in the grasp of what, for the region of the Allowee, were profound emotions.

"Ye see, somehow, Dank," she began after a moment's thought, "I'm sick sometimes o' bein' jest nobody down yer in Allowee County. Pap an' mammy—they think I'm jest stuck-up an' bigotty, but I ain't. I don't begretch nothin' to Jedge Burnley's folks, only I kin see plain enough that they have a heap better times than we-uns do. All we-uns do is jest gittin' up in the mawnin' an' fryin' a mess fer breakfast, an' then crawlin' roun', an' washin' up, an' such-like, an' then fryin' another mess fer dinner, an' then walkin' out, likely, down to Pappy's, or the Fo' Corners or such a matter, an' then fryin' another mess fer supper, an' then goin' to bed. Then the's

goin' to church, an' camp-meetin'. That's better; but
seems to me, they-uns gets a heap more outen livin' than
we-uns do."

"Likely," admitted Dank, yawning immoderately, but
without a thought of disrespect to his wife. "Most I
'low now, Rexy, is I've got to tote that truck to the Fo'
Corners an' git it started fer Memphis bright an' soon
in the mawnin',"—and Dank shuffled off to bed.

Direxia pondered over the coals a little longer. Then,
with a long sigh, she raked them up, and was soon asleep
beside her husband. She never approached him again
upon the subject of changing his vocation; but when the
carriages of the "quality" rolled by her humble cabin,
she would look after them longingly, and secretly cherish
a hope that had sprung up in her proud heart that her
children might enjoy this better living, of which she had
caught glimpses in her poor starved soul, even if she and
her husband were to be forever denied it.

When little Earl was six years old, the war broke out.
Dank Driggs was not very "f'erce" at first, as the Allowee
Folks expressed it. One night he and Direxia rode
over to T'rall to hear Judge Burnley and the other "lawyers" recite the outrages to which the South had been
subjected by the North, and to urge the young men to
enlist. Direxia came home burning hot.

"You-uns got to go, Dank," she said when they were
fairly started on the ride home.

Even her husband's phlegmatic temperament had been
stirred. He "reckoned likely" he should, "after a spell."

"You-uns got to go now," insisted Direxia, shrilly.

"Lord, Rexy," protested Dank, feebly, "who gwine
put in the craps fer you-uns? Ye'll starve, likely, lessen
I put to an' seed awhile."

Direxia yielded and gave him a fortnight's grace. Each night he was so weary with the incessant application which she required that he could not even get over to the Fo' Corners for his nightly dram—a serious loss to his comfort. At the end of the two weeks, though his work was far from done, as he declared, he enlisted with a recruiting agent who came around, and left Direxia to manage the plantation as best she might.

That year another little one came, suffered awhile and died. Direxia struggled on. The children helped her in the fields, and her house, which it had been her pride to keep neat, she left largely to manage itself. The second year Dank came home. He was heartily sick of soldiering, and sighed for the flesh-pots of his own home again, but there was a draft, and he found himself back in the field, where he staid until the end of the war, with only occasional and brief visits to the Allowee. Dank never rebelled against authority. Like so many of the Southern "pore whites," to which class he really belonged, though far better off than many of them, he was gentle and yielding to the point of effeminacy.

In 1865 Dank returned home for good—poor but happy. He wore a corporal's stripe on his sleeve, and felt mightily set up thereby. There was another baby now, and Direxia had managed the farm so well that it was in better condition than it had ever been under Dank's supervision.

One summer evening Dank was just starting for the Fo' Corners, when Direxia, who was getting worried at the habit of heavy drinking which he had acquired in the army, persuaded him to sit down outside a moment and listen to the reciting of a "piece" by Voylet who was growing up a bright and forward little maiden with more of beauty than her poor mother had ever possessed. Dank listened with a glow of fatherly pride, and after the child had been sent to bed, having lingered so long and so comfortably that he felt loath to rise, he sat on, smoking assiduously.

"Hit's mighty pleasant to have ye roun' again, Dank," said Direxia, contemplating him, if not with wifely pride, with at least some degree of affection.

"Hit's mighty nice to be here, Rexy," responded Dank with profound civility.

"I 'low you-uns did right well, comin' off a corp'ral so," continued Direxia, with a slight interrogative inflection in her tone.

"I reckon," rejoined Dank, complacently.

"I 'lowed ye'd come home a gineral, shore, Dank," pursued his wife. Then, seeing that she had offended him, she added hastily, "but hit's powerful smart in you-uns to git to be a corp'ral. They ain't many did so well in Allowee County."

Dank simply grunted.

"Don' you-uns git some lan' or—or somethin'—some extra pay o' yuther, fer bein' corp'ral, Dank, now the war's over?" she asked a moment later.

"Women folks is durn fools," remarked Dank, impersonally, taking time to blow out a cloud of smoke before he deigned to notice her question. "Why, gal, hain't ye sensed it that we-uns are mustered out now? They ain't no army no more. Lord! We hain't drawed no pay—not fer a year or more! I reckon we-uns 'bleeged to count ourselves lucky to git off with our skins, and to have a place to settle down on! 'Extry pay!' Wal— not much!"

But Direxia was not to be driven from her main point, even by such scorn as this.

"Dank, tell me this," she began a moment later, "an' I won't pester you-uns no more. Ain't a corp'ral as big as a jedge now?"

"Hit's diffrunt," began Dank, philosophically, after something of a pause.

"Yes, hit's diffrunt," she repeated, eagerly, "but ain't it somethin' like? Don't corp'rals go to Congress, an' git to be somebody more'n Allowee Folks?"

"Huccom ye sech a durn fool!" he cried savagely— for him—"I cayn't make out head nor tail to yer talk nohow. I 'low I'm allers goin' to live down yer on the Allowee now I've got back yer. Hit was good enough for my pap, an' your pap, an' hit's good enough fer me. Go to Congress! Lord! They ain't any Southerners goin' to Congress for one while, not ef they-uns up Nawth can help it, you bet! Congress! I 'low ye're goin' crazy, shore, Rexy!"

Dank rose and shuffled off to the Fo' Corners, whence he returned very drunk two or three hours later. The last spark of hope in Direxia's heart that the social position of herself and her children was ever to be bettered by her husband, was out.

She devoted herself now to the training of her children, and almost spoiled her health and her head in trying to help them—she had some dim notion of helping herself also—in the long evenings when Dank was away with his mates, and the younger children were asleep. Then a fifth child came, but, though Direxia tended him with feverish care, he sickened and died before he was three years old. The one next older, the brightest and prettiest of them all, a boy on whom she had set bright hopes, followed him. Earl was heavy-faced, gentle and forceless like his father; but Direxia would not admit even to herself that he was not so "likely" as "Voylet."

At fifteen Voylet was a beauty for the Allowee. She had learned, as her fond mother told her neighbors, everything that could be learned in the valley, and in the fall she was going to T'rall to school. By saving and pinching, in the true New England fashion—though Direxia might have stopped it if she had suspected that she was copying so reprehensible a model—she had amassed a little fund, to which she was constantly add-ing, by the most incessant labor, for the education of her children. No lawyer, nor anybody else, she was determined, should hold his head above her children, on account of superior knowledge. With an innate acuteness which seized and held fast the best of the con-clusions at which she arrived by slow and painful mental processes, she had discerned that education was the key to that broader existence which she coveted for her chil-dren, and she proposed to devote her life to securing it for them.

Her father and mother did not survive the war many years. They lived long enough to hear from their North-ern friends of the sad changes which had taken place during the five or six years which had passed since they had written last; and to learn, in the most chaste and ex-plicit New England plain speech, that they were regarded as "Rebs" of the blackest dye, and as cut off forever from the sweet influences of family affection. Eliezer retorted in kind, and he and Eunice gave up at last a hope which they had secretly cherished to go back to their old home some time and "see the folks." In the better land to which they departed soon afterward, a land to which they might have remained strangers for years to come if they had only staid under the shadows of the salubrious blue hills of the North, instead of subjecting their ignorant Maine constitutions to the miasms of the Allowee—in that better land, no doubt, their foolish quarrels were all settled.

Cyrus succeeded to his father's plantation, but the money which the old people had saved, considerably over a thousand dollars, despite the ravages of the war, fell to Direxia. She put it hungrily by for her children, though Dank thought he knew of other ways to spend it. Direxia, despite her love for him, on this one matter was adamant. Those children were going to be educated.

Cyrus had not turned out to be essentially different from the small planters around him. He drank more than was good for him, and his "shif'less" young wife, who had once been the belle of the Allowee, had faded in a few years to be a dragged-out-looking woman, with the clayey complexion and lustreless eyes which characterized the female portion of the Allowee folks. Her children were neglected, her house was worse even than the average of her neighbors', and Direxia hated to go to the poor cabin which her mother had kept spotlessly neat through so many years. But Cyrus did not seem to mind it.

"I've heern tell as how they's colleges fer gyurls nowadays, same as they is fer boys," Direxia told her husband one day, shortly after she learned of the amount of money which had come to her from her parents. "If they is, I reckon Voylet is goin'."

Dank had no opinion of this putting forward of wom-

an-bodies, and he said so, but Direxia was far in advance of him, and, indeed, of her entire section. Voylet
was going to have the best kind of an education that
was to be had, and if colleges supplied that, why, to a
college Voylet should go.

In the fall, as Direxia had "reckoned," Voylet went
to T'rall. A boarding-place was found for her in a respectable family who had moved into town from the Allowee. Friday nights some one drove in for her and
brought her home.

But one night in February, when the journey to town
had been made with infinite labor through liquid miles
of mud, Earl came home without Voylet. He brought
a lady-like note from that highly-educated young person, saying that the roads were so "turrible" that she
thought she wouldn't go home this week, especially
as she had an invitation to attend a concert the next
evening and was having a powerful good time.

Direxia sniffed trouble immediately. The next morning she went in person, and brought her daughter home.
She learned then, what she had dimly suspected before,
that Voylet's young affections were fixed upon a masculine object in the person of a journeyman plumber in
T'rall. Direxia wept and pleaded, but as the weeks went
on, she saw that there was no use in opposition. Voylet
was wilful and spoiled, the young man seemed a "likely
enough" sort of a fellow, and devoted to her. Dank
thought it was a heap better for "the gyurl to settle down
as gyurls should, stid o' settin' out to git a heap o' 'larnin'
they hadn't no use fer"—and, in the May following the
T'rall educational experiment, Voylet was married, and
after a trip to Memphis she "settled down" in a little
home of her own.

Now, Direxia concentrated all her hopes upon Earl. The boy was not stupid, and when he left the log school-house, where he had had a year of instruction from the best teacher that the Allowee had ever known, it was predicted that by a year more of solid study he might be ready to enter the college in the next county, to which Direxia's ambition had turned. The young teacher had taken the pains to tutor Earl out of school hours for a little extra pay, and had had a faculty of interesting the boy, so that he had really done well. He was accordingly sent to school in T'rall, just as his sister had been, only he boarded with her, and, to do her justice, she attempted to second her mother's projects. He worked through the year and came home in June, having accomplished his task.

That summer Cyrus wanted extra hands, and Earl went over to the old homestead and staid several weeks with him. He earned some money by this means, but he acquired a habit which was worse than any lack of money. Officious neighbors brought the news of it to Direxia. They thought she would not mind it much. Dank drank enough, heaven knew. But there were not so many hopes pinned to Dank as to Earl. Direxia was wild at the thought of her son's future being imperilled by a possible appetite for liquor, and she had long talks with the boy on the subject before he started for college in the fall. He made her many fair promises, but before another summer came around, he was expelled for getting into some scrape while he was not himself, and he came home to find his mother heart-broken.

The boy was sorry, but he was too shallow and too easy-going to feel his disgrace and her disappointment very long; and as Dank, who had had the "middlin'

poorlys" ever since his army life, and had not lived in
a way to get over them, sickened during the spring,
and was not able to do a stroke of work all the season,
the boy had his hands full. In the fall Dank died, and
poor Direxia mourned him sincerely. The next year
she and Earl managed the plantation together. He did
not conquer his habits, but he was fond of her, and,
with the overweening love of a mother, she had managed to forgive him, outwardly at least.

The year following, Earl was twenty-one. The wom-
en on the Allowee were old at forty, and though Direxia
was not much more than that, she felt that her life was
spent. She had cherished her poor little ideals, but she
had seen them shattered; and since Dank's death she
had felt that she had little to live for.

Earl, like all of the young fellows of the neighborhood, among whom he had lost none of prestige by his
escapades, spent every evening away from home, and
usually in the store at the Fo' Corners. He was regarded as an oracle among his companions. His language was good, and he knew more than any other
young man upon the Allowee. There had been some
talk about his studying law, but even his ambitious
mother did not encourage him to do so. She had a
blind feeling that, so long as he was at home where
she could look after him, he would not go quite to the
dogs. She was not so sure of it, if he should try to
shift for himself. Earl, though he enjoyed the distinction awarded him by his companions, seemed utterly
destitute of aspiration. It had seemed to be his duty,
after his father's death, to stay with his mother, and to
carry on the plantation as well as he could. He had
been content to rest in that place.

One night he came home soberer than usual. Direxia did not always sit up for him, but to-night she had happened to. His eyes were very bright, and he looked handsome, though he had never been thought so good-looking as his sister.

"I've got some news for you, mother," he began, almost before he had opened the door.

A sudden dread smote her heart. She had picked up some of the phrases of civilization from her children, but in her excitement she reverted to the old vernacular in which she first talked and in which she thought.

"You-uns struck me all of a heap, Earl," she began, tremulously, "but I 'low it's good news by yer looks."

"You're right it is," he rejoined, with smiling pride. "Jinny Powers is going to marry me. I've made her set the day already. I told her everything was ready here for her, and I knew you were lonesome. She says the wedding may come off the first of March."

It was now the middle of January. Direxia drew a quick breath. She could not even congratulate her boy, though the girl was well enough, and she could see that he was perfectly happy. She sat dumb.

"Speak out, mammy!" he cried, with a spice of masculine sternness in his tone. "Ain't you glad? Ain't I a lucky fellow? Half the boys on the Allowee are after Jinny—and she's going to have me!"

"Hit's powerful pleasant, I 'low," stammered Direxia, "I hope you'll make her a good husband, Earl—I'm shore I do—an' that she'll make you a good wife. I—I ain't so dreadful lonesome—'cept long o' missin' your pappy—an' 'tain't likely she's goin' to be like he was to me."

"Poor mammy!" cried the young man, too full of

happiness to reproach her for not entering more fully
into his joy. "You've had a hard time—but you'll like
Jinny and she'll like you, and we'll enjoy ourselves now,
you'll see."

But to Direxia the thought of having this giddy young
Jinny Powers come into her own home as the mistress
thereof was very hard. She went to bed weeping un-
reasonably, and all through the next day she could not
keep her thoughts on her work. Her shining kitchen!
There was none like it on the Allowee. Jinny Powers
would doubtless allow her mother-in-law the privilege
of keeping it clean in the future, as she had done in the
past—but Direxia was not sure that she should thoroughly enjoy that privilege under the changed conditions of her life.

Earl went off soon after supper the next evening, and
Direxia sat down beside the lamp and gazed into the
fire through the tears which rolled silently down her
cheeks from time to time. At last, from sheer weariness of her thoughts, she picked up the county paper,
published at T'rall, and glanced idly over its columns.
She regarded with pride the advertisement of the
plumbers for whom Voylet's husband worked. Then
she read a story, at the silly sentimentalism of which
the hard-headed—yet, after all, fiercely sentimental—old
woman sniffed disdainfully. Then she turned to a col-
umn of local advertisements, and one among them caught
her eye. She read it over several times. It said:
"Wanted, a matron for the new orphan asylum, at once.
Apply to Mrs. Judge Burnley."

"A matron!" reflected Direxia. "I don't exactly know
what a matron is. I reckon it's somebody to look after
the housekeepin' for them pore little things. I reckon

she'd likely have to see that the house was scrubbed clean, and the young 'uns too, an' see to the cookin' an' such-like."

"That yer would likely be powerful hard work," she pursued a moment later. "Hit's a mighty big buildin', that yer orphan asylum. I seen hit when I was to T'rall many a time. I 'lowed hit was nigh about finished up. Likely they're ready to move into it. They's a heap o' orphans, I heern tell, an' now hit's got too small fer 'em in the old place—pore little things, their pappies was killed in the war. I'd like right well to do 'em a good turn myself."

The next morning, Direxia put on her best mourning bonnet and shawl, and, harnessing a mule with her own hands, started for T'rall, with the dimmest possible ideas as to what she was going to do. She went at once to the grand residence of Judge Burnley.

It was well along in the twilight when Direxia and the mule were on their homeward way. There had been old neighbors of the Driggses in T'rall, to whom Direxia had referred Mrs. Burnley. They all testified to Direxia's capabilities as a housekeeper, in the Allowee meaning of the word. They told how she had run the farm when her husband had been away. They said " 'Meers Dank Driggs passed fer a powerful smart woman" up Allowee way.

Direxia was going to undertake to be matron of the great new orphan asylum, at a salary which seemed to her too munificent to be true. As she rode along, her thoughts kept time to the jogging of the old mule, something like this: "Wal, Rexy Driggs! what in time would Dank say if he was to know this yer? Likely as not he does sense it up thar"—and Direxia turned her face reverently toward the sky, "Like ʾs not he's a laughin' fit to kill, same as he uster, when he was tickled hyar. Wal, he wouldn't strike out to be a lawyer nor a gineral. He was boun' fer to be a planter down in the bottom of the Allowee, an' so he was. I ain't sayin' but it was best so," with a guilty thought that she was doing her kind, weak husband an injustice—"but I always did think that Dank Driggs could have took his place to be more 'count than ever he set up to be. Then I was powerful onhappy because Voylet up an' got married so—before she had come to bein' sensible, 's ye might say. I wanted Voylet to be like Jedge Burnley's gals, and them as they goes with, but she ain't. She's a nice gal—Voylet is—an' she takes powerful good keer of her babby—but she's a livin' along, fer all I see, not much better'n I always was on the Allowee—and I meant she should have something a heap better. I do' know as she was to blame. Likely she couldn't see it as I do. An' then thar's Earl. I always thought he was the likeliest boy in Allowee County. He mought have gone to Congress—he mought have been President likely, if—if——," Direxia could not name even to herself the cause of the failure of her idol to come up to her hopes of him. She sobbed aloud as she rattled over the rough road. "But——" gathering her strength with a long sigh—"likely he won't git much worse. Likely Jinny Powers'll change him. He's boun' to be the bigges' man on the Allowee, 'out'en he gits worse. But 'tain't what I planned fer him. An' now, after all, this projeckin' to git the res' to start out in the worl' an' be different— the old woman herself has had to do it fer 'em." She laughed to herself, doubtful as she really felt in her modest soul of her capacity to do the work which she had undertaken. "She's set out to be somebody, an' she don' mean to give up till she's wore to a plumb frazzle."

Direxia felt an exaltation akin to that with which a sculptor regards the shape of the clay toward which his thought has long been tending, but which has hitherto eluded his yearning touch. To her simple soul it was an ambition of the loftiest kind to become the matron of an orphan asylum.

For twenty years Direxia Driggs labored in the sphere to which she had been called by the chance reading of the T'rall paper that night. She became the pet of the directors of the institution, who numbered some of the leading women of the county. Her juicy idioms, her strong yet gentle character, her loving devotion to duty, made her the friend and favorite of them all. When she died in 188—, the mourning for her was more like the mourning for a great hero of the war than for "only a woman"—a plain, homely woman from the Allowee. She had instilled into the children who had been under her care her own lofty ambitions. She had lived to see some of them realize her hopes for them—hopes which had been almost as fervent as those which she had cherished for her own children, and which had ended so miserably. In the broader life which she had entered in her new sphere of labor she had found the happiness which she had hoped for. It had been a realization such as is seldom granted to mortals.

The lawn which stretches out in front of the orphan asylum is one of the most beautiful in the South. Magnolia and tulip trees, pink judas trees, bowers covered with the vines of the multiflora rose—all of the choicest products of that favored clime have been taught to grow there; but on a little knoll, clear and high amid this luxuriance of greenery and bloom, all the shrubs and trees have been cut away, and only the velvet grass is reverently allowed to grow. The knoll is crowned by a costly statue. It was carved by one of the foremost of living sculptors, and represents a woman in cap and spectacles—a homely, large-featured old woman—but with a look upon her face which is an inspiration to every-one who beholds it.

On the base of the statue, cut deep into the living stone, is the name "Direxia Driggs." "This woman," the inscription goes on to say, "though her lot lay always among the humble and afflicted, ever reached forward to the things which are before, and taught to all about her the sacred lesson that mortals should make the most of such gifts as the providence of God bestows. She rests from her labors, and her works, yea, even the praise of a mighty host of those for whom she unselfishly toiled, do follow her."

Those who know all of Direxia's pathetic story can-not behold without tears the beautiful memorial, in its inexpressible simplicity and dignity.

Voylet and Earl come there sometimes, and bring their children to gaze upon the statue. They often say dully, "It is monstrous strange how mammy was for pushin' us all on to be somebody," and shake their heads. Their hearts ache dumbly—even Earl's, under his sodden skin— for the pangs which they know they caused her. But it was not in them to be like her. They will be Allowee Folks to the end of the chapter.

Lyddy Washburn's Courtship.

"THE prettiest girl in Franklin County." That was what they called Lyddy Washburn. Brown-haired, blue-eyed, pink-cheeked, red-lipped, of a tall and slender figure, and a graceful and spirited carriage, the youngest and only surviving daughter of a well-to-do farmer—what wonder that from far and near suitors came for Lyddy Washburn's hand? But "Law!" said that young woman, many times over, "there ain't no hurry at all about my marryin' and settlin' down." Which in those days was rank heresy, Lyddy's mother having been married at fourteen, and all Lyddy's mates being settled in homes of their own, leaving that independent young woman to the tender mercies of a younger set of companions by the time she was twenty-two years old. But Lyddy tossed her head, looked in her glass, and sang the more blithely over her wheel and her churn.

"Now, Lyddy," her mother said one day, "why don't you marry Jotham Hunter? He's a likely young fellow as ever lived, and sets consid'able store by you."

"Jotham Hunter!" laughed Miss Lyddy. "Law, mother, he's got red hair!"

"Wa'al, his heart's right," pleaded Mrs. Washburn.

"No use, mother," said her fractious daughter. "You can't get rid of me yet awhile; and don't ever say 'Jotham Hunter' to me again."

"Wa'al, tell me one thing," said Mrs. Washburn, her ill-concealed anxiety making her voice sound strained and unnatural. "You hain't—now, Lyddy, you hain't, be you?—a-goin' to take Tart Taylor?"

A bright flush swept over Miss Lyddy's beautiful face.

"Who said I was a-goin' to 'take Tart Taylor,' Mother Washburn?" she said, a little sternly. "Better wait till I get a chance, I think! An' if I was a-goin' to 'take Tart Taylor,' I'd like to know what's the reason he ain't as good as Jotham Hunter?"

"Wa'al," said the old lady, slowly (she always began with "Wa'al"), "they do say that Tart can't keep from liquor; and though"—here Mrs. Washburn no doubt voiced the feeling of everybody in those days—"though every man must have his dram, yet there ain't no sense in gettin' drunk at every raisin' an' trainin' an' cattle show, as they tell on Tart Taylor; an' he's got his mother to take care of; an' no daughter o' mine, Lyddy Washburn, shall ever live with that cross-grained, ugly old Aunt Betty Taylor!" and the old lady—for she was well along in years, Lyddy being the youngest of thirteen children—stood up defiantly before her daughter, her excitement giving her unwonted courage.

Lyddy Washburn's temper was roused, and she glanced at her mother with a contemptuous expression, like the spoiled child that she was.

"You'd better be savin' your advice, mother——" she began, in a high, clear voice, when suddenly a long shadow fell across the room from the doorway, and "Cap'n Tart"—(Mr. Tertius Taylor was called "captain" from the fact that he was an officer of the militia)—stood before them, with his hat in his hand.

Mrs. Washburn tossed her head, and turned away with a stiff nod, while Lyddy, with a heightened color and unwonted nervousness of manner, welcomed the stately newcomer, whose military bearing and critical taste in the matter of his female companions had set half the girls in the county wild over him. It had been easy to see for some weeks now that Captain Tart had made up his mind to "have Lyddy Washburn," and that that captious damsel was more complaisant toward him than toward any of her other suitors.

It was now the middle of May. The lilacs were budded in the front door yard, and the apple trees pink with bloom—a dangerous time for young folks in the state of mind of these two, had thought cautious Mrs. Washburn, and, not approving the match at all, she had made up her mind to warn Lyddy in such a way that the immediate danger should be tided over; but by her precipitance she had ruined everything, and she felt it, for the girl's blushes had convinced her that Lyddy's heart was touched by Captain Tart's manly graces, and perhaps by that very wildness which often seems to captivate when it should repel.

"The fact is," said Mrs. Washburn, retailing the story to her husband that evening—"the fact is, 'Liakim, our Lyddy's in love with that ere Tart Taylor. What ails the girl?"

"'Tain't no use," said sensible 'Liakim Washburn, who was too sleepy to argue, and too fond of Lyddy to think of opposing her—"'tain't no use, Mirandy, a-meddlin' in love matters. What 'ud 'a' been the use, now, a-meddlin' 'twix' you an' me?" and with this half-facetious, half-tender reminiscence the old farmer took up his candle and went to bed.

That afternoon quite a scene had taken place between "Cap'n Tart" and Lyddy, and though they did not know it, they passed then the turning point of their lives; for

Lyddy Washburn's Courtship.

Lyddy, in her excited state, was just impressionable
enough, and enough roused in his favor, by her defense
of Captain Tart, to make this meeting the decisive one.
But she did not forget herself.

"Won't you come in, Cap'n Taylor?" she said, cor-
dially, and with apparent calmness.

"No, thankee," said Captain Tart, eyeing the old lady
uneasily; "I come to see you a minit 'bout suthin'. S'pose
you walk down the border with me, an' look at them
posies you was tellin' of down to Jerushy Willitts's."

So Lyddy got her sun-bonnet, and they strolled "down
the border," where some daffodils and wonderful hyacinths, the only ones in town, and sent to Lyddy from
Boston, were just then the horticultural wonder of the
neighborhood.

"By the way," said Lyddy, gradually recovering her
composure, "have you seen Jerushy Willitts since donation?"

"No, I hain't," said Captain Tart; "but I see Adonijah
Brewer this mornin', an' he said Loisy Pettingill was
a-goin' to hev a quiltin' next Wednesday, and o' course
you'll be a-goin'. I come to see ef you'd ride home on
my pillion, come night."

Lyddy hesitated. Captain Tart had never made so
bold an advance as this, and Lyddy thought of her
mother.

"Jotham Hunter hain't asked you, has he, Lyddy?"
said Captain Tart, his forehead gathering in a scowl.

"No, no," said Lyddy, hastily. "I hain't had no invite
myself yet, you know; but, law!" recklessly deciding to
follow her own wishes in spite of her mother, "o' course
I shall have, an' I might as well come home with you as
anybody, I s'pose. Here's the flowers."

"Purty, ain't they?" said Captain Tart, brightening up.

"Mebbe you'd like one for your button-hole," said Lyddy, the something within her which had been roused by her mother's words getting the better of her prudence. "Here's a pretty one"; and she broke off a little stalk which bore two twinkling blue stars, and twisting them with a sprig of southernwood which grew beside it, began to pin the posy on the lapel of Captain Tart's homespun coat. That ended the whole matter for the young man. Her bright hair was close to his shoulder, her pink face almost against his breast. His breath floated down in her face and her bosom heaved faster, as she made two or three efforts to fasten the refractory flowers, and the young man's eye glistened with a new tenderness. His heart was all aflame. He thought of the "quiltin'," and the ride home afterward, and could scarcely wait as he thought. He decided that he must ask her then the final question, and with her flowers breathing up perfume into his face, and the remembrance of her tell-tale blushes in his mind, he felt that her answer could not be "No." Then, after lingering a moment at the door, he walked away, his heart full of love, Lyddy, and anticipation.

Wednesday came, and as the "invite" had decorously preceded it, Lyddy Washburn, with a party of merry girls, walked, as was the custom, the two miles to Loisy Pettingill's, to the quilting, arriving there at two in the afternoon, and setting bravely to work at once upon the gorgeous quilt, which was to be the chief adornment of Loisy's "outfittin'" at her approaching nuptials.

The great "quiltin' bars" folded together fast, as skillful fingers deftly sewed along the lines of the intricate pattern, and by five o'clock, when supper was announced, the quilt was reduced to so small a compass that "Miss

Pettingill" insisted that everything should be put away before the young men came. "Loisy and the rest can finish it in no time to-morrow," said the hospitable lady, "and I'm afraid that ef you go ahead as you've been a-goin', you won't have no appetite for them sugar doughnuts I've been a-makin'."

"Law!" the girls all broke in, in courteous deprecation, "we hain't got along none; oughter 'a' had it off the frames an hour ago."

"You go 'long!" said Loisy. "That quilt's an awful big one, and amazin' hard to quilt; but I was bound I'd have one jest like Lony Travers's, and I did."

"Yes," said Lyddy, thoughtlessly, "and I mean to have one like it too."

"When is it goin' to be?" said Loisy, mischievously, while the curiosity of all made them gather more closely around Lyddy.

"Law!" said Lyddy, with a forced laugh, "I s'pose you didn't know that Uncle Dari Mallers and I was a-goin' to make a match."

"Uncle Dari Mallers" was the good-natured old hat-maker of the village, who had lived single all his life, because, rumor said, he had been jilted in his youth. He was a queer but popular old fellow, and Lyddy's joke, received with great laughter, diverted further attention from her matrimonial prospects, and they went out into the big kitchen to supper.

Such a supper! The "sugar doughnuts" adorned each end of the table, while a great " 'lection cake" stuffed with plums was the center-piece. Generous pitchers of foaming cider were scattered here and there, while cold pork-and-beans, flanked by "rye an' injun" bread, formed a prominent feature of the entertainment. Great light biscuit, clear maple syrup, rich preserves of citron, cookies full of caraway, fennel, and anise seeds, ginger bread, mince pies, apple pies, and squash pies—such was the feast which the delicate damsels who had officiated at the "quiltin'" were to taste before engaging in the revelry of the evening; and such was the digestion of the sex in the "good old times," that a doctor's bill, or even a nightmare, seldom followed the free enjoyment of these substantial dainties.

The evening came. The girls had previously gone up into the big front chamber, with its lofty, puffy bed and high, stiff bureau, to don such extra ribbons and trinkets as they had reserved for the edification of the young men who were expected shortly. Of course, they all had gold beads, and most of them big brooches containing a small painted likeness of some ancestor. There were several pairs of gold earrings; and the combs —the shell combs that towered half a foot above the smooth luxuriance of our grandmothers' coiffures—who can describe them?

One by one the young men were admitted at the clang of the great brass knocker—Jotham Hunter and Adonijah Brewer and Timothy Bassett and a dozen other brown-faced, square-shouldered young fellows who had never had a day's illness in their lives, and who, though they knew little Greek, were well versed in such branches as were taught in the district schools of their section, and, better than that, had the industrious habits and the unbending integrity which have made our country what it is.

Among the rest came Captain Tart, and more than one knowing glance passed around as it was seen that in his button-hole he wore, in observance of the May-time,

and in proud display of the favor of the most courted
girl in town, the hyacinths and southernwood which
everybody knew were given him by Lyddy Washburn.
He had preserved them carefully in water, and his love
had grown with every whiff which he had drunk in of
their intoxicating perfume.

Lyddy's heart beat faster with mingled pleasure and
indignation as she saw her gift thus openly flaunted before them all, and she instinctively talked faster to Adonijah Brewer, the prospective bridegroom; but she could
not long be angry, so utterly was her heart subdued by the
tenderness she felt for Captain Tart, and the manly beauty
of his face, which had won him the secret admiration of
every girl in Clearpond; and when he came up a few
moments later to beg her hand for a reel which was to
be danced in the great kitchen, she went tamely enough.
After the reel they "twirled the platter," and then the
apples were brought out, and Farmer Pettingill mixed a
bowl of his famous toddy, which he could make as no
one in all the country round. The glasses were filled and
refilled till the hilarity waxed rather noisy. Captain Tart
had drunk his glass at a draught. Then he looked up and
caught Lyddy's eye, in which there was a look that
stopped him as he was about to take more. She was very
pale, and hastily seeking her side, he said, tenderly, "Be
you sick, Lyddy?"

"No, no," said Lyddy, her color coming back in great
waves over her face. "The toddy's kinder strong; I
can't drink mine. You ain't goin' to drink no more,
Tart?" with a beseeching tone in her gentle voice which
went to the young man's heart.

"Not if you don't want me to, Lyddy," he said.

18

"Well, please," and she turned away. There were too many looking at them to talk any longer.

Jotham Hunter saw it all, and his jealous heart sank within him.

"Tart ain't a-drinkin' so much as common to-night," he remarked with affected carelessness to his neighbor, but loud enough to be heard all about him.

"No," said the other, a coarser-grained fellow than the rest, with a loud laugh, "but he'll be makin' up for it after he gits out o' Lyddy Washburn's sight."

"That's so," said Jotham Hunter, with angry emphasis, and with his face set toward Lyddy, who had heard every word, till her slim figure dilated and her eyes blazed at the young men in such a way that they were glad to drop the conversation at once.

After the toddy there was an uproarious game of "round the chimney," and though proud Lyddy Washburn did not always condescend to participate in the romping sport, she ran to-night, and received a kiss from Captain Tart, the memory of which thrilled her to her dying day; and then she set all tongues wagging by stubbornly refusing to catch Jotham Hunter—whose melancholy not even the toddy, nor the smiles of Jerusha Willitts, a young woman who affected him, could mitigate in the least.

Then it was nearing midnight, and the "quiltin' party" broke up, each young man taking his chosen "girl" to her home on horseback on a pillion behind him, and those unprovided for going in Farmer Pettingill's big hay wagon.

The stars were bright and the air cool and bracing, and the smell of the green earth and the apple-blossoms set young blood astir. Lyddy sat firmly on her seat, perhaps clinging a little closer to Captain Tart than necessity demanded, and they jogged slowly along till the merry voices of the rest were lost in the distance. Then the young man turned his horse into a lonely wood road which led home by a roundabout way, where they could talk without interruption.

"Oh, Tart!" said Lyddy, nervously, as she felt him give spurs to the horse when they neared the turning. "Be you goin' by the 'Lish Woodard farm? It's further."

"Why not?" said Captain Tart, as though that were the only thing to do. " 'Tain't muddy. I drove my cattle through there to-day, an', Lyddy," his voice growing deeper—"Lyddy, I've got suthin' to say to you."

She could not speak, for something seemed to suffocate her, and they rode on in an electric silence through the deep shadows of fragrant pines and hemlocks till they came to a secluded spot, when Captain Tart vaulted in his saddle and faced her, folding her in his arms as he did so. Lyddy was frightened. It was well understood in the village that Lyddy Washburn allowed none of the liberties which were not strictly considered improprieties among the young folks of the place, and no young man could boast that she had ever given him a good-night kiss, or allowed him to put his arm about her when going home from any of the parties which abounded during the gay country winters; and here, at twenty-two, she sat on Tart Taylor's pillion, pressed close against his breast, his handsome face caressing hers—and without a protest!

"Oh, Lyddy!" said Captain Tart, almost choking with the passion which overpowered him, "I can't wait another minute till you tell me you'll marry me. Oh, Lyddy, you will, won't you?"

Lyddy lifted her beautiful face to his and gave him a

kiss, and he knew that she was his. Then they said nothing for a long time, till they noticed suddenly that the
horse had stopped, and was leisurely chewing on an old
lilac bush which marked the spot where the " 'Lish
Woodard" homestead had once stood.

But they did not care. The stars, the night wind, laden
with the May sweetness—it was heaven itself that they
were riding through, completed by the kisses and caresses of an honest love. Captain Tart started up the
shrewd horse, which fell into an easy canter. Then he
said, anxiously, "Now, Lyddy, you'll ride on the pillion
behind me, come trainin', won't you?"

On the pillion behind Tart Taylor! On training-day!
Before everybody! Yes, she would do anything for him.
If he wished their engagement thus publicly proclaimed,
she was willing. So she told him "Yes," and her mind
went back to the training on the last Fourth of July,
when he rode at the head of the "milishy," so straight and
handsome that her heart fluttered at the thought that he
was now her lover.

Suddenly there was a low noise, which made the horse
start, and Captain Tart turn uneasily in his saddle. A
low, fiendish laugh, and a muttered "The devil!" were all
they heard afterward. Then there was a rustle in the
bushes, and Captain Tart put spurs to his horse. The
fleet creature darted on to the turning, when they rode
down the turnpike like the wind, till they reached Farmer
Washburn's great red house, where a light was burning
in the kitchen for Lyddy. She was all a-tremble when
her lover lifted her from the horse; but she saw no fear
nor tremor in his eye or on his firm-set lips.

"Why, Lyddy, dear," he said, folding her tenderly to
him, and soothing her with his great, rough hand, "didn't

you know who that was in the thicket? Why, Lyddy"
—he paused and choked a little—"that was—that was"—
she looked up at him in terror—"that was—my mother."

Then, before she could fairly enter the hospitable door,
he had leaped to his saddle, and was gone. The horrid
fright had shattered their love dream, and spoiled the
beautiful evening which should have been the sweetest
of their lives. Alas! it had done much more, but they did
not know it then.

The next morning, before Lyddy's shaken nerves had
half recovered their tension, her mother entered her
chamber and roused her from the uneasy sleep into which
she had only just fallen. Lucifer matches were then un-
known, and the flint and matchlock were the only sub-
stitute. If these failed, there was no resource but to ride,
sometimes for miles, to the nearest house and beg some
fire. Farmer Washburn was too rheumatic this morning
to ride, and the hired men, and the two of Lyddy's brothers who were still unmarried and at home, had eaten a
cold breakfast and were ploughing the "medder," and
could not leave. The fire was out, and Lyddy must get
up and ride a mile and a half, as fast as she could, to get
some coals.

She rose mechanically, and was dressed and on her
horse, with the foot-stove fastened securely beside her,
before she remembered that the nearest house, her brother
"Si" Washburn's, was to be reached ten minutes sooner
by passing over a section of the " 'Lish Woodard" road
than by the main highway. At the turning she hesitated;
then, ashamed of her foolish fears, she reined her horse
resolutely into the wood road, and was soon near the
scene of the dreadful adventure of the night before. She
could not help hurrying a little as she approached the

spot; but the bright rays of the six o'clock sun streamed through the trees and showed only the innocent under-brush below; so she rode on more quietly. Then her thoughts turned to her lover, and the caresses he had given her. It all seemed to her, in the bright morning, like a feverish dream; and a guilty blush suffused her pure face as she thought how he had embraced her, and of the sweet words that he had whispered in her ear.

Suddenly a shadow fell across the sunshine, and she was rudely roused from her tender reverie by the appearance of the woman whose demoniac laugh and ejaculation had chilled her blood the night before. She was haggard and unkempt, and had apparently been wandering all the night. As Lyddy looked at her, she could see that "Aunt Betty," from some cause or other, was almost, if not quite, frenzied, and she was about to put her horse to his speed, when the woman checked her by a motion of her hand.

"No, Lyddy Washburn," she said, in a harsh, angry voice, "you needn't run away from Tart's mother. She'll do ye no harm, though she heard all the billin' and cooin' last night, and she knows ye've stole her darlin' away from her—her darlin'! her darlin'!" and she wrung her hands wildly.

"He's all I've got, and little ye know, ye pink-faced girl, how I love him—the straightest and handsomest man in all these parts. But, mark ye, Lyddy Washburn" —and her voice took on an unearthly depth and stern-ness, "them red cheeks o' yourn'll be white, an' that shiny hair thin an' gray, before ye'll take my boy away from me. I feel it—I know it!"

"You may be sure," said Lyddy Washburn, her horror showing in her strained and excited voice—"you may be sure, Betty Taylor, that as long as you live, I shall never marry your son."

"Won't ye?—won't ye?" said Aunt Betty, in a kind of devilish glee. "I'll be sixty year come Michaelmas, but the Lord'll give me strength to live past ye both. Mark my words, ye proud young puppet! Mark me! mark me!" and flinging up her withered hands, she darted up the hillside with a savage cry, climbing the steep like a spider, until she was out of sight.

Lyddy Washburn rode on mechanically, got her fire, and was soon home again, but she could not have told a word that was said at her brother's house, nor anything of the people whom she saw after Aunt Betty left her. A dull loathing and horror possessed her, and her mother, noticing her pallid face and subdued manner, sent her—unheard-of proceeding!—peremptorily to bed right after dinner. Then Lyddy fell into a long, dreamless sleep, and though the night that followed was wakeful and uncanny, her fresh young nature soon rallied, and in a few days she had regained, to all appearance, her sprightliness and her beauty. But Lyddy Washburn was not the same. She had passed through a deep and a terrible experience, and it had left its mark upon her soul.

Captain Tart had come the next Sunday night to make his first regular "courtin'." Mrs. Washburn and good Farmer 'Liakim had been duly informed of the state of affairs, and had finally given a reluctant consent to the match, though Mrs. Washburn had wept many tears in private, in spite of her daughter's assurances that Captain Tart would "steady down" now, and that she would never, never marry him while his mother was living. She shuddered at the thought of this more than even her mother, who had only seen Aunt Betty "dressed and in

her right mind," though she had heard frightful stories
of her ungovernable temper and her disgusting profanity.
These, strange to say, had seemed to be a product of her
age, though she had always been a termagant. Her children were temperate and intelligent men and women
though only Tertius was left now to care for her, the
others having either died or removed to distant places.
He seemed to be enough, however, for she was utterly
bound up in him. The idea of his marriage had long
tormented her. As time went on, she had come to hope
that, like many of his race, he would never marry. But
she began to notice his preference for Lyddy Washburn.
She saw him cherishing her flowers. She knew he was
to escort her from the quilting, and she felt instinctively
that he would take her home by the secluded wood road.
There she had stealthily waited for them to come, had
seen her son's caresses, had heard the words which she
fancied were to part him from her forever, had listened
till, wrought almost to madness, she had uttered the cry
which had so startled them. Then she had wandered, in
a sort of stupid craze, till morning around the spot where
the fatal words had been spoken. There she had been
met by Lyddy on her morning ride; but the solemn determination that the girl had evinced in making her vow
had filled the agonized mother's heart with a fiendish
delight.

"I will not die!—I will not die!" she chuckled to herself as she climbed the hillside; and a superhuman
strength seemed to descend upon her with the oath she
took.

The Fourth of July came—a glorious, cloudless day.
The fife and drum ushered in the morning, and they
were accompanied by the peal of bells and roar of can-

non. The mustering ground was early crowded with the yeomanry of the county and their wives and daughters, while blue coats and brass buttons blossomed thickly in all directions. Before long the music started up anew, and the procession began to form, in which the militia were to march from the church green to the parade ground. It was growing late, but the captain had not come. All necks were craned to watch for him, when, lo! riding down the road came Captain Tart, his bright uniform becoming well his manly figure, while on the pillion behind him, in a dress of delicate green, with a silver feather—an heir-loom in her family—drooping above her lovely face, rode Lyddy Washburn. She sat straight and stately in her seat, and a murmur of admiration ran through the wait-ing crowd.

The drum beat, and the men formed in line, but just as they were about to march, someone passed a word along, and with lifted caps they sent up three tremen-dous cheers for the captain and his fair sweetheart. He had, indeed, restrained his appetite for liquor of late, and the match had come to be quite generally approved among the towns-people. The appearance of the young couple in such dashing and picturesque style at the "trainin'," completed the favorable impression, and even Jotham Hunter and a score of other disappointed youths were forced to admit that the Lord had evidently made Captain Tart and Lyddy Washburn for each other. The excitement caused by the advent of the handsome young pair was easily kept up throughout the day, and that "trainin'" was famous in the annals of the town as the most successful that had ever been known there.

Every Sunday night thereafter Captain Tart—steady now, and becoming a most successful farmer—came to

see Lyddy Washburn, and they settled down into the
ordinary ways of "courtin' "; and when the Fourth of
July came around again, Lyddy rode again on the pillion
behind her lover, and again the enthusiasm at their
appearance was unbounded.

But still Lyddy would not marry him. Another year
went round, and still she refused. He pressed her for
her reason.

"We've been courtin' long enough, Lyddy, dear," said
the honest fellow, pleadingly. "I've got a good farm, and
can take care of you. Let's be cried right off, Lyddy."

But Lyddy was determined, and by-and-by she told
him her reason. Then he urged her no more, while the
hateful old woman on the hillside chuckled to herself,
and nursed herself more carefully.

Every Fourth of July for five years Lyddy rode with
Captain Tart at the mustering. Then she grew ashamed,
and would go no more, and Captain Tart himself, a few
years later, resigned his sword and his cocked hat to
another.

The village folk talked and talked for a while over
the "long courtin' Tart Taylor was a-makin' of Lyddy
Washburn." Then it began to be accepted as a settled
fact, and ceased to excite remark.

Mrs. Washburn scolded and wept as Lyddy went on in
her thirties, and a little gray began to creep into her hair,
and her complexion lost its bloom; but though one or
two farmers boldly came to try their luck at wooing away
from Captain Tart the still beautiful woman, she was
pathetically true to her only love, who was equally stead-
fast in his devotion to her.

As time crept on, her father and mother passed away,
and she went to live with a brother, whose motherless

children she grew to love as her own; but still Aunt Betty lived on, growing tougher and heartier apparently with each successive year. There was something ghastly in the thought that they were waiting for her to die.

Then Lyddy Washburn began to grow old and wrinkled. She was over fifty, and her lover's rugged face, with its look of pathetic patience and unfaltering resolution, lost its handsome contour, and his hale figure began to bow with time and hard work.

But still the old woman lived on, with a defiant persistence which deepened Lyddy Washburn's secret conviction that she was a witch.

It was one lovely spring day, forty years from the time when Lyddy Washburn had pledged her word to Captain Tart to marry him, that the news was borne to the village from the hill farm that Aunt Betty, at the age of one hundred years, was dead at last. She had failed to outlive them, after all. For several days before her death she had been ailing, but no one had anticipated the end so soon, and she had dropped away suddenly at the last, as though the force of gravitation had at just that moment grown too strong for her hold upon the tree of life.

It was forty years from the Fourth of July when Lyddy Washburn, in her green habit and silver feather, had first graced the pillion behind her lover at the training, that she stood up in the church beside him, an old and wrinkled woman, and became his bride. The fire and passion of their early courtship had died away, but a holy affection had taken its place, which brought, at the last, genuine happiness to their blighted lives—blighted by the curse of a selfish and vindictive woman.